No flowers, by request

At a party in the comfortable little village of Woodstone, some twenty people are gathered in a pretty drawing-room, drinking wine and exchanging small-talk. Their enchanting hostess, Elizabeth Hamilton, moves about the room shedding her aura of radiant warmth on each of them – endearingly naive and disorganized Dodie; cool and intelligent Kate; Ruth, the local doctor; Steven, who runs the kennels next door; as well as on her good-looking, dependable husband David and her devoted father, Felix.

A pleasant, ordinary little gathering – but a few days later one of those present is dead, blasted with a shot-gun, and all the others are under suspicion. The small community at Woodstone is shattered almost as brutally as the victim's body.

As Detective Chief Inspector Finch – stocky, with the bluff open-air features of a farmer – starts his routine questioning, he becomes aware of several undercurrents in the apparently straightforward relationships among the party-goers. To an outsider, even one as astute as Finch, they seem no more than the minor antagonisms, jealousies and unspoken longings that are usual in any community – but concealed among them, he knows, there must be an emotion powerful and explosive enough to have led to murder . . .

June Thomson is a superb crime novelist who excels at portraying character and exploring motive, with 'finesse, subtlety, delicacy, discrimination' – to quote *The Times*. This, her thirteenth novel in the highly acclaimed series featuring Detective Chief Inspector Finch and set with loving precision in the East Anglian countryside, is as full of memorable characters, acute perceptions, and neatly timed surprises as her countless fans will expect.

Also by June Thomson

Not one of us (1972)
Death cap (1973)
The long revenge (1974)
Case closed (1977)
A question of identity (1978)
Deadly relations (1979)
Alibi in time (1980)
Shadow of a doubt (1981)
To make a killing (1982)
Sound evidence (1984)
A dying fall (1985)
The dark stream (1986)

June Thomson

No flowers, by request

CONSTABLE CRIME

Constable London

First published in Great Britain 1987
by Constable and Company Limited
10 Orange Street London WC2H 7EG

Set in Linotron Plantin 11pt by
Rowland Phototypesetting Limited
Bury St Edmunds, Suffolk
Printed in Great Britain by
St Edmundsbury Press Limited
Bury St Edmunds, Suffolk

British Library CIP data

For Ruth and John. With affection

I

'Come to lunch on Sunday,' Dodie had suggested. 'I'd love you to meet Mike.'

So Kate had accepted, taking the invitation at face value. At the time, there had been no reason to suspect Dodie of any ulterior motive, certainly not of trying to fix her up with a husband. Dodie was too warm and naive a person to be capable of such manipulation.

It was one of the reasons why Kate had taken to her in the first place, unlikely though such a friendship might appear, considering the two women had so little in common.

Unmarried at thirty-two, Kate Denby, as head of English at Framden Girls' High School, was well established in her career. Neat, dark-haired, competent, she was perfectly satisfied with her life, her modern flat in the town, her small circle of like-minded friends, even her lack of a husband. She had no wish to change any of it.

Dodie Pagett was her opposite, which might have been why Kate had warmed to her in the first place. She had joined the staff only at the beginning of that autumn term as a part-time teacher in the Art department, specializing in pottery and fabric-printing, and had never quite adapted to the routine of timetables and duty rotas. Cheerfully and endearingly disorganized, she had flung herself enthusiastically into the life of the school like, Kate thought, a large, brightly coloured beach ball thrown into some sedate backwater, scattering little heedless drops of water and raising cries of consternation from those around her.

Amused at the concept, Kate had decided to take Dodie under her wing although at times she felt that Dodie would have preferred to reverse their positions and become the mother hen herself, a role which, Kate admitted, better suited Dodie with her soft, little, plump figure, her untidy bundle of brown hair and her air of busy concern about others, including Kate herself.

'You really ought to get married, Kate!' she would urge. 'You're so attractive, I can't think why you haven't been snapped up years ago.'

Her warmth and genuine admiration prevented Kate from feeling exasperated at what in any one else she would have considered unjustified interference in her private affairs. But it was almost impossible to be angry with her; her naivety was too disarming – although later Kate realized that she should have been warned by Dodie's eager canvasing of marriage, dismissing it at the time as an artless desire to share her enthusiasms which included the merits of home-baked bread, brown rice and what Dodie referred to vaguely as 'country living'. It had all seemed perfectly harmless and innocent.

Dodie herself was married – to Mike who grew herbs on a smallholding at Woodstone, a village a few miles from Framden, packaging and selling them to whole-food suppliers although, reading between the lines of Dodie's accounts of their life together, related with the same ingenuous honesty over mid-morning coffee in the staff-room, Kate suspected that the business was not all that successful, which was why Dodie had taken up part-time teaching.

'I'm sure you'll like him,' Dodie had added confidently.

Meeting Mike on that Sunday, Kate had her reservations. To begin with, he was so disconcertingly like the photographs of the young D. H. Lawrence, tall, thin and bearded, that Kate wondered if his whole image of shabbily dressed ascetism, his air of being above such worldly concerns as making money, hadn't been carefully contrived in order to conform to some artistic ideal. He was also almost totally silent, another quality about him which exasperated Kate as being part of this pose. Pipe in mouth, he watched and listened as the two women talked together, a small smile tucked away behind the pipe and the beard, reducing, it seemed to Kate, their conversation to mere female chatter. It annoyed her.

His remarks, when he did deign to remove the pipe from his mouth to make some comment, had this same air of belittling everything and everyone, particularly Dodie.

There was an incident at lunch which, though trivial, summed up this attitude as far as Kate was concerned. It was obvious that Dodie had gone to a great deal of trouble over the meal, loading down the table with a variety of vegetarian dishes – bean stew, a choice of salads, cheeses, home-made bread and chutneys. When Kate remarked how delicious it all was, Dodie looked pink and pleased. It was then that Mike, tasting the French dressing, had laid down his fork and offered his only comment on Dodie's efforts.

'Not enough salt,' he said, 'and too much vinegar.'

And Dodie, like a fool, immediately apologized and, jumping up from the table, carried the jug away to the kitchen to make more.

Had she been in her place, Kate thought, she would have told him to do it himself if he knew so much about it.

The house also disconcerted her although Dodie had at least warned her in advance what to expect.

'It's a pair of old cottages we're doing up,' she had explained, 'although I'm afraid Mike's been so busy that nothing's finished yet.'

Even so, Kate had not been altogether prepared for the unplastered walls in the dining-room, the bare board floors, the total absence of doors to any room in the house, including the bathroom. To give Dodie her due, she had done her best to make the place look presentable by hanging lengths of her own hand-printed fabrics over the openings and by stuffing the rooms full of pottery, pictures and great jars full of wild flowers, which took away some of the starkness and discomfort of what would otherwise have been little better than a building site.

After the meal was finished, Dodie suggested a walk, to Kate's relief. She assumed that Mike would remain behind; might even offer to wash up the lunch things which she helped Dodie carry into the kitchen although, looking around her at the makeshift shelves and walls stripped down to the brick-work, there seemed to her little chance that Mike would suggest anything so practical and useful.

Nor did he intend to, for, as Dodie bundled herself up into her black woollen shawl, he went to stand by the front door, pipe in mouth and hands in pockets, looking scornfully patient, the image of a man kept waiting by the unreadiness of his womenfolk and, once they had turned into the lane, he emphasized this aloofness by striding off ahead of them.

It was a perfect October afternoon; too good, as Dodie had said, to waste indoors although it seemed there had been another reason behind the suggestion than the pure pleasure of a country walk.

'I want to call in on a neighbour,' Dodie explained. 'You don't mind, do you, Kate? It'll only take a few minutes.'

'No, of course I don't mind,' Kate replied, not even then, as Dodie gave her an oblique, oddly apologetic glance, suspecting Dodie of deviousness.

The lane led uphill towards a detached house on the crest, modern and undistinguished, which Kate might have passed without a second glance except it was evidently their destination for, calling to Mike to join them, Dodie pushed open the driveway gate and crossed the gravelled forecourt to the porch where she rang the bell, giving Kate no option but to follow.

The door was opened to them by a middle-aged man with an upright bearing and an air of courteous formality who invited them into the house, going ahead of them through the hall to a drawing-room overlooking a back garden, where Dodie introduced him to Kate as Felix Napier.

The introductions over, Kate sat politely waiting, still unsuspicious, as Dodie concluded her business with Felix Napier, something to do with a list of people willing to help with some church bazaar or other, and trying, as a mere friend of a friend, not to appear over-curious by looking too closely about her.

The room, like the house, was modern and stylistically too bland to convey much of the personality of its owner, Felix Napier, who himself was too conventional to be particularly noteworthy. With more time and opportunity to study him than the brief doorstep encounter had given her, Kate saw that he was in his fifties, with neatly cut grey hair which might once have been fair and which, together with his tweed hacking jacket, his cavalry twill trousers and beautifully polished brown brogue shoes, suggested to her the short-back-and-sides type all over, with whom she had very little in common. He seemed all of a piece with the room itself – the cream walls, the chintz-covered armchairs and sofa, the absence of books apart from some copies of the *Shooting Times* piled up tidily on the shelf of the coffee table.

The only object worth a second glance was a handsome yellow labrador which had been stretched out on the carpet in front of the fireplace as they entered and which, once they were seated, came across the room to lay its head in Kate's lap.

Felix Napier broke off what he was saying to Dodie to order the dog back to its place.

'I don't mind. I like dogs,' Kate said and went on fondling its ears, feeling slightly resentful at the man's command over the creature when all it had done was to single her out for attention.

It was then that Dodie, snapping shut her handbag and wrapping herself up again in her shawl, as if about to leave, said to Felix Napier, 'Do show Kate the view.'

Something about her voice and manner, a little too warm and eager, warned Kate that the situation was not what it seemed and that this casual call on a neighbour had been contrived by Dodie for the express purpose of introducing her to Felix Napier. Perhaps even the invitation to lunch had been part of the same plan, although Kate doubted if Dodie's capacity for deception was as well-organized as that. It seemed more likely that, having asked Kate to the meal, the idea of setting up the meeting with Felix Napier had occurred to her only later, in a muddled eagerness to spread a little happiness about her.

Felix Napier himself seemed unaware of any ulterior motive behind Dodie's request to inspect the view. With the immediate courtesy of a man trained to defer to a woman's wishes, he got to his feet and, sliding open the patio doors, ushered Kate out into the garden.

Nor, it appeared, was Mike part of the conspiracy for, glancing back as she crossed the threshold, Kate caught the tail end of a piece of pantomime going on between the two of them, Dodie pulling Mike back by the sleeve of his lumber-jacket to prevent him from falling into step, man to man, beside Felix Napier. Mike's expression of puzzled resentment could not possibly have been feigned.

Despite herself, Kate could not help feeling amused and she glanced sideways at Felix Napier's profile, wondering if he were still ignorant of what was going on. It appeared he was. There was nothing either in the erect, rather military carriage of his head nor the polite, non-committal smile on his lips to suggest he was doing anything other than his duty as a host.

Seeing him at closer quarters as they walked side by side, Kate realized that this lack of awareness was perfectly in keeping with the man. There was a guileless quality about him which would prevent him from questioning other people's motives, a form of innocence which, she could see, might make him vulnerable and which prompted her to say brightly, 'What a beautiful garden!', offering the compliment in the nature of an indirect apology for her own much sharper perceptions.

Although the remark was banal, it had at least the merit of being true. The garden was indeed beautiful. After the conventionalities of the house, it came as a surprise. On all sides there were roses, many still in bloom, lavishly planted in wide borders round a long sweep of lawn leading down to a semi-circular terrace which, like the prow of a ship, commanded an uninterrupted view over the valley.

Seeing it, Kate was inclined to forgive Dodie for her clumsy, if well-intentioned, attempt at match-making. The view was worth it. From the terrace, the landscape opened up in front of her, lying rich and replete in the Indian summer sunshine of that warm October afternoon. There was a sense of fulfilment about the shorn harvest fields of blond stubble, the hedgerows and trees ripening into red and yellow, the heaps of fallen leaves themselves, which reminded her of Keats' paean to autumn and those full, lazy days of grain and apples, sharpened by the scent of woodsmoke and the tang of early mist in the late afternoon air.

From this vantage point she was able to see the village of Woodstone as an entity, not as the sprawled and not particularly picturesque collection of houses which had been her impression on driving through it on the way to lunch with Dodie. It, too, had been garnered like the harvest, rooftops and church tower and gardens safely gathered in.

She was about to exclaim again in admiration when Felix Napier forestalled her. He was standing by her side, arms folded comfortably along the top of the balustrade, the dog seated beside him, as if for the pair of them this was a favourite and habitual resting-place.

'Magnificent, isn't it?' he remarked, turning to look at her and surprising her by the blueness of his eyes. 'And they say Essex is flat. Mind you, I doubt if you'll find another view to match this one in the whole county. It's the reason why I bought the place when I retired.' He made a small, backward gesture of his head towards the house, dismissing its banality. 'Can't say I was keen on that. But the view!'

'Yes,' Kate agreed, 'the view is certainly worth it.'

His unexpected loquacity as well as the brightness of his gaze surprised her. She had imagined his stiff, rather formal politeness to be a cover for shyness or an antipathy towards strangers, particularly women, but she found herself revising her original impression. He was more complex than she had at first thought.

'Felix built the terrace himself,' Dodie remarked as she and Mike joined them. They had been strolling more slowly down the garden, another ploy, Kate suspected, in order to give herself and Felix Napier a few moments alone together. 'Didn't you, Felix? It meant digging away tons of earth before he could start laying the flagstones.'

'Yes. Well,' he replied, straightening up. He seemed embarrassed by this attention and Kate saw his face resume its polite, non-committal expression. Turning the conversation away from himself, he went on, 'You can see your place quite well from here, Dodie,' pointing to where the gable end of Dodie's house was visible among the trees that surrounded it.

'And Elizabeth's.' Dodie picked the subject up happily. 'Elizabeth is Felix's daughter,' she added, for Kate's benefit. 'She's married to David Hamilton, the solicitor. Perhaps you've heard of him? His office is in Framden, right in the town centre.'

'Really?' Kate murmured. She was beginning to feel embarrassed herself by the situation. Mike, as usual, remained silent. Felix, too, had withdrawn and was standing back from the balustrade as if physically distancing himself both from the scene in front of them as well as Dodie's remarks about it, although it was, Kate thought ridiculously, *his* view after all. She felt Dodie was trying to draw her into a shared interest in

Felix Napier and his family concerns which she did not want to know about and which were none of her business, anyway.

But Dodie, quite oblivious, was continuing, 'She's got an exquisite house. You'd love it, Kate, if you saw it! It's full of the most beautiful things. She and David had it built, didn't they, Felix? Felix gave them some land next to the kennels he used to own. Look, you can see it over there.'

She was pointing down towards the village to a white house on the right, standing in a large garden, well back from the line of telegraph posts which marked the road. 'And that's where Felix used to live,' Dodie added, indicating a smaller, squarer, red-brick house closer to the road. Behind it were rows of low-roofed buildings which were presumably the kennels to which Dodie had referred and, now that it was pointed out to her, Kate remembered passing the place on her way through the village with its board announcing '*Woodstone Boarding Kennels*' at the entrance. A short distance past it, she had had to turn right into Brookhouse Lane which led to Dodie's place.

So Felix Napier had once owned the house and kennels, Kate thought. She wondered why he had given them up. He didn't seem old enough yet to retire.

Mike, who had taken the pipe out of his mouth, at last contributed to the conversation.

'How do you get on with your successor these days?' he asked.

'Bradley? Never speak to the man if I can help it,' Felix Napier replied abruptly.

It put an end to the conversation. Dodie gave Mike a reproachful look, although he seemed pleased at having been provocative. Seeing a small smile touch the corners of his lips, Kate felt her instinctive dislike of him deepen.

'If you've seen enough,' Felix Napier remarked, 'we'll go back to the house, shall we?'

It was said politely, but the implication was clear enough. The diversion was over; he wanted them gone.

They returned in silence to the drawing-room where Dodie had the sense to put an end to the visit.

'We really must be going,' she announced.

'Then I'll show you out,' Felix Napier replied, making no pretence at keeping them.

On the doorstep, he shook Kate's hand, his blue eyes looking into hers although Kate doubted if he saw her as an individual, certainly not as a woman. There was an opacity about the glance, as if good manners prevented him from registering her too positively. His hand in hers was cool and firm, the skin a little dry.

'Delighted to meet you,' he remarked. Quite clearly he had already forgotten her name.

And that was that. Breaking the clasp, he turned away to raise his hand in a more casual salute to Dodie and Mike as befitted close neighbours, and the three of them began walking down the gravelled drive towards the white-painted gate that led into the lane.

'Poor Felix,' Dodie commented almost before they were out of earshot. 'He's been so lonely since his wife died. He's such a nice man. Didn't you think so, Kate?'

'He seemed very pleasant,' Kate agreed. It seemed safe to say it. There was no likelihood she would ever meet the man again.

'Likes to play the squire,' Mike commented. He had stopped to knock out his pipe on the heel of his shoe, keeping the two women waiting.

'I don't think he means it,' Dodie replied, springing instantly to Felix Napier's defence. 'It's just the way he is.'

'And I can understand,' Mike continued, unable, it seemed, to let the matter rest, 'why he and Bradley are at loggerheads over the kennels. The trouble with Felix is he just can't let go, even though he's sold them. It's the property-owning instinct, of course.'

'But that's just not fair, Mike!' Dodie protested, the colour rising in her face. 'Felix only meant to be helpful, and you know what Steven Bradley's like. He can be very touchy.'

The conversation had begun to degenerate into that bickering exchange of remarks between husband and wife embarrassing to a third person, when, to Kate's relief, an MG sports car came sweeping up the hill towards them from the direction of the village, forcing them to separate and withdraw in single file on to the verge.

A few feet past them, it drew to a sudden halt at the side of the road and Dodie, breaking off her protest to Mike, went loping back at an awkward trot to speak to the driver through the open passenger window.

'Oh, Elizabeth, how lovely to see you!' Kate heard her exclaim with a naive, unfeigned enthusiasm. 'We've just been calling on Felix. Do let me introduce a friend of mine.'

As she spoke, she turned to beckon Kate forward.

Kate joined her reluctantly at the side of the car. The woman at the wheel was obviously Elizabeth Hamilton, Felix Napier's daughter, and, remembering Dodie's embarrassing attempt earlier to interest her in the father, Kate was far from eager to be drawn into further contact with the family. Besides, the circumstances of the meeting were hardly satisfactory, for in order to speak to the woman Kate had to squash in beside Dodie on the narrow verge and stoop half-double to reach the window of the low-slung car. It smacked too much to her of having to bend the knee at Elizabeth Hamilton's altar. Mike, she noticed, had hung back, refusing to join them.

The introductions over, they exchanged a few remarks about Kate's visit to Dodie's and what a splendid day she had chosen for a drive into the country; ordinary pleasantries which two strangers with a friend in common tend to make on such a brief acquaintance, while Dodie stood beaming at Kate's side, clearly delighted at the chance meeting which had brought the two of them together.

It was impossible for Kate to see much of Elizabeth Hamilton's features at such an awkward angle. She was on the far side of the car, leaning across the passenger seat. Besides, as an antidote to Dodie's eagerness, Kate was damned if she was going to show too much curiosity in the woman. All the same, she had an impression of someone young, fair-haired and beautiful. And also self-assured. It was evident in her voice, the set of her head and the manner in which her arm rested with an easy grace across the back of the passenger seat, suggesting a stylish self-confidence.

The next moment, almost as soon as she had registered these qualities, Kate deliberately withdrew, nodding good-bye before, straightening up, she walked back along the verge to where Mike was waiting, leaving Dodie to take a more protracted farewell. Shortly afterwards, the car drove away up the hill.

Dodie came puffing up to join them, looking pleased.

'Wasn't that lucky, meeting Elizabeth like that?' she asked of Kate. 'I didn't for a moment think we'd have the chance. I suppose she's on her way to visit Felix.'

'She's his only daughter?' Kate asked, feeling obliged to say something.

'Yes, she is, although I sometimes wonder if he wouldn't have liked a son – to pass the business on to, of course.' As she spoke, Dodie gave a hitch to her shawl, drawing it closer about her shoulders. It could have been merely for extra warmth, although Kate felt the action was defensive. Dodie and Mike were childless and Kate wondered if, by wishing an heir on Felix Napier, Dodie wasn't expressing a secret longing for a son of her own. 'Not that Felix has ever said so,' Dodie was quick to add. 'He thinks the world of Elizabeth. Nothing's too good for her. She and her husband are such a charming couple, I'd love you to meet them both. As you saw, Elizabeth's so vivacious and full of life. David's quieter; good-looking too, but more serious. You know what I mean? The type who listens sympathetically and makes you feel he really cares.'

'Perfect for a local solicitor,' Kate suggested lightly. Although she was grateful that the conversation had passed to this more agreeable topic, she had no intention of becoming involved, even on an impersonal level, with the Hamiltons – despite Dodie's attempts to share her obvious enthusiasm of them.

What were Elizabeth and David Hamilton to her? Kate thought. Or, come to that, Felix Napier?

All the same, listening to Dodie's remarks, Kate could not help thinking that Elizabeth Hamilton sounded spoilt, an absurd conclusion to come to when she had barely even met her. But she was aware of a stirring of envy of those women who, like Felix Napier's daughter, seemed born to be cherished and for whom life was always made easy; not that she would have changed places with her for the world.

They reached the gate of the cottage, Dodie going ahead of them to open the front door.

'Tea?' she suggested as they entered the sitting-room.

'I mustn't stay too long,' Kate replied. 'Let's do the washing-up and then I really ought to go.'

She was anxious to leave. However fond she was of Dodie, she had to admit that the afternoon had not been an entire success and she did not want to prolong it longer than necessary.

'No, tea first,' Mike said, settling the matter.

Giving Kate a quick smile, appealing for her understanding that, as the man of the house, Mike's needs were paramount, Dodie went into the kitchen to put the kettle on. After a moment's hesitation, Kate followed her, leaving Mike standing by the fireplace, which was nothing more than a hole in the wall where the mantelpiece and grate had been removed, slowly and comfortably filling his pipe with the infuriatingly self-satisfied air of a man who knows he has got his own way.

2

After the Pagetts and their guest had gone, Felix remained standing on the doorstep, reluctant to return to the house. His mind seemed to function more clearly in the open air. Indoors, he felt stifled by the walls and furniture.

In the old days, he thought ruefully, although the old days were in fact only a year ago before Helen's death and his decision to sell the kennels to Bradley, he had spent most of his time out of doors. But at that time, with one of those ironic twists with which life seemed to amuse itself, he had had no serious problems on his mind apart from the day to day running of the business. Life had been full of things to do. He had not needed to cast about for tasks with which to occupy his time.

But now that his physical space had contracted to this house and its garden, time had perversely expanded, bringing with it worries which he had all the leisure in the world to ponder over.

Helen's death was not a problem, in that sense. It was more a great hole in his life which he knew would never be filled but which he had learned to accept as he might have done a physical handicap such as blindness. He mourned her loss constantly but, little by little as a blind man learns to cope with his disability, Felix had come to terms with his grief. She was gone and there was nothing he could do to recall her.

Bradley presented a different problem because, Felix felt, there might be some way in which he could solve it, although God alone knew how.

It was largely his own fault, of course. If, after Helen's death, he had not decided to sell up, he wouldn't now be faced with the question of how to deal with his successor. David, his son-in-law, had warned him about it. 'Don't come to a decision too soon,' he had advised. 'Leave it for a few months.'

And he had been right. Felix could see that now. He had been in no fit state to decide anything so soon after Helen's death. At the time, however, it had seemed the right judgement to make. Once she had gone, he had wanted to erase as much as possible which might remind him of her, to start filling in the blank she had left with positive action. Selling up and moving out had seemed the best course to take.

He had been mistaken; he admitted that now. Equally foolish has been certain assumptions which he had drawn at the time and which he had had no right to make.

Put quite simply, it amounted to this: that Bradley would take over the kennels but, he, Felix, would go on playing an active part in running the business. Bradley, he had imagined, would be grateful for his help and advice, particularly over the breeding of labradors which had been Felix's own speciality.

But Bradley had seen it differently. To be fair to the man, he'd had every right to do so. They were his kennels now, after all, and Felix, in his more objective moments, could see that, had he been in Bradley's shoes, he would have resented the ex-proprietor turning up, expecting to have a say in the business.

But the man might have gone about it more – well, *respectfully*, Felix thought, searching for the right word. After all, he had lived in the village for nearly thirty years. The name

'Paddocks Boarding and Breeding Kennels' was well known over a wide area. His dogs and bitches had won many prizes at shows, and not just local ones either. And, apart from all of this, he was old enough to be Bradley's father and, on age and experience alone, he felt he was entitled to some courtesy.

But Bradley had approached the situation in quite the wrong way, almost as if he had set out to be damned awkward. Not only had he changed the name to just 'Woodstone Boarding Kennels', thus negating more than twenty-five years of hard work on Felix's part in building up its reputation, but he had given up breeding labradors on the excuse that it was not profitable.

Profitable!

Even now, standing on the doorstep with his own labrador, Percy, at his side, the last in a long line of pedigree dogs, some of them champions, Felix found anger rising in him again at the memory of that last confrontation with Bradley. The word seemed to sum up an attitude of mind which Felix utterly rejected. Nothing, it seemed to him, mattered these days unless it was financially successful. It was the triumph of a mean, money-grubbing instinct which was becoming more and more prevalent. All the old, true values of excellence and quality, of doing things simply for the pleasure of the task or the challenge it presented, seemed to have gone by the board.

He had told Bradley so in no uncertain terms, and the conversation had ended with Bradley walking to the door of the office, opening it and saying in an offensive manner, 'In that case, there's no point in discussing the matter further. I'd be grateful if you didn't turn up here again unless you happen to want my professional services.'

This last confrontation had happened three months earlier, since when Felix had not been near the kennels; and whenever he had chanced to meet Bradley in the village he had studiously ignored the man. The situation distressed him. He preferred to be on good terms with his neighbours. In a village, that counted for a lot. It struck him also as a meanness on his part which put him on much the same par as Bradley, although that hadn't stopped him from showing his dislike.

Damn Pagett! he thought. If he hadn't brought up the

subject of Bradley in the first place as the four of them had been looking at the view, he wouldn't be standing here now, brooding. But he had noticed before that Pagett had a knack of referring to painful topics. Although he never had much to say for himself in the course of ordinary conversation, when he did open his mouth it was usually to make some such remark; not that Felix suspected him of doing it deliberately. Lacking Kate's perspicacity, he put it down to an unfortunate lack of social grace on Mike's part which he regarded as a pity. He was very fond of Dodie, who was one of those warm, kindly, unpretentious women, but he found it difficult to feel at ease with her husband. There was something spiky about the man.

At that moment, Percy, who had been sitting motionless by his side with the patience of a well-trained dog, suddenly stiffened, his head and ears alert. He had evidently heard something. A few seconds later, Felix himself was aware of the sound of a car coming up the hill towards the house.

It was Elizabeth's. There was no mistaking the powerful thrum of its engine in low gear. Bradley forgotten, Felix hurried forward to swing open the gate which the Pagetts had partly closed behind them, before standing back to watch as she made the sharp turn out of the lane.

It never failed to amaze him that she was his daughter. Every time he saw her, he felt something of that same tremor of astonished delight he had experienced when he had first peered down at the shawled bundle soon after she was born, marvelling at the tiny hands, the sealed eyelids, the smooth curve of her forehead. It had seemed a miracle that he should be partly responsible for such perfection and, from that first moment, it had never crossed his mind to wish she had been a son. She was Elizabeth, uniquely herself, and he counted it a privilege to have fathered her. He was not even disappointed that he and Helen had had no other children. The fact that Elizabeth was their only child had only served to confirm her special qualities and to allow him to concentrate on her alone that steady, unchanging beam of his love which had lighted up his own life as well as hers.

Indeed, she seemed a creature of light. Hurrying forward as she parked the car and got out of the driver's seat, he was struck again by this ability of hers to radiate brightness about her. It wasn't only her fair skin and hair, which swung round her shoulders like a shining bell, nor the vivid blue of her eyes which she had inherited from him and which in itself was another miracle; the brilliance seemed to emanate from somewhere inside herself as a joy and a pleasure in living and being loved, which illuminated everyone and everything about her.

As she kissed him on one cheek, he was conscious of a brightening of his own mood which she was always able to evoke, as if her mere presence carried with it its own vivacity, vitalizing the air about her. The scent she wore, some fresh, flowery essence, the warmth and softness of her cheek, the faint rustle of her silk sleeve against his, all combined to heighten his own awareness and to lift his spirits and, as she tucked her hand into his arm and they walked together into the house, he felt his own steps grow quick and light in response.

'This is a pleasure,' he said. 'I didn't expect to see you this afternoon.'

'I've come to ask you to dinner this evening,' she replied. 'You will come, won't you, daddy? I need cheering up.'

'I can't believe that.' Although he was flattered both by the remark and by the invitation, he couldn't take her seriously. She spoke lightly, smiling over her shoulder as she walked towards the patio doors to look out at the garden, Percy following at her heels.

'Oh, but I mean it,' she said. 'David's been so busy I've hardly seen him all day. I've been so dull. Do say you'll come. David would enjoy it, too. You can talk about rough-shooting and rights of way and how the country's going to the dogs.' She softened any implied amusement at the conversation the two men might indulge in by speaking in a teasing manner and by adding, as she bent down to rumple Percy's ears, 'Although if it's anything like you, you lovely old thing, it can't be that bad, can it?'

The dog, with a devotion matching only his love for Felix, thumped his tail against the parquet in response.

Felix hesitated before replying. Like all conversations with Elizabeth, he was not quite sure where to start. There was a mercurial quality about her which made it difficult to pick on any one aspect of what she had said. Should he refer first to her invitation to dinner? he wondered. Or the fact that David had been working all day, and on a Sunday, too? Or had she meant to hint, by mentioning the subject of rough-shooting, that he should ask his son-in-law out for an afternoon with the guns? They both enjoyed the sport but Felix had not liked to suggest a meeting as David had seemed so busy with his own business affairs.

Even the reference to the right of way could have a particular significance of its own. When he had given David and Elizabeth the land adjoining Paddocks on which to build their house, he had rather foolishly done nothing about the pathway which led behind the property through the spinney and which gave access into Gade's Lane, running roughly parallel to the main village road. At the time, it hadn't seemed important. He himself still owned the kennels and, as David had agreed – and, after all, he was a solicitor – it was unlikely to cause any difficulties between members of the same family. Besides, none of them made much use of the right of way. But, since Bradley had taken over the business, it was possible that some dispute had arisen. He was the type who would insist on his rights. However, that brought him back full circle to the unpleasant subject of the man and his own relationship with him, and Felix didn't want to distress Elizabeth by referring to it.

It was better, he thought, to stick to more personal, family matters which concerned only themselves, and he said, 'Of course I'll come to dinner. You know I always enjoy an evening with you and David. But I don't want to be in the way, my dear. If David's so busy, wouldn't it be better to leave it for another time?'

As he spoke, he was aware that he was voicing his own major concern – that of becoming a nuisance. He had been more conscious of this possibility since his wife's death. When Helen had been alive, the relationships had been equally balanced; he and Helen, Elizabeth and David. Now that he was alone, he felt that the equilibrium had shifted, leaving him vulnerable to the temptation, unless he was very careful, of becoming too intrusive in the lives of his daughter and son-in-law, another reason behind his decision to sell out to Bradley. He wanted desperately to avoid that trap. In fact, he tended to go to the other extreme by making himself less conspicuous in the relationship than he might normally have done. But he loved his daughter too much to take the risk of becoming a burden and was grateful that neither she nor David had ever once made him feel that he was in the way. In that respect, he was lucky in his son-in-law. Of all the men who had fallen in love with Elizabeth and whom she might have married, David was the one man Felix himself would have chosen for her, had he been asked for an opinion. If he had ever wished for a son, Felix would have wanted one very like David, honest, dependable, utterly trustworthy. He could only thank God that Elizabeth had possessed the good sense to see those qualities in him.

She was saying, 'No, do come tonight, darling. You can cheer David up as well. I know he'd love to see you. I'll get him to open a bottle of claret for you.'

'But should he be working so hard?' Felix asked, picking up one of the other subjects which she had referred to so lightly and ignoring the claret, although David was something of a connoisseur of wine. 'Can't Dunbar take some of the burden off him?'

Dunbar was David's partner in the firm and, as senior, should, in Felix's opinion, be prepared to shoulder more of the work.

'Ralph's getting a divorce,' Elizabeth told him.

'A divorce!' Felix was distressed as well as surprised. Any mention of the subject always upset him. It was one of his hobby-horses, which he had to be careful not to ride too hard when talking to others, although he genuinely believed that many of the country's problems were caused by a breakdown in family life. Couples were too quick to put an end to their marriages. After all, it was largely a question of give and take and, when children were involved, a matter of duty as well to try and make a go of things.

'Sheila's left him,' Elizabeth explained quickly. 'But don't let it upset you, daddy. The marriage had been on the rocks for years. Anyway, with Ralph rather taken up with his own affairs for the time being, David's been left with more than his fair share of the work; added to which, poor old Wilfred Chitty over at Millbridge really can't cope any more, so David's had to go over there once a week to help him out.'

'Surely they'd do better to close down that branch?' Felix said. 'I can see that in the past, when few people had cars, it was useful for the local farmers and shopkeepers to have a solicitor's on their doorstep, but these days most people can get into Framden quite easily. It can't be financially worthwhile to keep two offices going.'

As he said it, he was aware that he was expressing much the same value-judgement as Bradley had done over the breeding kennels, and he was exasperated with himself for having allowed such a thought to cross his mind, let alone voiced it out loud. Perversely, some of his anger was directed at Bradley as well, although this was hardly fair. All the same, the man had the infuriating ability to keep cropping up whatever the topic of conversation.

Elizabeth seemed unaware of his reaction.

'I think they will close it down eventually,' she replied. 'It's simply a question of waiting until Chitty retires, which can't be that far off now.' To his relief, she changed the subject, raising a hand to point towards the garden. 'Just look at your roses! Aren't they beautiful?'

'I'll pick some for you,' Felix said, crossing the room to find the secateurs which were kept handy in the top drawer of the bureau.

'But you never pick the roses for yourself!' she protested, laughing. 'You always say they look better growing than in a vase.'

'For you, my darling,' he told her, smiling back at her and managing to match her vivacity with a touch of his own, 'I'm prepared to make the sacrifice.'

Opening the patio doors with a flourish, he flung out an arm, inviting her to step into the garden where he began cutting at the flowers with an extravagance which surprised even himself, recounting their names as he did so.

'Belle Blonde, Pascali, Joyfulness,' he announced, moving from bed to bed. 'And Fragrant Cloud,' he concluded, laying the last rose in her arms and watching as she lifted it to her face to breathe in its perfume.

'It's beautiful,' she said.

'Then it's a fitting tribute,' he replied a little awkwardly. He always found it difficult to pay her compliments, lacking that easy grace to make it natural, but he went on trying, feeling that he needed to put into words his love for her. To leave it unspoken would have been a betrayal of them both.

She accepted both the flowers and the compliment with a spontaneity and a teasing affection which saved him any embarrassment, hugging his arm and remarking, 'Do you know, you're nearly as nice as Percy?' at which the dog, which had followed them into the garden, looked up at them both and flapped his tail on hearing his name.

'Nearly?' he asked, as they walked arm in arm up the lawn towards the house.

'You haven't such long, floppy ears as he has,' she said laughing and then, changing the subject before it became too forced, she added, 'By the way, I understand you had visitors this afternoon?'

'Did I?' He sounded uncertain.

'The Pagetts?' she prompted him. 'I stopped and spoke to Dodie on my way here. She said they'd called on you.'

'Oh yes, of course, the Pagetts,' Felix said. In his delight at Elizabeth's visit, he had forgotten all about them. 'Yes, they did drop in for a short time. Dodie brought the list of people willing to help with the Christmas fair.'

'And also a friend, I gather?' Seeing his look of surprise, she continued, 'A dark-haired woman, in her thirties I suppose? We were introduced briefly.'

'That was a colleague of Dodie's. She teaches English at the same school in Framden. Kate somebody or other. Denby? Daulby? I forget which. Why do you ask?'

He was intrigued to know why Elizabeth should show interest in a woman whom she had only just met and whom he himself could not recall in any detail, except for a quality of directness and freshness about her which he had rather liked at the time but which he had forgotten until that moment. It rose again briefly in his mind, associated absurdly with mint. But that was the image she evoked: uncomplex, aromatic but at the same time slightly astringent. How ridiculous such mental connections were!

'I thought she looked different,' Elizabeth was explaining. 'Intelligent, too, I should imagine. She reminded me of Ruth.'

'Ruth? Oh, you mean Ruth Livesey. Yes, I suppose there is some similarity, now that you mention it,' Felix agreed. He could see Elizabeth's point. Both women had dark hair and shared a certain air of brisk independence, although in Ruth Livesey's case there was a much more practical and no-nonsense quality about it which, Felix assumed, arose from her medical training. Secretly, he was a little intimidated by her and was thankful that, on the rare occasions when he had been ill, he had been treated by Dr Wade and not by his young woman assistant whom he had taken into the practice in the last eighteen months.

'By the way,' Elizabeth was adding, 'David's changed doctors. He's asked to be taken off Dr Wade's list and has signed on instead with a GP in Framden who practises holistic medicine.' But before Felix could raise any objection – was it wise for David to register with a GP who lived so far away, and did holistic medicine anyway bring such great advantages? – Elizabeth, with that swiftness of mind which made it hard for him to keep up with her, had jumped ahead of him to an entirely different topic.

'I think I must give a party before too long,' she said. 'It's ages since we had people round for drinks. Do you think, if I asked Dodie nicely, that she'd bring her friend?'

'But why?' Felix asked, bewildered.

'Why not?' Elizabeth countered. 'She looked fun.'

'Fun?' he repeated. It had hardly been his impression of the woman. Intelligent, yes. He was prepared to give her that. Probably interesting to talk to as well, especially as she taught English and had presumably a knowledge of books and literature. But 'fun' was not the word he would have used to describe her.

'Well, interesting, then,' Elizabeth said, choosing the same epithet as himself. 'And, as I said, different. There're so few people round here who are.'

Felix made no comment, although he wondered, as he had

done many times in the past, if Elizabeth didn't find village life restricting. Quick herself, eager and full of vitality, she couldn't have much opportunity of meeing like-minded people. She always kept herself busy, of course. Being Elizabeth, she was too fond of life to find it boring, involving herself in many of the local activities although at times Felix thought he detected an amused, slightly frivolous air about the manner in which she discussed them, as if she found it difficult to take them seriously. For his own part, being asked to chair a committee, such as the one organizing the church Christmas fair, was something of an honour.

Which reminded him, he must ask her if she would run a stall again this year.

But before he could broach the subject, she had continued, her mind still on the party, 'I shall ask the Pagetts, of course. That goes without saying. And Ruth Livesey, as well as one or two people from Framden, including that nice man who runs the antique shop behind the Town Hall. And then there's Steven Bradley.'

'Oh,' Felix said.

Elizabeth looked at him sideways over the armful of roses, her face bright with laughter.

'You're not still cutting him dead, are you, daddy? How silly! He's really rather pleasant when you get to know him; a bit abrupt, I agree, but a lot of that's defensiveness.'

'I found him downright rude,' Felix said. It was better, he felt, to come straight to the point and speak his mind.

She stopped and made him turn to face her.

'Now, listen,' she said. 'I'm going to scold you as Mummy would have done and for exactly the same reason – because I care about you, you silly old thing. You really can't go on like this, you know. I can see it's making you unhappy and I feel I must do something about it. So I shall invite Steven Bradley to the party where you'll meet him and be extra specially nice to him. Will you promise me that?'

'My dear Elizabeth,' Felix began, feeling harassed. It was so difficult to deny her anything and yet he felt he ought to make a stand. After all, principles should count for something.

'Promise me!' she urged. 'Say you'll bury the hatchet over a gin and tonic.'

The absurdity of the image amused him as she had intended, for she laughed with him.

'All right, my darling, I promise,' Felix said, 'although it will have to be a very large gin. Now are you satisfied?'

He knew she was pleased because, as she took his arm again, she squeezed it close to her side.

'That's my boy!' she replied.

It was the same response that her mother had always made when she had wanted to show pleasure and affection, a teasing reference to Felix's own manner of addressing a favourite dog, and he felt the painful hollow of loss and regret open up again in his chest.

That's my boy!

If he could have withdrawn his promise to Elizabeth, he would have done so. Although he rarely examined his own motives, he was aware that, in an odd way, he had needed his dislike of Bradley to sustain him after Helen's death. His anger and hostility had been like a sharp disinfectant, cleansing the open wound and allowing it to heal. Take that away and the sense of bereavement would go on quietly festering somewhere close to his heart.

Strange, he thought, how therapeutic animosity could be in certain circumstances.

But he had given his word and there could be no going back. Besides, there was no opportunity. They had re-entered the house and Elizabeth was saying, 'I must go, darling. I'll see you later this evening. Come about seven o'clock.'

And then she was gone so quickly that he barely had time to follow her to the front door, where he kissed her and stood waving with the dog at his side as she drove off, still breathing in the scent she wore, mingled with the fragrance of the roses.

When her car had turned into the lane, Felix walked slowly back into the hall, closing the front door behind him, aware that the house seemed more empty and silent than ever. Her departure always had this effect as if, by withdrawing her presence, she took with her all light and colour, leaving behind only a nothingness.

To fill it, he entered the study which opened off the hall. Few people had been inside it. He even discouraged Elizabeth from using it too often, although she seemed to realize, with a sensitivity of perception for which he was grateful, that this part of the house, like talking too much about the death of her mother, was private and inviolate. It was here that he kept his books. In the old days, an euphemism he often used even to himself when referring to the time before Helen died and he had sold out to Bradley, the books had always been kept in the sitting-room at Paddocks, arranged on public display, as it were. After her death and his move to this house, he had preferred to have them hidden away in this small study although there was plenty of space for bookshelves in the drawing-room.

Like his antipathy towards Bradley, Felix had not considered the reasons for this decision at any depth. It had just seemed right at the time.

Now, as he entered the room, he was aware that the books represented a process of conciliation and inner healing which could only be achieved in silence and isolation. It was as if they breathed out a balm of their own, the opposite to the sharply stinging restorative of his dislike for Bradley but just as beneficial.

He smiled wryly at the idea. It seemed an afternoon of self-revelation which was not exactly welcome, especially as he had the uncomfortable feeling that women were responsible for both: Elizabeth, of course, by extracting that promise from him over Bradley, and the friend of Dodie's, Kate whatever her name was, although in her case the connection was not so clear except in a very generalized association with books and literature.

All the same, as he selected a volume from the shelves and sat down in the armchair, the memory of her presence stirred briefly as he turned the pages and began to read:

> It may be possible to do without dancing entirely. Instances have been known of young people passing many, many months successively, without being at any ball of any description, and no material injury accrue to either body or mind;

> but when a beginning is made – when the felicities of rapid motion have once been, though slightly, felt – it must be a very heavy set that does not ask for more.

He forgot her soon in the pleasure of *Emma*, feeling himself relax in the chair as the words flowed into him.

Around him as he read, the room, too, seemed to settle down and re-arrange itself into an old, familiar setting. It was like putting on a comfortable, well-worn jacket which was moulded exactly to fit. Here were his favourite possessions, not just the books but his winged chair, the Chippendale desk, Helen's collection of lustre-ware arranged in the bow-fronted cabinet, the T'ang horse on the mantelshelf above the fireplace, in front of which the dog was lying, sprawled out asleep on its side, ears and tail flaccid.

Yes, almost like the old days, Felix told himself as he read on.

3

'Perfect afternoon,' Felix remarked for the second time. He felt the need to say something because David was strangely quiet; not that he was the type of man to talk freely at the best of times. Thank God, Felix added to himself.

With someone like his son-in-law, it was possible to maintain a natural and companionable silence. But the quality of that silence had changed recently. Felix had noticed it at dinner the previous Sunday evening when he had thought David seemed drawn and tired, his youthful features which had preserved the diffident, studious good looks of his undergraduate days suddenly much older and harassed-looking.

Overwork, Felix had decided, which was why he had suggested that the two of them went out rough-shooting the following Saturday afternoon. 'Bag a few pigeons,' he had continued. 'It'll do you the world of good, especially if this weather lasts.'

With Elizabeth adding her own persuasion, David had finally

agreed and, by a piece of good fortune, Felix's wish had been fulfilled, the Indian summer continuing throughout the week in an unbroken succession of warm, golden days, persuading Felix to reiterate his comment.

The repetition of the remark was, however, not only intended to break the silence but to express his own simple pleasure. The afternoon was indeed perfect and to comment on it out loud, even for a second time, seemed to confirm the fact.

The two men, with Percy at their heels, were walking across the fields behind the village, over land which belonged to George Baxter who owned Gade's Farm and who had given permission for the afternoon's sport. The shooting rights were an agreement between Felix and Baxter going back many years, which benefited both men, Baxter from the assistance of another gun in keeping down the crows and pigeons, Felix from the sport itself – although in this particular instance he was more concerned with getting David away from his desk and out into the open air than in the size of the bag. If they potted nothing more than a brace or two of pigeons, he would be well pleased with the afternoon.

There was a smoky-gold light which hung in the air, softening the landscape and lying like a translucent net over the trees. In contrast, the air was as crisp and as dry as the earth and fallen leaves which crunched under their boots with a rich, satisfying sound.

To their right stood Gade's Farm, lying as if washed up and abandoned between the slope of the fields, a Noah's ark of barn roofs and gables visible among the trees.

To their left, it was possible to look down the slight incline towards the lane which ran in a loop behind David and Elizabeth's house as well as Paddocks, Felix's former home, before rejoining the main village street about quarter of a mile further on opposite the church.

Felix glanced in that direction and then deliberately averted his eyes. He was near enough to be able to pick out the lines of exercise pens and kennels as well as the office and outbuildings behind the house which he himself had designed and had built when he first took over the property, and he recalled with a pang the excitement and sense of commitment of those days, the anxiety about getting planning permission, the hours spent with the architect, the feeling of achievement on the day the builders finally moved in. He and Helen, he remembered, had opened a bottle of champagne in celebration.

It was on the tip of his tongue to make some comment about Bradley. It would have been easy enough. All he had to do was ask David with seeming casualness, 'How do you get on with Bradley these days?' After all, they were neighbours. David and Elizabeth's house stood on the adjoining plot of land that Felix had made over to them before their marriage and on which their own place had been built.

But he stopped himself in time. Since Elizabeth had extracted that promise from him, he had begun to feel that Bradley was a taboo subject. Better let sleeping dogs lie, he said to himself. All the same, he wasn't looking forward to the party and having to be pleasant to the man. It went against the grain.

Instead, he decided to refer to the party which in itself was non-controversial.

'Elizabeth's still going ahead with her "do" next Saturday?' he asked. She had talked about it over dinner the previous Sunday.

'As far as I know,' David replied.

He stopped to raise his gun to his shoulder and take aim at a pigeon which rose suddenly from the winter wheat ahead of them, and Felix also halted, watching critically as the double barrels followed the flight of the bird before David pulled the trigger. At his side Percy stood motionless, waiting for the command to retrieve.

The pigeon fell in an explosion of sound and feathers. The smell of burnt powder was flung into the air, adding its own smoke to the vaporous, golden light.

'Not bad,' Felix remarked as he sent the dog forward. It was the highest compliment he was prepared to pay to any fellow sportsman, although secretly he wasn't all that impressed with David's ability in handling a gun. It was literally rather a hit-or-miss effort, largely because David didn't practise enough in Felix's opinion. He ought to go out rough-shooting more regularly. A few times a year wasn't enough.

The dog came back, high-stepping over the furrows, ears

bouncing, the mass of blood and feathers held tenderly in his mouth, to drop the dead pigeon at Felix's feet. Stooping down, he rubbed a hand briefly over Percy's head before picking up the bird and putting it in the canvas bag he carried slung over one shoulder. It already contained half a dozen pigeons, not a bad result from the afternoon's sport, although he wondered what to do with them. In the old days, Helen would have made a casserole of pigeons' breasts in a red-wine sauce. But now that he was on his own, Felix couldn't be bothered with fiddling about with the preparation. It was easier to grill himself a chop. He doubted if Elizabeth would want to go to all that trouble either, although Baxter would probably welcome the game if only to pass on to a dealer in Framden for a couple of pounds – another example of the profit-making instinct which he had so deplored in Bradley.

Suddenly the afternoon lost its pleasure. The light was going, anyway. The sun had begun to sink low behind the trees of Gade's Wood ahead of them, outlining the branches now that the foliage was thinning. Leaves fell even as he watched, turning in the air in a slow, melancholy, downward drift. He could feel the damp striking up from the ground through the soles of his boots.

'Call it a day?' he suggested. 'We'll walk as far as the wood, shall we, and go back along the footpath?'

This route varied the walk, saving them from returning across the fields by the way they had come, although Felix made the suggestion for another reason as well.

The footpath had been Helen's favourite walk, especially in the months just before her death when, because of her heart condition, a long country tramp had been out of the question. It had been close enough to the house to make it easy to reach, too – another advantage, for an opening in the hedge at the back of Paddocks led directly into Gade's Lane and from there it had been simply a matter of strolling along it for a short distance before striking off along the path which led to the wood.

Felix had accompanied her on that walk on many occasions, especially in that last spring just before her death, matching his stride to her slower pace and sharing her delight in the signs of new growth everywhere – the clumps of primroses growing along the edges of the path and later, as the spring advanced, the bluebells lifting moist, juicy stems and leaves above last year's dead litter of bracken to spread in drifts underneath the trees, like patches of sky.

'That's fine by me,' David replied. 'You'll come back to the house for tea, of course. Elizabeth's expecting you.'

He had broken the gun after firing it and was carrying it crooked over his right arm.

'Delighted,' Felix replied, 'although I shan't stay long.' He wouldn't want to outstay his welcome. As he spoke, it crossed his mind that there was still one cartridge left in David's gun, although he refrained from mentioning it. They were walking towards the wood, keeping to the edge of the adjoining field which had been ploughed and drilled with winter wheat. The chances were that as they approached the trees they might stir up a pheasant from the undergrowth and David would make use of that last shot.

His own gun was loaded and he tucked the stock close to his side, sending the dog forward with a gesture to flush out any game, his own eyes and ears alert for the tell-tale clatter of wings and upward dart of movement against the darkness trees as a sitting bird suddenly took flight.

Steven Bradley drew his car up outside Ruth Livesey's gate and switched off the engine, although he did not immediately get out.

Instead, he remained seated behind the wheel, contemplating the front of her house. She was at home. He could see a light in the hall shining out through the glass panel in the door and a crack of brightness at the sitting-room window where the curtains had not been quite closed.

The decision to call on her had been made on impulse. After completing the rounds of the kennels, making sure that everything was secure for the night, he had returned to the house where he had been suddenly struck by its silence. Normally he did not mind. Given the choice, he preferred to be alone. But a quality about the evening, the light from the dying sun slanting in through the window and the mist gathering like smoke among the trees, had filled him with a strange and unaccountable melancholy. He had suddenly wanted company and, in particular, hers.

It was an urge which exasperated him with its vague, irrational longings. Why her, for God's sake? She was not even particularly attractive. Short, square-browed with dark hair cropped close to her head, she made few concessions to feminine beauty. In fact, on first meeting her, soon after he had moved to the village, he had disliked her. There was a quiet, ironic watchfulness about her manner, as if she were silently summing him up and dismissing him, which he had found disconcerting. When he had registered at the surgery, he had made damn sure that he was put on Dr Wade's list of patients, not hers. He had no intention of submitting himself to her small, cool, professional hands.

And yet, seeing her about the village and meeting her on various occasions, he had found his opinion of her subtly changing, almost against his will, not that Dr Livesey had made any attempt to influence his attitude. But, little by little, he had found himself thinking that perhaps, after all, she possessed an attractiveness of her own. Even though he still could not call it pretty, her face had a strength about the jaw and forehead and a directness in the level brows and dark eyes which, despite himself, he came to admire. She was the type, he decided, who wasn't afraid to speak her mind and that kind of honesty was, in his experience, rarely found. There was, too, a no-nonsense practicality in her manner which matched his own. She got on with the business of living without complaining or wishing things were different, his attitude exactly.

It was this frankness of hers which had given him the excuse to call on her. He wanted her opinion about a letter he had written but which he had hesitated to send. On one level, his motives were entirely genuine. He would indeed welcome her comments as a newcomer to the village like himself, who had no partisan feelings about the matter. On another level, however, he knew that such reasoning was only a subterfuge to visit her and that he was perfectly capable of coming to a decision on his own.

But, having given into the impulse to drive to her house, it seemed absurd to turn the car round and go home, although he got out of the driver's seat reluctantly, slamming the door behind him with more force than was necessary, expressing his exasperation with himself.

She was surprised to see him standing on the doorstep, raising her eyebrows at him although she invited him inside.

'Come through to the sitting-room,' she said, going ahead of him.

He followed awkwardly. The cottage was tiny, a doll's house of a place, better suited to her proportions than his for he was a big, ungainly man, broad-shouldered and more at ease, anyway, in the open air than indoors. Ducking his head to accommodate the low doorway, he was suddenly aware of his physical size, feeling clumsy and big-booted, although the homely clutter of her sitting-room comforted him a little. Like his own, it was untidy, with papers strewn across a plain, workmanlike desk where a metal reading lamp was angled to shine down on them, while a couple of baggy armchairs were drawn up on either side of the fireplace.

'Sit down,' she told him.

'No, I mustn't stay long,' he replied. Absurdly, now he was there, he wanted to be gone as soon as possible. Fishing in his pocket, he took out the sheet of paper. 'I called to ask your opinion of this.' As she unfolded it and began to read, he continued, 'I'm not sure whether I ought to send it. It could make things a bit awkward with the Hamiltons and I don't want that to happen. On the other hand . . .' He broke off as she finished reading and looked up from the letter. 'What do you think?' he asked quickly. 'Does it sound reasonable to you? I mean, you know them both but you're not exactly involved very closely with either of them, and as an outsider . . .'

He stopped again. It wasn't at all how he had intended expressing himself, although to his relief she seemed to understand his meaning.

'I can give an unbiased opinion,' she remarked, concluding the sentence for him. Handing the letter back, she went on, 'I can't see anything objectionable in it. After all, you're within your legal rights, and as David Hamilton's a solicitor I imagine he'd be prepared to discuss the suggestion objectively. If there is a problem, it won't come from him. It'll be from his father-in-law.'

'Oh, Felix Napier,' Steven Bradley said gloomily. He folded the letter up and returned it to his pocket, aware that she was watching him with an amused interest.

'You're still not on speaking terms with him?' she asked.

'He does a sharp right-about-turn whenever he sees me coming,' Bradley replied. She began to smile and he smiled back, grateful for her ability to make him see the funny side of the situation. 'Yes, it is ridiculous,' he agreed. 'If only he'd be prepared to talk to me, I'd willingly apologize. I admit I was damn rude to him, although it was infuriating having him keep turning up at the kennels. I know my ideas are different from his, but I've had to make changes. You can't run a business these days on sentiment. It's not a word that figures much in my bank manager's vocabulary.'

'Why don't you speak to Elizabeth Hamilton?' Ruth Livesey suggested. 'She and her father are very close and I'm sure, if you asked for her help, she'd smooth things out.'

'Yes. Well.'

Bradley let it pass. He wasn't sure that he wanted to involve Elizabeth Hamilton in his controversy with her father although she had always been friendly towards him and, as his immediate neighbour, had made him feel welcome. For this, he was genuinely grateful. At the same time, he had the uncomfortable feeling that there were certain subtle dangers in being drawn too closely into her orbit. Recognizing her physical beauty, he was aware of the old, fatal attraction of the moth for the flame and, naturally cautious where women were concerned, he had hung back. Besides, he knew his own limitations, and making himself charming and sociable was not one of them. And that, he suspected, was what Elizabeth Hamilton expected of him.

It was another reason for his growing admiration for Ruth Livesey. Her relationships would be, he imagined, as uncomplicated and as forthright as herself, although he doubted if any man had so far attracted her very deeply. He had the impression that she was too discriminating and critical to commit herself easily.

'So you think I should send the letter as it stands?' he asked, changing the subject back to the one which had brought him there in the first place. 'You wouldn't suggest any changes?'

He realized his mistake as soon as he finished speaking. She gave a quick gesture of impatience at what she took to be his obtuseness.

'Haven't I said so?'

'Yes, I suppose you have,' he agreed. He felt awkward again, too big and clumsy for the tiny room. He had intended rounding off the visit by suggesting he bought her a drink at the White Hart, or by asking her over to the kennels one morning for coffee as a form of thanking her for her advice, but he could see that he had fumbled the situation and lost his chance. 'Well, then, I'd better get going,' he added, making a balls-up even of his exit line as he moved towards the hall. 'Thanks for your help.'

'Any time,' she said in an ironic voice and, as he left, she shut the front door briskly behind him, leaving him with the uncomfortable realization that he had been a fool to come.

Felix sat forward in one of the armchairs in Elizabeth's drawing-room, rubbing his hands to get the blood moving before holding them out to the head of the log fire. For the sake of the pale carpet, he was in his stockinged feet, his boots having been abandoned in the kitchen together with poor old Percy, although Elizabeth had sweetened the dog's exile with a plate of liver.

He was alone in the room, Elizabeth having gone out to prepare tea while David was in the study, answering a telephone call which had come for him almost as soon as they had re-entered the house from the afternoon's shoot. It seemed he was not to be left in peace even on a Saturday.

As he waited for their return, Felix looked about him, familiarizing himself again with some of the better pieces of furniture from Paddocks which he had given to his daughter and son-in-law when he had sold up to Bradley and moved out. He didn't exactly regret having parted with them. At the time, it had seemed the right decision to make. He had wanted to take as little as possible with him to remind him of his former life and, besides, he had the gratification of sharing in Elizabeth's and David's pleasure in owning them while he was still alive to enjoy it. After his death, and theirs too, although he did not like to think about such things too deeply, he assumed the furniture and porcelain would be passed on in turn to their children – at least, he imagined they would start a family one of these days – and it gave him added pleasure to think that his grandchildren might be sitting in a room, perhaps like this one, surrounded by the same objects which had been handed down to him through his own grandparents.

So many generations! he thought.

The room was beautiful, a perfect setting for the antiques. In fact, they looked better than they had at Paddocks where the rooms had been smaller and it had not been possible to display them to advantage. Now, placed in Elizabeth's pale, exquisitely simple drawing-room, the rosewood seemed to glow more deeply, the *famille rose* china taking on richer subtleties of colour against the white walls. But Elizabeth had always had this gift of endowing everything about her, even inanimate objects, with some of her own beauty.

She entered the room at that moment and Felix broke off his train of thought to help her place the tray on the low table in front of the fire. 'Walnut cake!' he said appreciatively,

She patted his wrist affectionately. 'Made especially for you this morning.'

'Do you remember . . .' he began and then hesitated. He didn't like to play this remembering game too often, although seeing the familiar furniture about the room had reminded him of other occasions of tea taken round the fire, when Elizabeth had been a child, at which walnut cake had also been a special treat. The china was Helen's, too – the Coalport set.

He was spared the embarrassment of having to complete the sentence by the arrival of David, who came in holding an envelope and frowning a little at the front of it.

'It was lying on the hall mat,' he explained. 'Someone must have delivered it by hand.'

'Whose writing is it?' Elizabeth asked, looking up from pouring tea for the three of them.

'Steven Bradley's, by the look of it,' David replied. He

sounded distracted as he tore open the envelope and took out the letter it contained. Having read it, he passed it to Felix without any comment, although Felix was aware that David was watching his face as he waited for his reaction.

'*Dear David*,' he read, noting that the handwriting like the man himself, was large and awkward, lacking refinement. '*I should be grateful if you could spare a few hours at some time in the near future to discuss with me the right of way over my land. I have been thinking over the possibility of extending the kennels by building a boarding unit for cats and, should planning permission be granted, it might be necessary to cut down part of the spinney and to consider closing off the access into Gade's Lane for reasons of security.*

'*Naturally, I shall take no action until I have discussed this fully with you and your wife. Yours sincerely, Steven Bradley.*'

'The damned nerve!' Felix said, putting down the sheet of paper. He didn't know at which part of Bradley's letter to direct his anger first – at the proposed closing of the right of way, the removal of the spinney, or the new boarding unit. Cats! And to think that Bradley had refused to go on running the breeding kennels! The whole business was so bloody outrageous that he could barely articulate his rage.

'Let me read it,' Elizabeth requested, holding out her hand and, as he passed the letter to her, Felix was at last able to speak with some coherence.

'You'll refuse, of course,' he said, addressing David. 'The man can't deny you access to the lane. That right of way is marked on the plans. He knew damned well it was there when he bought the premises. As for cutting down the spinney . . .'

'He says only part of it,' David pointed out.

'And it is very overgrown in places,' Elizabeth added. She had finished reading the letter which she placed in her lap.

Felix looked at them both, baffled by their reaction. Their reasonableness seemed to him a form of betrayal.

'But surely you're not going to agree to any of these ridiculous suggestions?' he demanded.

'I'll have to talk it over with Bradley, of course,' David replied. 'Quite honestly, I can't see the point in turning the man down flat when he's had the courtesy to let us know about his plans well in advance.'

'But the right of way!' Felix protested. 'He can't by law close that without getting your permission.'

'David knows that, daddy,' Elizabeth put in. 'After all, he is a solicitor. He's dealing with rights of way and footpaths and that sort of thing every day of the week.' She spoke lightly as if trying to defuse the situation. 'Besides, we hardly ever use the path, do we, David?'

'We used it this afternoon' Felix interrupted. 'Anyway, that's not the point. The fact is that a right of way has existed for God knows how many years and yet Bradley, a relative newcomer to the village, thinks he has the authority . . .' He stopped abruptly, afraid he might say something he would regret later. 'As for this new unit he proposes building,' he continued, taking up the other point which also rankled, although he could not bring himself to specify its exact use, 'all I can say is, I shall write to Bradley myself, expressing the strongest objections.'

'You'll do no such thing, daddy,' Elizabeth said. Her tone of voice was sharp, startling Felix and also David. Felix saw his son-in-law look at her in surprise and, he thought, a little impatiently – as if annoyed that she had chosen to take part in what was, after all, men's affairs. 'I shall be very cross if you do. The decision is between David and Steven. It's their property now and they must be left alone to discuss what's done with it on their own. As far as the right of way's concerned, I don't think it really matters, do you, David?' She looked at her husband in quick appeal. 'If we need access into the lane, we could always make a new opening in the hedge at the end of our garden although we so rarely use the existing path anyway, it's hardly worth the trouble. As for the spinney, if David makes it clear that the best of the trees are to be left standing, I should have thought that getting rid of some of the undergrowth would improve it. All those nettles and brambles are a dreadful eyesore. You could write that into an agreement couldn't you, David? I mean about the trees.'

'Yes, of course,' he replied, although he didn't sound as enthusiastic about the idea as she did. 'I'd also make sure that the boarding unit, assuming it was built, was well screened off from our part of the land with a new hedge of fence. But I'd need to think about it first before talking it over with Bradley.'

'There, you see, daddy!' Elizabeth remarked, smiling at Felix. 'It's not as bad as you imagined, is it? Now have some walnut cake and cheer up.'

Felix accepted the proffered plate, although he found it more difficult to comply with her other suggestion. It was impossible to cheer up. He felt oddly humbled by her remark about the property being David's and Bradley's, although she was quite correct, of course. He had resigned all legal rights to it when he had divided up the land, handing over the deeds first to her and David and then, on completing the sale of the rest of the premises, to Bradley. All the same, it wasn't easy to give up the sense of continuing ownership. Some roots went too deep to be entirely eradicated. He was disappointed and hurt that she could not appreciate this fact and that she and David seemed to be taking Bradley's side over the matter. Their attitude struck him as disloyal, although he would never dream of telling them so. All the bitterness and anger was directed at Bradley who, after all, had been responsible for the whole affair in the first place. Despite his promise to Elizabeth, Felix was damned if he'd apologize to the man. It was asking too much.

As if aware of his thoughts, Elizabeth said coaxingly, 'You'll be nice to him, won't you, daddy, when you meet him at the party next Saturday? You promised you would be. Remember?'

Felix put his plate down carefully on the table and sat upright, trying to modulate his voice so that he, too, would sound reasonable and dispassionate.

'I'm sorry, Elizabeth,' he said with controlled and deliberate politeness, 'but if that man is a guest in your house, then I shall have to decline the invitation. I have no wish to meet Bradley under any circumstances. And now I think I ought to be going. Don't get up. I shall see myself out. Thank you for the tea, my dear. The walnut cake was delicious.'

He rose to his feet, aware of their faces turned towards him, Elizabeth's expression hurt and surprised, David's sombre. He hated leaving them on this note of disagreement but it was a matter of principle and, for that reason, he was prepared to risk their disapproval.

At the same time, he was pleased with the way he had handled the situation. He had remained calm and in control although, as he padded across to the door, he could have wished he was not in his stockinged feet. They hardly lent the right touch of dignity to his departure.

4

Kate's first reaction was to refuse the invitation to Elizabeth Hamilton's party when Dodie told her about it at mid-morning break at school the week before.

'But I hardly know her!' she protested. 'Why should she ask me?'

She suspected that Dodie had somehow persuaded the woman to include her among her guests on the strength of that fleeting roadside meeting the other Sunday in order to re-establish Kate's acquaintanceship with Felix Napier, brief though that had also been; although Dodie assured her that she was as much surprised as Kate herself. She certainly seemed genuinely astonished, as well as gratified on Kate's behalf, by the invitation.

'I honestly don't know. It seems she took a liking to you when she met you on that Sunday afternoon. Oh, do come, Kate,' Dodie urged. 'It'll be fun. Elizabeth's parties usually are.'

In the end, Kate agreed, more out of curiosity than for any other motive, intrigued to meet again a woman who, after the mere exchange of a few pleasantries, should consider her worth further acquaintance. After all, to be picked out in this manner was a form of flattery. A charming note from Elizabeth Hamilton which Dodie delivered the following day, written presumably after Dodie had voiced Kate's objections, finally persuaded her to accept. It, too, had urged her to come. 'Both David and I love meeting new people,' it had concluded. On reading it, Kate had capitulated. It seemed churlish to do otherwise.

So she found herself on the following Saturday evening, the

night of the party, back in Woodstone and following the Pagetts into the hall of the Hamiltons' house where Dodie introduced her to her unknown host and her hostess whom she hardly knew any better.

Seeing Elizabeth Hamilton at closer quarters, Kate was aware of the charm implied in Dodie's warm enthusiasm for the woman, and which Kate herself had been conscious of during their brief introduction the previous week. There was an animation about Elizabeth Hamilton which turned even the prosaic business of shaking hands into a special occasion, for she possessed that magical quality of making each individual feel that he or she was uniquely welcome.

'I'm so pleased you could come,' she said, holding Kate's hand in both of hers as she spoke. 'I told Dodie she mustn't let you refuse.'

Yes, it was a form of magic, Kate decided, smiling back. And she had been right, too, in thinking that Elizabeth Hamilton was beautiful, although her beauty was only the physical manifestation of her appeal. It was in her vivacity, her easy self-confidence, her ability to radiate little currents of light and air around her with every gesture, that her real attraction lay.

She shimmered; there was no other word for it. Later, as the party continued and Elizabeth moved about her drawing-room among her guests, Kate found herself watching her on several occasions, trying to analyse what gave her this special charisma. It was this shining quality of hers, she decided; not just of hair and eyes and skin but in the sheen of her dress, the sparkle from her earrings and the loops of fine gold chains round her throat, the bloom of light which seemed to surround her.

In contrast, everyone else seemed solid and dull, earthbound mortals who stood about the room, feet firmly planted on the carpet while Elizabeth fluttered among them, visiting each in turn.

Even her husband seemed prosaic although, on meeting him, Kate had liked his serious, dark good looks. She could understand now Dodie's remark about his ability to listen. He had the habit of leaning slightly forward when in conversation, as if anxious to catch every word that was said to him, his expression intent. He was perhaps a little too earnest. Kate could not imagine him taking anything lightly, although when he gave one of his slow smiles, his features became almost boyish. He had certain youthful mannerisms as well which had their own appeal – a trick of brushing his hand over the back of his head or of running one finger round and round the rim of the glass of wine he was holding, as if he found its circle comforting in some way.

There were about twenty people in the room, most of them from the village although a few were, like her, from Framden. Dodie, taking on the role of deputy hostess when Elizabeth Hamilton was busy elsewhere among her guests, introduced Kate to some of them – a small, dark-haired woman with very straight, sarcastic eyebrows who was, Kate gathered, one of the local doctors, and a tall, awkward man, Steven Bradley, the Hamiltons' next-door neighbour who had taken over the kennels from Felix Napier.

And Felix Napier himself, of course. Dodie made quite sure that Kate was re-introduced to him. Holding Kate firmly by the elbow, she steered her across the room to where he was standing on the far side, looking, as Kate had to admit, rather distinguished in a dinner jacket and black bow tie.

'You remember Kate Denby?' Dodie asked.

'Of course,' Felix Napier replied, holding out a hand and directing his bright blue gaze at her. 'I'm delighted to meet you again.'

The remark wasn't made entirely out of politeness. Felix was genuinely pleased to see her. It was relief, mostly. As a stranger to the village and therefore ignorant of any local gossip and tensions, she gave him the opportunity to talk naturally without having to keep up the ridiculous pretence that, despite all appearances to the contrary, he was not avoiding Steven Bradley's company.

In spite of his determination to refuse an invitation to Elizabeth's party if Bradley was to be among the guests, he had been coaxed by Elizabeth into changing his mind although, now that he was there, Felix regretted having been persuaded to come. He had even shaken hands with Bradley and exchanged a few remarks with the man before, with a brief nod, he had moved away with the excuse of getting himself a glass of white wine. Since then he had been careful not to trespass on that part of the room where Bradley had installed himself, deliberately choosing his own circuit so that their paths did not cross, although he had felt uneasy that other guests, who knew them both, must have been aware of these evasive tactics.

The arrival of Dodie's friend, Kate Denby – and he listened carefully to the surname this time to make sure of getting it right – was therefore in the nature of a diversion. He could now turn his back on Bradley and engage her in conversation, secure in the knowledge that she knew nothing about his quarrel with the man.

He was pleasantly surprised, too, at her appearance. When he had first met her, he had not considered her remarkable enough to remember afterwards any detail about her. But, concentrating his attention on her now in his effort to forget Bradley, he saw that she was, after all, rather attractive although he couldn't for the life of him understand why Elizabeth had compared her to Ruth Livesey. There was nothing intimidating about Dodie's colleague; none of that sharp, cropped edge which he found so antipathetic in the Livesey woman, although both of them were obviously intelligent. Dodie's friend Kate Denby had a much more engaging air about her, amused and ready to be amused, with an alert, interested expression and dark brown hair which, if he remembered rightly, hadn't been worn in this loose, casual style at their first meeting but more – and he fumbled for the right word – tucked back. She had a good neck, too, he noticed. It was always the first detail about a woman's appearance to catch his attention; that, and the hands. Her neck was firm and steady, holding her head at an agreeable relaxed angle, neither too aggressive nor defensive, while her hands were expressive without being over-mobile. He disliked fidgety women. They made him nervous himself.

'I believe you teach English,' he remarked which, if not exactly original, at least had the merit of setting the conversational ball into motion, although he had to cast about in his mind for some other comment to add. It was years since his own schooldays, and he assumed that the curriculum had changed. They probably studied more modern writers these days, James

Joyce and Iris Murdoch and Tom Stoppard, not the classics which had formed the backbone of his own studies. 'Does that include pupils who are going in for the examination – what's it called nowadays? It was School Certificate in mine.'

'GCE O Level,' Kate corrected him. 'Yes, I teach that, and A level as well – Higher School Certificate as it used to be called. In fact, it's not all that different. They still have set books to study, as well as précis and comprehension.'

She made the remark in order to close the gap between them, for Felix Napier seemed over-conscious of his age as if trying to set himself apart as a man well past his prime, which wasn't the case at all.

'Good Lord! Set books!' He sounded surprised. 'I remember we did *Henry IV, Part One*, the Romantic poets and *Persuasion*.'

'Then it's very much the same,' she assured him. 'This year it's *Hamlet*, and *Pride and Prejudice*, although the poetry's a modern anthology. No Keats and Shelley, I'm afraid.'

He was quick, she noticed, to pick up the reference to Jane Austen.

'*Pride and Prejudice?*' he repeated. 'I'm pleased to hear it, although I shouldn't have thought she'd have much appeal for today's youngsters. How do they take Miss Austen's humour?'

'Much as any other pupils have always done, I imagine,' she replied, amused by his old-fashioned courtesy in the use of the name 'Miss Austen', as well as by his assumption that contemporary schoolchildren were totally different from those of his own generation. 'The brighter ones appreciate the irony, although it takes some explaining to the more obtuse.'

'Marvellous writer!' Felix Napier commented, half to himself.

'I enjoy reading her,' Kate agreed, surprised by his obvious enthusiasm. She hadn't imagined that this man with his country-squire air, vaguely doggy and horsey, would have appreciated an author like Jane Austen – which in turn made her just as guilty as he, she realized, in jumping to conclusions.

So much, she thought, for first impressions. She had obviously been quite wrong about him.

'You've read the new edition of her letters?' Felix Napier was asking. 'It was published only a few weeks ago. There's a very good introduction; well worth reading.'

'No; I haven't been able to get hold of it yet,' Kate replied. 'I've tried the library in Framden and the bookshops, but none of them had a copy. They've promised to order one but it may take some time.'

'Then you must borrow mine.'

'I wouldn't dream . . .' Kate began. As she disliked lending her own books, his offer seemed too generous and impulsive.

'It's no trouble,' he assured her. 'I could post it to you or, if you prefer, you could drop by the house any time you're visiting Dodie and pick it up.'

Kate hesitated, glancing across the room to where Dodie was standing with her husband, talking to Elizabeth Hamilton, and was suddenly disconcerted by the expression on Mike's face. He was watching Elizabeth with a look of such longing and desire that Kate was startled by it. Neither of the two women seemed aware of it. Dodie, happily oblivious, was laughing at someone Elizabeth was saying, throwing back her head as Elizabeth joined in the laughter. Their shared amusement seemed to make Mike's expression appear even more shockingly licentious. His bearded face, Kate thought, looked like a satyr's positively goatish.

Distracted by it, she turned back to Felix Napier, saying quickly, 'Yes, thank you, that's very kind of you.'

She had meant the remark to refer to his offer to post the book to her and was further confused when he seemed to take her answer as an acceptance of his invitation to call at his house for he replied, 'Whenever it suits you, although I suppose, as you're teaching, it'll have to be at the week-end?'

It was too late to draw back. To do so would not only add to the confusion but make her appear discourteous and Kate, trying to gather up her thoughts, had no option except to say, 'It's half-term holiday next week. I could call any day.' She recovered enough good sense to add, 'Would Tuesday afternoon suit you?'

She knew that the Pagetts were going out for the day on Tuesday to visit Dodie's sister in Ipswich, Dodie having mentioned the arrangement at school. It seemed the simplest way out of an already embarrassing situation. At least if she made it Tuesday, Kate thought, she wouldn't be obliged to call on Dodie and, by explaining the reason for her visit to Woodstone, add yet another complication; although the decision caused her a pang of guilt. By avoiding Dodie, she felt she was adding her own form of betrayal to Mike's.

'Come for tea,' Felix Napier suggested.

'Yes, thank you,' she agreed.

'You know where I live, of course?'

'Yes,' she repeated.

She felt incapable of saying anything more on the subject and, to give Felix Napier his due, he was sensitive enough to be aware of this for, apart from remarking, 'I'll expect you about three o'clock, shall I?' he referred no more to the proposed visit, shifting the conversation to another topic.

Shortly afterwards they were separated anyway, Elizabeth Hamilton coming up to them and leading Kate away to be introduced to a man who ran an antique shop in Framden and who, it seemed, was enthusiastic not only about the furniture in the room – 'Some splendid pieces! Fetch a small fortune on the open market' – but about their hostess as well.

'Isn't she marvellous?' he asked Kate.

'Yes, isn't she?' Kate agreed, trying to match his eagerness with her own and to suppress a small stirring of envy at Elizabeth Hamilton's ability to attract men's attention like bees to a honey-pot.

First Mike and now this man, she thought. And Elizabeth Hamilton wasn't even trying as far as she could judge, merely moving about the room being vivacious and charming to everyone, men and women alike.

She did not mind this stranger's interest in Felix Napier's daughter as much as Mike's. It didn't imply the same quality of betrayal, and as they talked Kate glanced across at Dodie several times to reassure herself that she was still unaware of Mike's treachery. But, to Kate's relief, Dodie was chatting away cheerfully to whoever was listening and quite clearly enjoying herself.

Dead old Dodie! Kate thought with affection. She was wearing one of her ethnic dresses, an Indian print with dabs of gold paint spattered across the fabric, too bunchy in the skirt to be flattering, her gypsy ear-rings which swung every time she turned her head and kept getting caught up in her hair, and a long necklace of hand-carved wooden beads which were looped across the ample curve of her breasts to bump against her stomach.

Seen objectively – or perhaps with Mike's eyes? Kate asked herself – she cut a freakish, slightly ridiculous figure in comparison with Elizabeth Hamilton's gleaming elegance, although as the thought crossed her mind Kate felt angry with herself for having committed another small act of disloyalty. Excusing herself from the man with the antique shop, she crossed the room to Dodie's side, slipping a hand into her arm.

'You're not going already?' Dodie asked, pleased at the sign of affection as well as disappointed at Kate's obvious intention to leave.

'I must, Dodie. I don't want to be too late getting back to Framden. I've got a pile of sixth-form essays still to mark.'

'But it's half-term next week,' Dodie protested. 'You'll have all the time in the world to catch up with marking. Do stay a little longer.'

'Shall we meet for coffee one morning over the holiday?' Kate suggested, turning aside Dodie's appeal to her to stay. 'What about Wednesday morning at Frazer's at, say, eleven?' and giving Dodie's arm a final squeeze, she moved away to say good-bye to Elizabeth and David Hamilton, noticing that some of the other guests, including the woman doctor with the short dark hair and Steven Bradley, the Hamiltons' neighbour, had already left. Felix Napier was still there but on the far aide of the room with his back to her, which relieved her of the obligation of taking her farewell of him. As for Mike, she merely nodded to him as if to an acquaintance before going into the hall and up the stairs to collect her coat from the Hamilton's bedroom.

She had to dig about to find it under a pile of other coats which had been placed on the bed. And what a large, comfortable bed it was, too! It seemed symbolic of the Hamiltons' marriage, Kate thought, in its expansive, agreeable contentment, feeling the mattress give softly under its deeply flounced cover of glazed chintz. Her tweed coat with its small, neat collar and sensible pockets seemed out of place in such a setting, and as she put it on, buttoning it up briskly, she knew, without so much as glancing at her reflection in Elizabeth Hamilton's long mirror, that she herself didn't 'go' with the room either, with its silk-shaded lamps and crystal fittings.

The notion struck her as absurd and she smiled as she went to the door and let herself out on to the landing.

It ran in an L-shaped gallery along two sides of the upper floor, allowing her to look down into the hall, and as she walked along it towards the top of the stairs she was aware that two other people, Felix Napier and his son-in-law, David Hamilton, were standing at its foot talking together. Rather than disturb them, she retreated back towards the bedroom, overhearing only part of their conversation.

Felix Napier was saying, 'I'm delighted you've changed your mind about Bradley's proposal, David. It's about time someone put that confounded man in his place.'

'It's not quite as you think, Felix. There's something else that's come up which I can't discuss with you now.'

As she reached the bedroom door, Kate heard Felix Napier say, 'Oh?' on a note of surprise, before adding, 'Shall I ring you on Tuesday? We could talk about it then.'

'No, not Tuesday. I'm over at Millbridge on Tuesdays.'

'Of course. I'd forgotten. I'll make it Wednesday then . . .'

At that point, the door closed behind her and Kate heard no more. By the time she had waited a few minutes and re-emerged from the bedroom, they had gone. At least, David Hamilton had disappeared, presumably back to the drawing-room to rejoin his guests. Felix Napier was at the front door on the point of letting himself out, although as Kate appeared at the top of the stairs he paused and waited for her.

'You're going, too?' he asked, stepping aside to allow her to leave first. 'Enjoyed the party?'

'Yes, very much,' Kate replied. 'It was charming of your daughter to ask me.'

She hoped he wouldn't engage her on the doorstep in a last little burst of small talk. It was one of those cold, clear nights with a breath of frost in the air, a fact which Felix Napier seemed to appreciate as well for he remarked, 'It's too chilly to keep you standing about. Goodnight, Miss Denby. I'll look forward to seeing you on Tuesday afternoon,' and, with a courteous wave of one hand, he crossed the drive to where his Range Rover was parked. Getting in, he drove away.

Kate waited until his car had reached the end of the drive and had turned left before following after him, taking the righ-hand turn towards the village and the main road to Framden.

Glancing up at his rear mirror, Felix saw the tail lights of her car disappear in the opposite direction.

Nice woman, he thought. He was looking forward to Tuesday and the chance to talk to her again about Jane Austen.

But at the moment, he had more urgent considerations on his mind. Although he was delighted at David's decision to turn down Bradley's proposal, he was puzzled about the 'other consideration' which David had hinted at and which had caused him to change his mind. As far as he could see, there was only one – stopping Bradley from getting his own way and, with the law on his side regarding the right of access, Felix couldn't for the life of him think what other reasons David might have been referring to.

He knew what he'd do if he were in David's shoes – write a stiff letter to Bradley refusing to allow the footpath to be closed and, at the same time pointing out that he would object strongly to planning permission being granted for any new building. And that would be that.

All the same, he felt a twinge of conscience as the thought crossed his mind. His conversation with Elizabeth and David the previous Saturday afternoon after the shoot had made him realize that to others his attitude could appear unreasonable. Perhaps he was reacting too strongly and his dislike for the man was beginning to take on the nature of a witch-hunt? He didn't want to hound Bradley; simply to put him in his place. Perversely, now that David seemed about to refuse Bradley's request, Felix was more inclined to come round to the other point of view and see the situation as Elizabeth had pointed it out to him. After all, if they used the footpath only infrequently, did it matter all that much if it were closed?

He broke off his thoughts, concentrating on slowing down and changing gear before taking the sharp right-hand turn into Brookhouse Lane which led up the hill past the Pagetts' place to his own house.

The answer was, he told himself, that he really had no right to interfere, a change of heart he couldn't exactly account for himself, although it had something to do with Miss Denby, Dodie's friend. For some extraordinary reason, he saw her face quite clearly for a second or two, smiling in agreement as they talked about Jane Austen. A certain remembered quality about her expression, pleasant, agreeable and – he searched his mind for the right word – eminently *sensible*, seemed to make all this fuss about Bradley appear rather mean-minded and trivial.

Were Bradley and the kennels so important to him after all? Life had to go on.

All the same, he was intrigued to know what had made David change his mind and he looked forward to discussing the matter fully with his son-in-law when he rang him on Wednesday.

Bradley carried his glass of whisky into the sitting-room and put it down on the desk among the clutter of bills and papers – his excuse for leaving the Hamiltons' party early, although it had the merit of being partly true. It was getting near the end of the month, the time when he usually did his accounts. He wrote a few cheques, addressed the envelopes to put them in, and then abandoned the task. The rest could wait until the following day. The sound of cars leaving the Hamiltons' place next door disturbed his concentration and reminded him of the evening's failure from his point of view.

He didn't much care for parties at the best of times and would have declined the invitation if he hadn't been anxious to show neighbourliness, especially towards David Hamilton, and simply by turning up to remind him of the letter which he had delivered by hand the previous Saturday. He had heard nothing in the meantime, apart from a typewritten acknowledgement sent through the post on Hamilton's office paper, merely stating that the matter regarding the right of way was under consideration and agreeing that the two of them should discuss it further. It had been couched in the formal language that solicitors tend to use, although the closing words 'Yours sincerely, David Hamilton' had been written by hand.

Nothing more had been said that evening either, Hamilton simply remarking, 'I haven't forgotten about your letter, Steven. We must get together some time.' Not that Bradley had expected a full-blown discussion there and then. But he had hoped for a more positive reaction, if only a suggestion of a definite date when the two of them could meet.

Hamilton's attitude exasperated him for what he took to be its delaying tactics. It was typical of solicitors, he thought angrily. They seemed incapable of getting a move on, although in this particular instance he suspected Felix Napier might be responsible for the lack of action. Bradley could imagine him getting a lot of quiet satisfaction out of frustrating his plans over the kennels out of sheer bloody-mindedness.

Flinging down his pen, he got up abruptly from the desk in a sudden excess of impatience, swallowing down the rest of the whisky before going into the kitchen and letting himself out of the house by the back door.

It was a cold night but the sharpness of the air did nothing to cool his anger.

Damn David Hamilton! he thought, tramping past the kennels to the far end of his land. And sod Felix Napier!

He was angry also with himself. If he hadn't gone to that bloody party, he wouldn't have had to shake hands with the man and pretend to be friendly; not that Napier had put himself out to be sociable. Apart from that brief handshake and a couple of conventional remarks, Napier had deliberately avoided him for the rest of the evening. It must have been obvious to everyone.

Even Ruth Livesey's presence hadn't been much of a comfort. Although they had talked, their conversation had been impersonal, mainly concerned with her difficulty in getting a replacement from the local garage for a cracked wing-mirror on her car as if, by choosing such a banal subject, she had been deliberately trying to keep him at arm's length. She, too, had left early, even before he had done, giving the excuse that she was on call the following day – although he suspected that, like him, she didn't much care for such social gatherings.

He reached the spinney and crunched along the path over the fallen leaves to the gap in the hedge which bounded his property and which opened out into Gade's Lane, where, with a gesture of angry defiance, he kicked out at the piled-up brambles and small branches which he had cut down during the week and had left at the side of the path, scattering them into the opening. If the Hamiltons were so bloody anxious to preserve the right of way, then they could sort that lot out, he thought. As they hardly ever used the path anyway, it would be a calculated act of unfriendliness to refuse him permission to close it. How the hell could he build the new unit unless the property was completely enclosed and secure? No insurance company would give him cover while that gap remained, especially as the new unit would be so far from the house. It was simply inviting intruders.

Turning abruptly on his heel, he walked back the way he had come, noticing lights in the upper windows of the Hamiltons' house, all he could see of their place above the high fir hedge which separated the two premises. The brightness streamed out, illuminating the branches of the nearby trees and giving a festive lustre to the mist which was beginning to gather, as if the building, like Elizabeth Hamilton herself, had the power to generate its own radiance. It seemed to symbolize the comfort and contentment which people like the Hamiltons and Felix Napier took so much for granted; that easy disregard for the needs of others outside their immediate circle. Even the number of lighted windows suggested a carelessness about such mundane, everyday concerns as the quarterly electricity bill which ordinary individuals like himself had to bear in mind.

It was all very well for them, he thought bitterly. They had it made.

Well, he wasn't going to give in that damned easily over the right of way. He'd wait a few days and then tackle David Hamilton again on the subject; although, remembering Ruth Livesey's advice, it might be better to play a more subtle game and get Elizabeth Hamilton on his side first, even though such deviousness went against the grain.

5

The following Tuesday morning, the weather broke in a sudden violent storm of rain and wind, marking the end of the Indian summer. It took Steven Bradley by surprise. He had begun to work on the spinney soon after he had fed the dogs. On Tuesdays the kennels were closed for business to make up for the fact that they were open over the week-end, including Sundays, and Bradley usually spent part of this day off catching up with chores around the grounds.

He had decided to carry on with the task of clearing the undergrowth in the spinney although he could very well have left it. He had still had no response from David Hamilton nor seen anything of his neighbours since the party on Saturday. He had done nothing, either, about approaching Elizabeth Hamilton, having decided not to seek her out. If they met, he might casually introduce the subject of the right of way, but he felt the ball was now in Hamilton's court and he was damned if he'd put himself in the position of seeming over-eager. He'd rather sit it out until Hamilton made the next move, although by continuing to clear the spinney he hoped he would give Hamilton the hint that he hadn't given up. The job needed doing anyway. The brambles and nettles were beginning to spread across the path.

He enjoyed the work. The task of hacking a way through the tangle of small bushes and briars suited his mood. It had a satisfyingly destructive quality about it and it amused him to rake the pile of debris close to the opening into Gade's Lane so that the gap was partially filled in although, aware of the legal niceties involved, he was careful not to close it off completely. He wasn't going to give David Hamilton the opportunity of protesting that he had contravened the law by denying him his right of access.

The wind began to rise, driving the clouds before it, and the first few heavy drops of rain fell as he was dragging the last bundle of brambles and nettles towards the hedge. Picking up his tools, he ran towards the house, stopping to lock up the kennels on his way. By the time he had done this, the storm had broken in a tumult of wind and driving rain.

There was no chance of finishing the spinney and he decided to go into Framden, instead, for a couple of hours. He needed more dog biscuits, anyway, which he could pick up at the Cash and Carry, as well as one or two items of personal shopping. He would also, he decided in a sudden flash of inspiration, remembering his conversation with Ruth Livesey at the Hamiltons' party, try to get a new wing-mirror for her car. If he went to the Renault dealer's in the town, he'd probably pick one up for her without any difficulty. He could then phone her when he got back and offer to put it on for her. She, too, had her free day on Tuesdays. With a little luck she would be at home and might be willing to come round to the kennels so that he could fix it straight away. If he timed it right, she might even be persuaded to stay for tea.

He'd stop off at Frazer's while he was in Framden, he added to himself, and buy a cake, just in case. The prospect of seeing her filled him with a sense of pleasurable anticipation. As an excuse, the idea was better than the one he had used of asking her advice over the letter to Hamilton.

Stopping to put the pruning knife and the bill-hook away in the small store-shed behind the office, he stripped off the heavy padded jacket he was wearing and the leather gloves, protection against the briars and thorns, and left them there as well. They were wet through and he didn't want to take them into the house in that condition, not while there was a chance that Ruth Livesey might call later in the day. Without stopping to lock the door, he ducked through the rain to the house where, after a quick wash and change, he got into the car and set off for Framden.

Some few hours later, Kate Denby also drove through the rain, only in the opposite direction away from Framden towards Woodstone in time for tea with Felix Napier.

It was just her luck, she thought, as she waited at the end of

Market Street for the traffic lights to change, that the weather which had been perfect all the weeks she had been at school should choose to break up at the beginning of half-term, just when she was free to enjoy it.

It was sod's law, she decided, putting the car into gear as the lights turned to green. In such a downpour, there was no chance of enjoying the view from the end of Felix Napier's garden for a second time.

As the thought crossed her mind, she caught a glimpse of Elizabeth Hamilton, Felix Napier's daughter, walking along on the opposite side of the road, fair hair gleaming even on such a grey afternoon, the yellow umbrella she was carrying adding its own touch of summer to the drag, wet street.

There was no opportunity to wave even if Kate had wanted Elizabeth Hamilton to be aware of her presence, which didn't much trouble her one way or the other. The line of traffic was moving forward and Elizabeth Hamilton had turned into Bruton Street, on her way, Kate assumed, to the library. Apart from being a short cut into the town centre, there was nothing else in that particular side road to attract a passer-by except for a few little shops, and as she headed towards the roundabout on the outskirts of the town Kate dismissed the incident as one of those small coincidences which happen from time to time but which are of no real significance.

The drive to Woodstone which she had been looking forward to was spoilt by the weather. The countryside looked desolate, its colours drenched, the verges littered with pieces of broken branch torn down by the wind during the morning when the storm had been at its height.

Passing Dodie's house, Kate felt a return of that pang of guilt which she had experienced when she had first arranged this meeting with Felix Napier at his daughter's party, knowing Dodie would be in Ipswich. It was an underhand way to behave, even though in the long run it saved embarrassment and explanation. It also struck Kate as ironic that, despite her intention not to let Dodie draw her into any involvement, here she was driving up Brookhouse Lane towards Felix Napier's house for an afternoon of tea and Jane Austen.

Sod's law again, she thought, plus my own stupidity.

It was still a comfort, nevertheless, to see that Mike and Dodie's house seemed to be shut up and that there was no sign of Mike's battered old van on the forecourt. At least in this one respect she seemed to have played her cards with some finesse.

Felix Napier welcomed her into the house with the same courtesy which she had come to realize was as much part of him as his erect carriage and direct blue gaze. He was, as her mother would have expressed it, one of nature's gentlemen; an absurd phrase but one which summed up the essence of the man. And no bad thing either, she found herself thinking.

They had tea in the drawing-room, overlooking the wet garden where a few bedraggled roses still clung on, although there were more roses in the room itself, arranged in a bowl on a low table where the tray was already waiting for her arrival, set with a silver tea-set and two very beautiful china cups and saucers. A log fire was burning in the fireplace and the combination of silver, china, flowers and flames made the room look less conventional than it had seemed on her first visit.

All the same, it was a surprise to be taken after tea was finished into his study. He showed her in shyly, like a schoolboy displaying a secret treasure, Kate thought, uncertain if it would be properly appreciated. But it was evident that the heart of the house, and his, too, was here in this room, and it seemed to her typical of the man that he should have chosen to put on public show in the drawing-room the conventional, formal side of his nature only, preserving the hidden, secret part for this smaller, private place.

It was lined with shelves of books and contained a few good pieces of antique furniture – a desk, a comfortable armchair, a cabinet of china, and another fire spouting flames into the chimney opening, a setting in which the dog Percy was evidently at home for, as they entered, he followed at their heels, going straight over to the hearth and lying down with a grunt of satisfaction in front of it as if in his accustomed place.

While Felix found the book of Jane Austen's letters which he had promised to lend her, Kate ran one hand gently over the T'ang horse which stood on the mantelshelf, enjoying the sensation of drawing its shape through her fingertips.

'It's beautiful,' she remarked, feeling the need to express her admiration if only to let him see that she was aware of the special privilege he had shown her by inviting her into this sanctum. Few people, she realized, would be allowed to visit it.

He turned, the book in his hand. His expression was difficult to read for, although he was smiling, the blue eyes contained a more distant, pained look as if he were remembering some past unhappiness.

'It's one of the few pieces I kept when I sold up,' he explained. 'I wanted Elizabeth and David to have the other things.'

So the antique furniture which the man from Framden had so much admired in Elizabeth's drawing-room had originally belonged to Felix Napier. Lucky Elizabeth! Kate found herself thinking. To those that have shall be given. She was certainly one of those people on whom life seemed to shower its gifts. The yellow umbrella which Kate remembered bobbing along so confidently through the rain in the direction of Bruton Street took on a symbolism of its own as that special, protective aura of good fortune which Elizabeth Hamilton seemed to carry with her everywhere, like her own personal patch of bright sunshine.

She was about to mention the brief glimpse she had caught of Elizabeth Hamilton in Framden on her way there, but Felix Napier was opening the book to show her its contents and Kate let the opportunity pass. It was a trivial incident, anyway; hardly worth mentioning.

'You see,' he was saying, turning over the pages with the careful eagerness of the genuine book-lover, 'it's extremely well produced and the index is excellent. It's the first thing I look at when choosing a reference book like this. If the index isn't up to scratch, I won't buy it.' Selecting a page, he gave her a quick, oblique glance over the top of the volume, inviting her to share his pleasure as he added, 'Listen to this. It's a letter she wrote to her niece, Fanny Knight, and is one of the best examples, I think, of her observation and wit.'

He began to read and Kate, who had taken the armchair by the fire at his invitation, settled back to listen, one hand fondling Percy's head, amused at his obvious and rather touchingly naive delight in sharing his enthusiasm while, at the same time and almost against her better judgement, finding herself drawn into the comfortable contentment of the firelit room, the rain shut away outside the window and Felix Napier's pleasantly modulated voice reading out loud to her.

It was dark and still raining when Dodie and Mike returned from Ipswich.

Scuttling through the downpour to open the front door before Mike got out of the van, Dodie was grateful to be home.

The visit had been a failure even before it began. At the last minute Mike had discovered that the van was low on petrol, and he had gone slamming out of the house to drive down to Leverett's garage to get the tank filled. The weather hadn't helped, either. It meant that, instead of going for a walk as she had planned, they had been forced to remain all day shut up in Fran's little house with the two children, also on half-term holiday, and this had got on Mike's nerves. Dodie loved the children; it had been partly the reason why she had chosen that particular week to make the visit, so that she could see them. And Fran, too, of course. She and her sister had always been close, although Dodie could understand how this family proximity, she and Fran chatting away non-stop and the kids being noisy as children always are when they can't go out to play, had made Mike grow more irritable and moody as the day progressed. He had hardly spoken to her on the drive home.

To make up for it, because Dodie felt she was in some obscure way responsible for the failure of the visit, even for the rain, she was more than usually cheerful, scurrying about to turn on the lights and put a match to the fire so that the sitting-room would look warm and cosy, before going through into the kitchen to heat up the vegetable soup which she had prepared in readiness for their return.

It should have been all right. The fire burned up cheerfully enough and they ate their supper in front of the blaze. But Mike refused to be coaxed into a better frame of mind and in the end Dodie gave up. Knowing him, the mood might continue for days, hanging over the house like its own dark raincloud, taking the joy out of everything.

Clearing up the plates after the meal and carrying them

through to the kitchen, Dodie dumped them in the sink, feeling a sudden, rare surge of anger on her own behalf.

Oh, let him go hang! she thought. It wasn't my fault that it bloody well rained and the kids made a racket. What else did he expect?

She was angry, too, at the kitchen. Fran's was properly equipped, all fitted units and nice flat working-tops. Even though it was small, helping Fran to get lunch had been a pleasure. Not like this damned place, she thought, dashing a piece of hair out of her eyes and looking about her at the makeshift shelves and the unplastered walls which Mike had intended covering with pine boarding. But that was three bloody years ago and he still hadn't got any further than putting up the battens.

Sod him! Sod the whole stupid house!

All the same, she was disappointed when, having finished the washing-up, she returned to the sitting-room to find him putting on his anorak.

'You're not going out?' she asked. 'Not in all this rain?'

'I thought I'd have a drink at the White Hart,' he replied casually, although he was careful not to look at her, Dodie noticed, and was making a great to-do about knocking out his pipe, showering ash over the rug.

'Please yourself,' Dodie said with an off-hand air.

Her reaction took him off guard. Even though she didn't turn to look at him, she could feel his surprised hesitation as he stood for a few moments, adjusting to her indifference before letting himself out of the room.

He can put that in his pipe, Dodie thought and started to laugh at the aptness of the image.

She heard him slam the front door shut and then the sound of the van engine as it coughed into life.

Let him go. She didn't care.

All the same, it didn't prevent her from glancing up at the clock and noticing that it was nearly half past eight so that it would be at least another two hours before he came home; and meanwhile, despite everything, the place seemed very empty and lonely without him.

6

Later that evening, Steven Bradley also checked the time, glancing at his watch. It was nearly a quarter past ten, almost too late to try ringing Ruth Livesey again, although, out of stubborness more than anything else, he decided to make one last attempt. If she still wasn't at home, he'd give up.

Since he had returned from Framden at two o'clock he'd been phoning her number on and off all afternoon and evening, the words he would say to her rehearsed over and over in his mind so many times that he knew them by heart.

'I've managed to get hold of a wing-mirror for you,' he'd say. *'Why don't you drop by and let me fix it on for you? It'll only take a few minutes and it'll save you having to take the car to the garage.'*

He'd even bought a chocolate gateau at Frazer's, hoping she'd come for tea. That had been a bloody waste of money, but it was just his luck, he thought angrily, as he dialled her number yet again. Nothing seemed to go right for him.

He heard the phone ring and ring in what he thought must still be an empty house, and was about to bang his receiver down when hers was lifted and he heard her voice, sounding a little sharp as if she were annoyed at receiving a call so late on her day off. 'Who is it?'

'It's me,' he said foolishly, surprised and unprepared. 'Steven Bradley.'

'Yes?' she asked, giving him no help at all and listening in silence as he stumbled through his prepared excuse.

'Although it's too late to put the wing-mirror on now,' he concluded. 'What about another day? Tomorrow perhaps?'

His reference to the time made Ruth Livesey look at the clock on her sitting-room mantelshelf. It was almost ten-fifteen. She had not long returned home from a tiring day in London and had hoped to go straight to bed. The last thing she wanted was to cope with Steven Bradley's overtures of friendship, however well meant.

He was like some over-eager dog, she thought, bounding up, ready to jump up at her with his great paws but easily sent away with his tail between his legs by a sharp word.

Aware of this, she said in a friendlier voice, 'That's very kind of you, Steven, although there was no need to go to all that bother. I had a new mirror put on the car this morning. But I'll pay you for the one you've bought, of course.'

'I wouldn't dream . . .' he began and then broke off to add unexpectedly, 'Good God! What was that?'

He sounded so startled that she asked, 'What's the matter?'

'I don't know. I've just heard a bang outside, like a gun going off. The dogs are kicking up a hell of a racket.'

'Then I'd better ring off,' Ruth replied, seizing the opportunity to replace her receiver.

Steven Bradley put down his own. He was exasperated that the call had ended so abruptly with no chance of making arrangements to meet her. He suspected, too, that she had been relieved by this.

All the same, he couldn't have just ignored the noise, nor the fact that it had disturbed the dogs.

Grabbing up his waterproof which hung on the back door and picking up the torch, he let himself out of the house.

It was dark and still pouring with rain. He could see the long shafts of it slanting down in the beam of the torch as he went the rounds of the kennels, checking they were securely locked and settling down the dogs which took several minutes.

No one was about and there was no sign that anybody had attempted to break in. There were no lights visible, either, in the Hamiltons' house and he assumed they were out for the evening.

Having inspected the last kennel, he turned back. There was no point in walking down as far as the spinney – there was nothing there worth stealing; although as he reached the outbuildings behind the house he locked the door of the shed which he had omitted to secure that morning, without bothering to look inside.

Whatever the noise was, and he was convinced now that it had been a car back-firing, it had been some distance away.

Re-entering the kitchen he hung the waterproof behind the

door to drip on to the tiled floor and, replacing the torch on the shelf, went into the sitting-room where he poured himself a whisky, exasperated by the whole bloody stupid business.

Not only was he wet and cold but he had lost the chance of fixing up a meeting with Ruth Livesey in yet another balls-up which would make it even more difficult and embarrassing to contact her again in the future.

Hours after Kate Denby had left, taking with her his copy of the Jane Austen correspondence carefully wrapped up in a clear plastic bag to protect it from the rain, Felix made himself supper and then returned to the study where he stayed for the rest of the evening, reading *Emma*, although from time to time he raised his head to look up at the gap in the bookshelves opposite him where the edition of Jane Austen's letters had stood. Its absence pleased him. He liked to think of the book in Miss Denby's possession, and of her pleasure in reading it.

And eventually, of course, she would bring it back; in person, too. He had taken care to make small overtures in this direction before she left. 'Don't bother to post it,' he had said. 'Drop it in at the house any time you're visiting Dodie, although there's no hurry.'

That way, he had made sure of seeing her again but not for several weeks. The book itself did not invite hasty reading, rather a slow, indulgent study – and, besides, Felix preferred the pleasure of anticipation. He had never been the type of man to rush his fences.

Percy stirred in front of the fire, some inner clock telling him that it was close to bedtime and he hadn't yet had his nightly run. Glancing up again, Felix saw that the dog was as usual correct and the time was indeed just after a quarter past ten.

'Come on then, old chap,' he said, putting aside the book and rising from his chair. 'But it'll have to be a quick gallop down the garden on your own tonight. I'm not turning out in this rain.'

He could hear it still falling outside behind the drawn curtain, beating on the glass.

With the dog at his heels, he crossed the room towards the door, just reaching it when the telephone rang; he turned back to take the call from the study extension on the desk, wondering who could be phoning him at that time of night.

It was from a kiosk. As Felix lifted the receiver, he heard the sound of the pay signal, then the rattle as a coin dropped, before Elizabeth's voice came on the line.

'Daddy? It's Elizabeth. Listen, darling, I've got a puncture. Could you possibly drive out and pick me up? Sorry about this but I've tried phoning home and there's no answer. Perhaps David's out, or is in the bath. I'm at that little village a mile from the T-junction. Do you know where I mean?'

'Yes, I know it,' Felix said. He couldn't remember the name either; it was a tiny place, more of a hamlet consisting of nothing more than a row of houses, a petrol station and, he assumed, a telephone box. He spoke hurriedly, anxious lest the money should run out before the conversation was finished. 'Where shall I pick you up? At the kiosk?'

'No; better make it at the car. I've left it in a gateway on the far side of the village. It's more comfortable for waiting in than this awful little kiosk. It smells, and there's no light.'

'You must be soaking wet,' Felix said with quick concern, thinking that she would have had to walk from the car to the telephone box in all this rain.

'I'm not exactly dry,' she agreed and laughed. 'Do be quick, there's a darling.'

'I'll come at once,' he assured her.

'Bless you,' she said and rang off.

Felix replaced his own receiver before hurrying into the hall to collect his heavy shoes and mackintosh from the downstairs coat cupboard and shutting Percy up in the kitchen. He would have to wait for his run. As he left for the front door to go out to the garage and back the car out, fretting at the delay these preparations had caused, Felix could hear the dog whining uneasily at this sudden change in routine and scratching to get out.

It was about a ten-minute drive in daylight. At night and in such a downpour it took longer, although Felix drove as fast as he dared, anxious about Elizabeth waiting out there somewhere in the darkness and the rain at the side of the road, soaked to the skin, no doubt.

At the bottom of the hill, he turned left into the village, passing first Paddocks on the right where he noticed the lights were on downstairs although Elizabeth's house next door appeared to be in darkness. Perhaps David was out after all, Felix thought. It was Tuesday, the day he went to the branch office in Millbridge, although it seemed strange he shouldn't yet be home; unless, of course, he'd been called out after his return.

The village itself was deserted; not a soul about. Once past the church, the road straightened out and about half a mile further on he came to the T-junction where the main road to Framden led off to the left. Turning in that direction, Felix drove on for a couple more miles until the headlights of the Range Rover picked out the little huddle of houses which marked the anonymous hamlet, the garage, closed of course, and the telephone kiosk standing, together with a pillar box, just beyond it.

Once past the hamlet, Felix slowed down, keeping a watch on his right for Elizabeth's MG.

It was drawn up facing him on the opposite side of the road in a gateway about a quarter of a mile from the hamlet.

Felix flashed his headlights at it, signalling his arrival before making a three-point turn and drawing up behind it.

He got out, Elizabeth also climbing out of the driving seat of her car and coming to meet him, her coat and hair dark with rain.

'You've been quick,' she said, 'I've only got back myself a few minutes ago from the phone box.'

Her comment prompted Felix to look at his watch, Elizabeth herself glancing at her own watch as he did so.

'It's half-past ten,' he said. 'I came as soon as I could,' adding in protest, 'Do get back in the car.'

'Oh, darling, I can't get any wetter than I am now,' she said, amused by the situation as well as his concern. 'I'm sorry to drag you out but, as I said on the phone, I tried ringing David first but there was no answer. Come and inspect the damage.'

She led the way round the MG to the rear near-side wheel

where, as he crouched down in the wet grass, Felix could see in the light of his own headlamps tht the tyre was flat.

'That's what caused it,' he commented, pointing to a large, bent nail which was sticking out between the treads.

'I know,' Elizabeth replied. 'I had a look myself and tried putting on the spare but I couldn't get the jack to fit properly because of the bumps in the verge. It wobbled. That's when I decided I'd better try phoning for help.'

'You tried to change the wheel yourself!' Felix sounded outraged.

'I'm not exactly helpless, you know, daddy,' Elizabeth replied, the note of amusement again in her voice.

Felix straightened up as he came to a decision.

'I'll run you home,' he said. 'I'm not keeping you waiting about here while I change it. You'll get pneumonia. We'll leave the car here for the time being – it's not causing an obstruction – and get the chap from Leverett's garage to fix it tomorrow. If not, I'll come out again and do it myself.'

'All right, darling,' Elizabeth agreed. 'It seems the best thing.' Locking up her own car, she followed Felix back to the Range Rover where he helped her into the passenger seat. 'No Percy?' she added, turning round and seeing the wired-off back section was empty.

'I left him at home,' Felix explained, starting the engine and drawing out past the gateway.

'Poor old thing!' Elizabeth said. She might have been referring to the dog or her MG, both abandoned by their owners.

'What were you doing out so late?' Felix asked as they headed back through the hamlet towards the T-junction.

'I've been in Framden most of the day,' Elizabeth replied. 'It's Tuesday, my aerobics class, remember? I have told you about it. I go every week with Cynthia.'

'Oh, the Fuller woman,' Felix said, trying not to sound disapproving. She was an old friend of Elizabeth's although Felix had never taken to her. She had recently been divorced, too; another reason why he didn't much care for her.

'Anyhow, it's not all that late,' Elizabeth continued. 'It was only half-past ten when you came to pick me up.'

'I call it late. I'm usually in bed before eleven,' Felix replied.

He slowed down at the T-junction to turn towards Woodstone and was silent for a few moments as he looked to the right for oncoming traffic before continuing, 'What were you doing all day in Framden anyway? I thought your class wasn't until the evening.'

'The usual things,' Elizabeth said. 'The library; lunch at Frazer's; some shopping, which incidentally I've left on the back seat of the car but never mind. Having my hair done, which was rather a waste considering the weather.' She laughed and pushed back her wet hair with one hand, the same gesture she used to make when she was a child. 'Then tea and sympathy with Cynthia – her tea, my sympathy; followed my aerobics and a country walk in the rain which I hadn't planned.' While she had been speaking, they had driven through the village and turned into the driveway to her house. 'You'll come in for a nightcap and to say hello to David?' she added quickly.

'Just a very quick one then,' Felix agreed.

'A drink or a hello?' she asked in a teasing manner as the Range Rover reached the end of the drive and drew up outside the front door.

There was no light on in the hall, a fact which Felix commented on as they went up the steps.

'Perhaps David's already gone to bed,' he remarked.

Elizabeth said over her shoulder as she put her key into the lock, 'Oh, not yet, daddy. David never goes to bed before midnight. No; he's either out or still working in the study. He often forgets to put the lights on if I'm not there. He gets so absorbed in what he's doing.' As they entered and she switched on the lights, she called out confidently, 'David, are you in? I'm home! I've brought Felix with me. Come and say hello.'

For some unaccountable reason the silence in the house made Felix suddenly uneasy, although the crack of light showing under the study door to the right of the staircase suggested that David was inside the room.

Then why didn't he reply? Felix asked himself.

But he had no time to say anything out loud. Elizabeth was crossing the hall, slipping off her wet coat as she walked and throwing it down over the arm of the chair which stood beside the telephone table before approaching the door to the study.

What happened next became confused in Felix's mind as a sequence of events although individual images remained very clear like a series of snapshots taken over an interval of time.

Somehow he must have crossed the hall himself although afterwards he had no recollection of having done so. All he could remember was pushing Elizabeth to one side and opening the door, positioning himself between her and the oblong of light as if he already knew what the room contained. He might almost have been expecting it – the sprawled figure, which he didn't at the time think of as David's, lying on its back between the desk and the doorway, feet pointing towards him, one arm flung out, a dark, spreading stain blackening the chest and spilling out across the carpet.

Behind him, he heard Elizabeth give a little cry like a bird and the next moment he had got her into the drawing-room where he poured her a brandy, although afterwards he had no clear recollection of that sequence of actions either, only of Elizabeth sitting in one corner of the sofa, holding a glass in both hands and looking so small that he hardly recognized her, and their footsteps making a double trail across the pale carpet, his in a single file going to the drinks cabinet and back.

Something about the dark, wet marks brought him sharply to his senses. They were as much a violation as the body, David's body, lying in the next room in its own blood. It was time for action.

'Stay here,' he told Elizabeth in that tone of voice he sometimes used to Percy, and, like the dog, she obeyed him, looking up at him without speaking as he left the room.

Outside in the hall, Felix moved with a businesslike, automatic briskness, all emotion suspended, telling himself what to do.

First shut the study door.

He closed it, taking care not to look inside the room at the horror it contained.

Now phone Dr Wade.

As he dialled the number, he remembered Elizabeth had told him that David had re-registered with another GP in Framden, not that it made any difference. Wade would have to come, regardless. Felix did not propose waiting while some man he didn't know drove the eight miles from the town, although he was aware there was no real urgency. David was dead. No one could have survived that chest wound.

Mrs Wade answered the phone. Dr Wade was already out on a call, she explained. A patient had had a heart attack.

Felix cut her short. 'Then put me through to Dr Livesey's house,' he demanded. He knew it was possible to ring through directly from the surgery.

'It's Dr Livesey's day off,' Mrs Wade began.

'Put me through at once. This is an emergency,' Felix ordered, raising his voice. God damn the woman to hell!

He heard the click as the call was re-directed and then the telephone ringing in Dr Livesey's house. It rang and rang before it was answered.

'This is Felix Napier here,' Felix said when the receiver was at last lifted. 'There's been an accident at my daughter's house. Please come immediately. It's most urgent.'

He replaced the reciever just as she said, 'Of course,' in that cool voice of hers which never seemed to show any emotion although, to give the woman her due, she was at the house within minutes. Felix only had time to return to the drawing-room to tell Elizabeth that the doctor was on her way and to pour himself a whisky before the front door bell rang and there she was at the top of the steps, wearing an unbuttoned raincoat, her medical bag in her hand.

'In here,' Felix said, escorting her across the hall and opening the study door but taking care to keep his face averted.

She stood on the threshold for a few seconds without speaking, looking at the scene inside the room and then turned towards him.

'I'm so sorry,' she said quietly.

'He's dead, of course,' Felix replied. He took her remark to mean just that, although he hardly needed her professional judgement to confirm what he already knew.

'Have you phoned the police?' she asked.

'No, not yet.'

It was odd, Felix thought, that it hadn't occurred to him to do so.

'Then I think you should,' she told him.

'I'll do it now,' he agreed, and walked away towards the telephone leaving her to go inside the study alone and shut the door behind her.

As he looked up the number for the police station in Framden and dialled it, something else occurred to him for the first time.

How had David died? It was not suicide. Felix knew enough about guns to know that the wound was not self-inflicted. Besides, there was no weapon by the body. As the telephone rang at the police-station, he recalled the scene briefly – David lying on his back between the desk and the door, the stretch of carpet all round him quite empty apart from the spreading stain.

Someone lifted the receiver. A man's voice said, 'Framden police station. Can I help you?'

Felix drew himself up, pulling back his shoulders and straightening his spine.

'I want to report a murder,' he replied.

7

Detective Chief Inspector Jack Finch of Chelmsford CID stood just inside the doorway of the room, surveying the body and its setting with a contemplative air, hands clasped behind his back like a farmer at an auction. The stance suited him. He had the stocky build and the bluff, open-air features of a countryman, apparently guileless but revealing nothing of his real thoughts as he looked about him, gaining his own first impressions before McCullum, the police photographer, and the fingerprint experts moved in with their equipment.

Wylie, the scenes of crime officer, had made his own examination. So, too, had Pardoe, the police surgeon, who had already left in compnay with Byrne, the local Inspector from Framden who had been first called out on the case.

Byrne had known the dead man, having met him on several occasions, and had been able to give Finch some background details which, as he stood in the doorway, the Chief Inspector ran through in his mind, summarizing the facts.

Name: David Hamilton; married; young – in his early thirties; local solicitor in an old, thriving Framden firm; keen; conscientious; well-liked with a wide clientele; no known enemies.

Some of it Finch might have deduced for himself simply by looking about him.

The room was comfortable if a little austere, equipped more as an office than a study, with a modern desk on which an angle-poise lamp was shining down on to some papers neatly laid out on the surface; a swivel chair; shelves containing law book; all of it suggestive of a man who was well-organized and professional in his attitude to work.

Between the desk and the door, David Hamilton's body lay on its back, the soles of the leather slippers pointing towards the Chief Inspector, the head turned to the left, revealing a youthful profile although the lines which were beginning to mark the forehead and to gather between the eyebrows showed that he was older than the boyish features might have indicated at first glance.

It was also possible to make certain deductions from the corpse itself, although Finch preferred not to look too closely at the dark hole which had once been the left-hand side of the man's chest. From what he knew about such wounds, he guessed that Hamilton had been killed by a shot-gun fired at fairly close range, an opinion which Pardoe had agreed with when he had examined the body and one which the pathologist's report would probably confirm.

Hamilton had been shot, moreover, as he had got up from his desk and faced his killer. The angle of the swivel chair, turned towards the door, suggested this. So, too, did the position of the body. He had, Finch imagined, taken a few steps across the room before the blast from the shot-gun had flung him backwards.

The weapon had not yet been found, although a group of men with Detective Sergeant Boyce in charge was at that moment making a search of the house and the garden.

The clothes the dead man was wearing, a dark grey sweater

and navy cords, were casual but of good quality and of the type that a man might choose for an evening at home, while the soles of the leather slippers were clean and dry, as Finch discovered when he took a few paces inside the room and squatted down to examine them more closely. It certainly didn't look as if Hamilton had been outside since he had put them on.

Nor was there any sign of a forced entry. On first arriving, Finch had made a quick tour of the Hamiltons' house and had found no evidence that anyone had broken in, while the study itself seemed undisturbed. Even the papers on the desk were laid out tidily as Finch saw for himself when, rising to his feet, he stepped over the dead man's legs and crossed the room. A half-finished letter, written by hand but on paper bearing the printed heading of the firm of solicitors, Dunbar & Hamilton, and addressed to someone called Steven, lay on the desk top immediately in front of the chair, a pen laid neatly beside it. It would seem likely, therefore, that not only had David Hamilton been writing the letter just before he died but he had probably known his killer and had not been disturbed by the sudden, unexpected arrival of a stranger bursting into the room – although Finch was prepared to keep an open mind on this particular point. All the same, the position of the pen seemed significant. It hadn't been flung down in a hurry and, as McCullum knocked and entered the room with his equipment, Finch asked the tall, laconic Scotsman to take a few shots of the desk and its content as well as the body before leaving the room to let the man get on with his job.

Crossing the hall on his way to the drawing-room to interview Felix Napier, the dead man's father-in-law who had first discovered the body, as Inspector Byrne had informed him, Finch looked quickly about him.

Here was money, he decided, noting the rich-looking rugs on the parquet floor, the expensively framed collection of watercolours which marched step by step up the staircase wall, the huge copper bowl of yellow and bronze chrysanthemums which stood on the telephone table, discerning in these details a woman's hand. Hamilton's study had shown a more severe, masculine taste.

The same elegance and style was evident in the drawing-room, although Finch's attention was directed not so much at the furniture and paintings as at the figure of a man who was seated in an armchair by the fire, a whisky and soda in his hand, and who rose to his feet as the Chief Inspector entered.

Felix Napier looked drawn and tired but that did not prevent him from stepping forward with a military briskness, back and head held straight, to shake Finch by the hand and to look him directly in the face with a bright blue gaze, very much man to man. *I shall tell the truth*, that look and handshake seemed to be saying, *but I am not necessarily impressed either by your rank or your professional authority*.

Indeed, Felix Napier's first impression of the Chief Inspector was not favourable. The man looked – well, not to put too fine a point on it – more like a farmer, and not a gentleman farmer either but a tenant who did his own mucking-out. The shabby raincoat which he was wearing had seen better days; so, too, had his shoes, while his voice as he introduced himself had, if not an Essex accent, then the soft intonation of the countryman, pleasant enough but hardly suggestive of a brisk professionalism.

'Do sit down, Chief Inspector,' Felix Napier said, indicating a chair and watching with barely disguised impatience as Finch slowly removed his raincoat, folded it and laid it down across the arm.

It was quite clear to him that the Chief Inspector would have to be brought up to the mark, and Felix fretted at the prospect of a long, rambling interview with Elizabeth upstairs in a state of shock, although Dr Livesey, thank God, was with her, David's body still lying in the study, and nothing yet done that he could see to make a serious start on the investigation although the police had been tramping about the place for the past half-hour. Percy, too, worried him. The dog was still at home, shut up in the kitchen and, judging by Finch's unhurried manner, the Lord alone knew when he would be allowed to leave and take Elizabeth with him.

He plunged in himself, anxious to get matters moving.

'I assume you'll want a statement from me, Chief Inspector,' he began, 'so I'll come straight to the point. I returned with my daughter to the house at approximately twenty to eleven and found my son-in-law dead. I immediately telephoned my GP but, as he was out, his assistant, Dr Livesey, came in his place within a few minutes. I then rang the police at Framden. While waiting for them to arrive, I made a brief inspection of the house, assuming an intruder had broken in, but found nothing – although, I ought to add, the back door was unlocked. I think I should also point out that when my daughter and I first arrived all the lights in the house were out except for the reading lamp in David's study, so it seemed feasible that someone could have assumed the place was empty, let himself in by the back door, and then panicked and shot my son-in-law when David disturbed him.'

It was basically the same statement which he had already made to the Inspector from Framden, and one which Byrne had seemed to accept for he had replied, 'You could very well be right, sir.' But that hadn't stopped him from sending for the Chelmsford CID, and this worried Felix.

But, damn it all, the facts fitted the theory and yet there was Finch, sitting back in his chair, listening with a bland, non-committal expression behind which Felix thought he could detect a sceptical air.

'You don't agree with me?' he asked abruptly. If the follow had other ideas as to how David was murdered, then let him come out with them. In the time that had elapsed since he had first found his son-in-law's body, Felix had passed from the shocked horror of disbelief to a determination to bring whoever was responsible to book as soon as possible. There had been no time for grief. That would come later. All that mattered for the moment was to get the investigation under way.

'It's much too early for me to come to any conclusions,' Finch replied, remembering the pen laid down so tidily beside the half-written letter and wondering why Felix Napier seemed so anxious to establish the theory that an intruder was to blame. But he picked up one point from Napier's statement. 'So your son-in-law was alone in the house?'

'Haven't I said as much?' Felix Napier demanded testily and then, regretting his impatience, added, 'I'm sorry, Chief Inspector. I've already made a statement to Inspector Byrne and I imagined he had passed on the facts to you. I apologize for any discourtesy.'

Finch nodded, accepting the apology but taking care not to admit that he had indeed received a full account of Napier's statement from Inspector Byrne, preferring to hear it again first-hand from Napier himself.

'Then I must put you in the picture about exactly what happened,' Felix Napier continued. 'I gather from my daughter that David was alone this evening. She herself was in Framden until quite late. On the way home, she had a puncture and tried phoning David first. But as there was no reply, she rang me instead.'

'What time was this?' Finch asked. If David Hamilton had not answered the phone, it was possible he was already dead and the timing of the call could be important.

Felix Napier looked harassed at the interruption although he seemed to grasp the point of the question for he replied, 'It was very shortly after a quarter-past ten. I happened to glance at the clock seconds before the phone rang. I – we, that is – assumed David was having a bath or had been called out to a client, although that would have been unusual. Anyway, to get back to the point, Elizabeth rang me from a call-box on the Framden road . . .'

'You're quite sure the call came from a kiosk?' Finch broke in again to ask.

'Yes, of course I am.' Felix Napier sounded affronted. 'I heard the pay signal as well as the sound of the coin dropping. I don't know what you're suggesting, Chief Inspector . . .'

'Merely checking the facts,' Finch replied with a peaceable air. 'Go on, Mr Napier. Your daughter rang you?'

'And I drove out to pick her up. As it was raining hard, I decided not to change the wheel but to drive her home. It was, as I've already said, about twenty to eleven when we got back here. The lights were off in the hall and, as I discovered later, in the rest of the house.'

'Was this unusual?' Finch asked, picking up the same word which Felix Napier himself had used earlier in his account.

'Not necessarily,' Felix Napier replied. 'We simply assumed that, if David was at home, he had been so engrossed in his work that he either hadn't bothered to turn the lights on or hadn't had any reason to leave the study. I might add that this was typical of my son-in-law. He was an extremely hard-working young man, highly professional in his attitude.'

Felix added the last remark deliberately, not only because it was true but as a small rebuke directed at the Chief Inspector who, as far as he could see, lacked any similar drive. He was also careful when referring to David to use the past tense. After all, facts had to be faced.

'My daughter called out to David to join us for a nightcap,' he continued. 'I could see there was a light showing under the study door and, when David didn't reply, I opened it and found him lying on the floor.'

'You were uneasy?' Finch suggested.

Felix looked at the Chief Inspector with a sharpened interest. As far as he was aware, there had been nothing in his voice or manner to indicate that sense of disquiet which he had felt at the time and which Finch, for all his apparent intertia, had nevertheless been perspicacious enough to pick up.

'Yes, I was,' he admitted. 'I don't know why. The house seemed too quiet and oddly empty.'

As an explanation, it would have to do. Felix could not describe his feelings more accurately but the Chief Inspector seemed to accept it for he nodded briefly before asking, 'You touched nothing?'

'No; I didn't even go inside the room. I could see from the doorway that David was dead.'

'And when your daughter telephoned you from the call-box you were alone?'

'Yes, I was,' Felix replied, 'although I don't see what that has to do with the inquiry.'

'I assume her car is still where you left it?' Finch continued, ignoring the remark although he made a mental note of the fact that Felix Napier would appear to have no alibi for at least part of the evening, which could be significant if he were correct in thinking that Hamilton had known his murderer.

'It's in a gateway about a couple of miles along the Framden road past the T-junction,' Felix replied. He couldn't see the point of that question, either, unless the Chief Inspector was concerned about traffic regulations, however trivial such a consideration might be in a murder investigation. He added quickly, 'It isn't causing an obstruction. I was careful to make sure of that before we decided to leave it there.'

'We' again, Finch thought, noting Felix Napier's repeated use of the plural pronoun which suggested that not only were he and his daughter very close but something more besides – a sense of identification as if the two of them shared similar thought-processes which could not be distinguished.

'About your daughter,' Finch began but got no further. Felix Napier bristled up at once.

'If you are about to suggest, Chief Inspector, that you question Elizabeth, I shall raise the strongest objections. She is lying down upstairs, recovering from shock, and is in no condition to make a statement.' The blue eyes were positively glaring.

This was exactly what Finch had been about to suggest but he was spared a confrontation with Felix Napier, at least for the time being, by the arrival of Detective Sergeant Boyce who, having tapped at the door, put his head briefly round it to announce, 'If you could spare a moment, sir, we've found something outside which we'd like you to look at.'

Finch got to his feet and, picking up his raincoat, followed the burly, broad-shouldered Sergeant across the hall and down the passageway which ran alongside the stairs, past a new brightly lit kitchen, towards the back door which was set open. The passage was carpeted, a fact which the Chief Inspector had already noted with disgust on his own quick tour of the house soon after his arrival, so there was no chance of finding footprints, assuming the murderer had entered by this route.

The lights from the kitchen were strong enough to shine out into the garden, illuminating a paved patio area where several uniformed and plain-clothes men were standing in the rain which was still falling heavily, forming an interested cluster round an object lying on the flagstones to the right of the doorway and mid-way between it and the point where the patio gave way to lawn.

They fell back as the Chief Inspector approached, although

he was conscious of their feet a few yards from him as he squatted down to examine their trophy.

It was a double-barrelled shot-gun, the stock nearest to him, the barrels, glistening with rain, pointing away, as if it had been hurriedly thrown down by someone leaving the house by the back door.

As he crouched over it Finch was aware of other details, of the sense of a large garden which extended into the darkness beyond the brightly lit area where the gun was lying, of a high fir hedge over to his right, the scent of which he could catch in the wet air, and, behind it, another house, only the roof and chimneys of which were visible, showing up as bulks of denser darkness against the sky.

So there was a neighbour, Finch thought, who might have heard or seen something – although the house was some distance away and was well-screened from the Hamiltons' place.

It was Boyce who voiced the theory already put forward by Napier. 'What do you reckon?' he asked. 'Someone tried breaking in and Hamilton disturbed him?'

It was a tempting theory, especially if, as Napier had said, the lights had been out apart from the one lamp in Hamilton's study. To anyone approaching the house from the rear, it would have appeared unoccupied and in darkness. Finch could understand why Boyce as well as Napier had jumped to the same conclusion.

He straightened up.

'No, I don't think so, Tom,' he replied, 'although whoever shot Hamilton may have wanted us to believe just that. I'll explain later why it doesn't work as a theory. Get Napier out here. I'd like him to look at the gun before it's removed.'

When Boyce had gone, Finch sent the other members of the team about their own tasks, Kyle to fetch McCullum, the photographer, Barney together with Johnson and several of the uniformed men to examine the rest of the garden, although he did not expect them to find much. A full-scale search would have to wait until daylight.

As the men moved off, Finch followed them a few paces into

the darkness, feeling the lawn give soggily under his feet, the damp spreading up through the soles of his shoes.

It was a wild night of gusting wind and fragmented clouds which went tearing past above the tree-tops, lit by patches of paler light where an almost invisible moon seemed also to be carried along by the storm, flashing momentarily in and out against the racing sky.

The house, when he turned to face it, looked solid in comparison. Modern, white-painted, the rear façade was now brightly illuminated, lights shining out not only from the kitchen and drawing-room but from a bedroom window where presumably Elizabeth Hamilton, the dead man's widow, was recovering from the shock of his murder.

Despite Napier's objections, he'd have to get a statement from her, Finch thought, although he was not looking forward to it with much relish. Even after more than twenty years in the force, he had not yet learned to cope adequately with other people's grief.

As the thought crossed his mind, he saw Napier emerge from the back door, accompanied by Boyce, and he walked forward to join them.

Napier noticed the gun at once, bending down quickly to examine it before straightening up again. 'It's David's,' he said simply.

There was something about his manner which told Finch that this was not all Napier had to say and he was about to forestall him by replying that it was not yet established that this was the murder weapon when Napier brushed his objection to one side.

'No doubt you'll have it tested but, as far as I'm concerned, the answer is obvious. My son-in-law was shot; a gun – his gun – is found just outside the back door. The two facts must be linked. I'm equally convinced that your expert will find that only one shot was fired, and for that I blame myself entirely.'

'Indeed, sir?' Finch asked in his official, non-committal voice, wondering what the hell Napier meant by this last remark. 'What makes you say that?'

'I was out rough-shooting with my son-in-law about ten days ago,' Felix Napier replied. He had drawn himself up and was looking at a point a few feet beyond the Chief Inspector's left shoulder, his blue eyes screwed up in concentration as he attempted to remember the exact sequence of events which had occurred on that Saturday afternoon, while at the same time trying not to recall other more painful details – the sunlight falling across the furrows, the smoky tang of autumn in the air and the sense of male camaraderie as he and David had walked together towards Gade's Wood. 'We'd bagged two or three brace of pigeons earlier on and David had reloaded. I remember he fired one barrel after that, but the light was going and so we decided to call it a day. I meant to remind him that he still had one cartridge left in the gun but it slipped my mind. When we got back to the house, there was a phone call waiting for him and he went straight through to the study to take it.'

There had been other diversions as well which he did not think were worth mentioning – Elizabeth's exclamations over their muddy boots, the flurry to take them off and keep the dog contained in the kitchen, his own eagerness to recount the afternoon's events.

'And what happened to the gun?' Finch was inquiring.

Damn the man! Felix thought. It was the same question he was asking himself. What had David done with the gun and why in God's name hadn't he reminded him of that cartridge left in the breach? He would never forgive himself for that omission.

'He took it through with him into the hall,' Felix said, pointing along the passageway. 'I remember he was still carrying the gun in his right hand. Elizabeth had objected to him leaving it in the kitchen. But he must have put it down somewhere because, just before I shut the door to keep the dog in, I saw him going into the study and he didn't have it with him then.'

With Finch at his heels, he had taken a few steps along the passage, before stopping abruptly at the point where it broadened out into the main hall. There, in the angle formed by the newel post and the side of the staircase well, was a small alcove in which stood a tall, narrow, brass container, cylindrical in shape, filled with walking-sticks, collected presumably for their ornamental heads.

'He put it in here,' Felix Napier announced.

'You're sure of that?' Finch asked.

'Not a hundred per cent, but there's nowhere else he could have left it between the kitchen and the study,' Napier replied, not unreasonably.

'But wouldn't he have taken it out and unloaded it when he came to clean it?'

'Not necessarily. David wasn't a keen shot. He rarely went out with the gun. Normally, it would have been kept in the study, locked up in the gun-safe, but on that Saturday afternoon, with that phone call coming just as we got back, I can only suppose he intended to leave it here only temporarily and then forgot about it. He had no *routine*, you understand.'

It was said with the faintly disparaging air of the expert speaking of the amateur, a criticism of his dead son-in-law which Napier himself seemed aware of for he added quickly, 'He'd been very busy recently and if he did put it in this,' indicating the container, 'he'd probably not notice it.'

Which was a valid point, as Finch had to agree. The container was tall enough to take a shot-gun with only a few inches of barrel showing above the rim and was placed moreover in the alcove out of line of the main lights in the hall.

'And don't you see,' Felix Napier was continuing, 'if someone let himself in by the back door, he could have picked up the gun on his way through to the hall and then used it to kill my son-in-law when he was disturbed.'

The intruder theory again, Finch noted, although he refrained from pointing out that if David Hamilton had failed to notice the gun it was unlikely that a potential burglar in a strange house, and one which was supposed to be in darkness, should have discovered it lying so conveniently to hand. If anything, such a supposition would tend to support his own theory – that the murderer had been acquainted with his victim; and, not only that, but had also known exactly where the gun was to be found.

'Yes, I understand, sir,' he replied in the same non-committal tone which Felix Napier was beginning to find infuriating. There was another quality about the Chief Inspector which angered him. He disliked being proved wrong and yet he was being forced to change his opinion of the man. Despite his shabby shoes and unhurried air, Finch was a damn sight more intelligent than he had originally given him credit for, an uncomfortable conclusion to have to make.

'And was that particular Saturday the last time you saw your son-in-law?' Finch continued.

'No; I saw him last Saturday. He and my daughter gave a party which I went to.'

'At which friends of theirs were also present?' Finch inquired. He seemed more concerned with the collection of walking-sticks in the container than in Napier's reply, bending down to examine the head of the one facing him in the shape of a fox's mask although he was careful, Felix noticed, not to touch it, keeping his hands clasped behind the back of the quite disgraceful raincoat he was wearing. 'So you'd be able to give me a list of their names?'

'I don't see why,' Felix began. He was about to add that surely this was unnecessary – none of David's friends could possibly be implicated in his murder – when the Chief Inspector straightened up and, turning to face him, added, 'And I take it you and your daughter wouldn't object to having your fingerprints taken as well as hand swabs?'

'Hand swabs?' Felix Napier demanded.

'For powder stains,' Finch explained. 'It's routine in a case involving firearms. I shall also need the clothes you and your daughter were wearing this evening for forensic testing.'

'But it's outrageous!' Felix replied, raising his voice and was further outraged when, at this point, the telephone in the hall rang and, without so much as a by your leave, Finch waved aside Napier himself as well as Gilmore, the local policeman, who was on duty at the front door, before, crossing the hall, he picked up the receiver. It seemed, Felix thought angrily, that he was not permitted to answer the phone in his own daughter's house. And in front of Gilmore, too.

'Yes?' Finch said and waited.

'David Hamilton?' a man's voice said in a doubtful tone on the other end of the line.

'Who is it?' Finch asked.

'It's Steven Bradley,' the voice replied. 'Is something wrong? I saw cars arriving a little while ago and what with that and the shot I thought I heard earlier . . .' The voice broke off to add more sharply, 'Who is that? It's not Felix Napier, is it?'

'No, Mr Bradley,' Finch replied cheerfully. He had already picked up the man's Christian name – Steven – the same as the one used in the letter which Hamilton had been writing shortly before he died. 'I'm Detective Chief Inspector Finch of Chelmsford CID. I assume you're the Hamiltons' next-door neighbour? Yes? Then I shall be round to see you very shortly.'

He replaced the receiver immediately, giving Bradley no time to ask any further questions, and was about to set off in search of Boyce to inform him of this new development in the case when Napier put out a hand to detain him.

'I take it that was Bradley?' he asked, his voice full of disapproval, aware that Gilmore was listening but angered to the point where he no longer cared. 'What did he want?'

'Merely concerned as a neighbour about what was going on,' Finch replied. He had no intention of telling Napier about the rest of the conversation concerning the shot Bradley thought he had heard. That was for Boyce's ears alone.

'Damned impudence!' Felix Napier retorted in such a violent tone that Finch was taken aback. Although Napier had struck him as a man of strong opinions, this impatience was usually held in check by an even stronger sense of good form; except in Bradley's case, it seemed. 'I wouldn't have put it past him to phone up about that blasted right of way! I only hope to God David did what he said he would do last Saturday and turned the confounded man down.'

And with that, he pushed past the Chief Inspector and went into the drawing-room, shutting the door pointedly behind him.

Finch made no attempt to follow him. Instead, avoiding the eyes of the local bobby who had been watching the scene with undisguised interest, he went out through the back door to find Boyce.

Whatever the business was regarding the right of way, it was evidently of sufficient seriousness to arouse passions, at least on Felix Napier's part.

Interesting, thought Finch.

Under the circumstances, it might be more useful to hear

Bradley's side of the story first before tackling Napier on the subject, while at the same time interviewing the man about the shot he said he had heard.

Might as well kill two birds with one stone, he told himself, and then grimaced wryly at the inaptness of the image.

8

When the front-door bell rang shortly after he had made the telephone call, Bradley was relieved to find only two detectives, both in plain clothes, standing on the step, one a stocky, fresh-faced man, the other taller and broad-shouldered. He had been expecting several uniformed officers who would come swarming into the place and he had regretted ringing the Hamiltons' number. He had done so partly out of genuine concern and a sense of neighbourliness but partly, as he admitted himself, out of curiosity.

Why in God's name were all those police cars turning up next-door at that time of night? It was then that he remembered the noise he had heard earlier and he had decided he ought to find out what was going on, although he had not expected the police to respond so promptly.

'Detective Inspector Finch and my Detective Sergeant, Boyce,' the shorter of the two men was saying.

'You'd better come inside,' Bradley replied in a grudging manner, opening the door wider to allow them into the hall.

'We're both rather wet, I'm afraid,' Finch said with an apologetic air at which Bradley merely shrugged, as if this fact didn't matter, as he preceded them down the passage to the back of the house.

'You can hang your things up here,' he said, indicating a row of pegs already bulging with coats and waiting impatiently as the two men stripped off their wet mackintoshes before following him into the sitting-room.

Finch had already taken Bradley's measures on the doorstep. He was a tall, ungainly man with an awkwardness that was more than just physical clumsiness although he seemed ill-adjusted to his size. He didn't even seem at home in his own sitting-room which was a curious mixture of styles, the Regency-striped wallpaper and the delicate plaster cornice contrasting oddly with the shabby armchairs and a plain, brown-painted deal desk on which papers lay about haphazardly together with a bag of dog biscuits, stamped 'Sample', and the wing-mirror from a car.

'Sit down,' he told them.

Finch took the chair nearest to the fire, holding out his hands to the blaze, and leaving Boyce, whom he had briefed quickly before their arrival, to open the questioning. The Sergeant's heavy, official manner was, he felt, best used as an opening gambit. Besides, he had a card of his own up his sleeve which he wanted to save until later.

'I believe you said you heard a shot earlier this evening, sir?' Boyce began. He had produced his note-book and a pen which he held poised over the page with a business-like air. 'What time was this?'

'Now hang on a moment,' Bradley protested. 'I said I *thought* I heard a noise which could have been a shot. It would have been a minute before quarter-past ten, I suppose. It disturbed the dogs so . . .'

'You run a kennels, I believe?' Finch put in pleasantly. He and Boyce had noticed the sign hanging beside Bradley's gate as they had walked round to his house from the Hamiltons' place.

'That's right.' Bradley seemed relieved by the interruption. 'Although I haven't been here all that long. I took over from Felix Napier about a year ago.'

'Ah, Mr Napier,' Finch remarked softly although he added nothing more to the comment except to say, 'Go on, Mr Bradley. You said the noise disturbed the dogs.'

Bradley paused to look at the pair of them and then appeared to recover a little self-confidence.

'What's all this about?' he demanded. 'What happened at the Hamilton's place tonight?'

'There's been a shooting accident,' Finch explained.'

'Who to? David Hamilton?'

Now why should Bradley jump to that conclusion? Finch thought and was further intrigued when, as he affirmed this fact with a nod of his head, Bradley continued, 'Is he dead?'

'I'm afraid so,' Finch said, watching for Bradley's reaction.

'Good God!'

The man seemed genuinely shocked by the news although it could have been a clever piece of acting, or relief that Hamilton was, in fact, dead. If the gun had been fired from a darkened hall into a room only partially lit by a desk-lamp, Finch thought, Hamilton's murderer might well have panicked and fled before making sure that the shot was fatal and that his victim was not still alive to give evidence against him. It was, of course, still too soon to make such assumptions, but all the same it could be significant that Bradley had been so eager to telephone the Hamiltons' place to find out what was happening.

'Go on,' he repeated as Bradley, who had sat down abruptly on the upright chair by the desk, appeared to have forgotten that he had been in the middle of his account.

'Oh , yes, as I was saying.' Bradley still seemed distracted, running a hand over his rough brown hair before continuing. 'I rang off and went outside to quieten the dogs down and check round the kennels. I didn't see or hear anyone and, as everything seemed all right, I assumed what I'd heard had been a car back-firing. Anyway, after I'd made sure no one had tried breaking in, I went back indoors.' He trailed off a little lamely.

'You said you heard nothing when you went outside to the kennels?' Boyce asked. 'What about a car driving off from the Hamiltons' place?'

Bradley shook his head. 'If there was, I didn't hear it. The dogs were kicking up a hell of a racket. It took me about five minutes before I could settle them down.'

'Can you see the Hamiltons' house from here?'

'No,' Bradley replied and then corrected himself. 'At least, only the roof and part of the upstairs although, if the lights are on, they shine through the hedge. As a matter of fact, I noticed the place was in darkness when I went outside to check, and I assumed the Hamiltons were out for the evening.'

'Know them well?' Finch asked casually.

the Sergeant's questions and the notebook in which he was writing down everything that was said.

'Fairly well. I mean we're not close friends but we get on all right as neighbours.'

'What about Felix Napier, Hamilton's father-in-law?'

'Oh, him,' It was said in a weary, resigned voice as if Napier was the cause of some long-standing grievance with which Bradley had come to reluctant terms. 'I'm afraid he and I don't hit it off at all.'

'Oh? And why's that?' Finch's tone was interested and commiserating but still casual, inviting further explanation. Bradley seemed eager to have a sympathetic listener.

'As I've already explained, I bought the kennels from him about a year ago. I gather his wife had not long died and he wanted to retire. It wouldn't have been so bad if he'd done just that – retired, I mean. Instead, he seemed to think he still owned the place. He was round here every few days, ostensibly to give advice, but as far as I was concerned he was sticking his nose into what was now my business. In the end, I lost my temper with him and told him to clear off.' He gave a small, rueful smile. 'I'm afraid we haven't spoken since. Napier avoids me whenever he can, although we did exchange a few polite remarks at the Hamiltons' party on Saturday.'

'So you were there?' Finch asked with the same interested air. 'Were there many guests?'

'About twenty, I suppose; mostly local people, although there were a few from Framden.'

'And everything went off well?' Finch put the question casually at the same time feeling in his pocket for the plastic envelope containing a single sheet of paper which he held in one hand. He saw Bradley was watching him, his expression more wary.

'I don't know what you mean,' he said.

'The question of the right of way didn't come up?'

There was a small silence and then Bradley replied, 'Oh, that. No, it didn't. Hamilton said nothing to me about it, except that we ought to meet to discuss it. In fact, I've heard nothing definite from him, apart from an acknowledgement, since I wrote to him about ten days ago.'

'It seems Hamilton intended replying to you this evening,' Finch remarked. He had taken the letter from his pocket which, before coming to interview Bradley, he had shown to Boyce and which the Sergeant had slipped inside the plastic envelope in readiness for fingerprint testing. 'Shall I read it to you?' he continued and, taking Bradley's silence for assent, he began, '"*Dear Steven, I am sorry I have not given you a definite answer to your letter concerning the right of way across your land. Although I can understand your concern over the access into Gade's Lane on the grounds of security, I am afraid I cannot give permission for the opening to be closed off. Under normal circumstances, I might have agreed. However . . .*" And there the letter ends,' Finch explained.

Bradley's reaction was immediate. As if unable to contain his anger, he got abruptly to his feet, moving with surprising agility for a man of his awkward size.

'But it's ridiculous!' he burst out. 'Hamilton hardly ever uses that path! It's just sheer bloody-mindedness.' He broke off suddenly, aware of what he was saying and remembering too late that Hamilton was dead. He was conscious also that the two men were watching him closely, Finch with a bright-eyed curiosity, his Sergeant with a much more morose and suspicious expression.

It was Boyce who resumed the questioning.

'You didn't telephone Mr Hamilton tonight or call round to see him?' he asked. It was the theory which he and Finch had discussed on the way there.

'No, I bloody well didn't!' Bradley exclaimed. 'I haven't seen him since last Saturday and, as I've already told you, nothing was said then about the right of way. I had no idea he was going to refuse me permission to close it.'

'Could we look at it?' Finch asked, getting to his feet as he spoke as if expecting Bradley's agreement.

'What, now?' he protested.

'If you don't mind, sir.'

'But it's dark and bloody well pouring with rain.'

'We've brought torches with us,' Finch said with a maddeningly cheerful air, going over to the door and fetching his own and the Sergeant's raincoats from the pegs in the hall.

Bradley shrugged and gave in, leading the way into the kitchen where, with bad grace, he unhooked his own waterproof from the back door, thrusting his arms into the sleeves before, picking up a torch from the windowsill, he clumped his way outside where Finch paused to flash the beam of his torch round quickly, getting a rough idea of the lay-out.

They were standing on a concreted area, surrounded by outbuildings – storehouses by the look of them, although Finch realized he would need to look at the place again in daylight to get a better idea of the premises. There was no time, anyway, to take in more details for Bradley was striding off ahead of them into the darkness.

It was still raining and their torches lit up only patches of the grounds which were extensive, although Finch could only get an approximate impression of their size. A broad concrete path led the way towards the kennels, long, low buildings set out on each side of it, each with its own pen surrounded by high, chain-link fencing. As they passed, a few dogs began to bark or whine inside the separate units which housed them, Bradley calling to them to be quiet.

On their left, the high fir hedge which separated Bradley's land from the Hamiltons' was not visible, although Finch could guess its position from the presence of lights from the house behind it, twinkling intermittently as the wind stirred the branches. He could also see the shape of the roof against the sky.

In that fact, at least, Bradley was right. It wasn't possible to see much of the Hamiltons' house from his own property, only the upper storey.

The concrete path ended and was replaced by rough grass over which they tramped in silence for several seconds before Bradley halted and directed the beam of his torch to the left towards the hedge.

'There's a gap there,' he said. 'That's where the right of way runs from the Hamiltons' back garden. It leads along here.'

He had gone ahead of them again, following a faint track in the grass which led into a small spinney where someone, presumably Bradley, had been clearing the undergrowth. Broken twigs and small branches, the ends showing white where they had been cut, littered the ground, and at the far side of the spinney, where the path ended and where an opening showed in the hawthorn hedge which formed the boundary of Bradley's property, larger branches had been piled up to form a barrier, although a narrow space had been left in the middle, just wide enough to allow one person to squeeze through.

Bradley appeared to be about to scatter the pile with his foot but Finch moved forward to stop him.

'Leave it just as it is, Mr Bradley,' he told him. 'I take it that you put the branches here?'

'I wanted to close the gap up a bit,' Bradley muttered. He seemed embarrassed to be caught out in this piece of attempted illegality although he had been careful, Finch noticed, not to close off the opening completely. Bradley evidently knew his common law regarding rights of way. It was also an interesting example of his own bloody-mindedness, of which he had only a little earlier accused Hamilton.

'Anyone could get through on to my land,' Bradley was adding, as if anxious to explain his action.

'Exactly!' Finch remarked pleasantly and, walking forward, stepped sideways through the gap. He could see in the beam of his torch that the opening had once been much wider and had been closed off with a gate, for the supporting posts were still in position. Between them, the grass verge had been cut back and hard-surfaced – with gravel, as Finch discovered, bending down to examine it, although it was so thickly overlaid with dead leaves and the broken debris from the undergrowth which Bradley had cut down that there was no chance of finding footprints or tyremarks on it, a conclusion which Boyce confirmed when he pushed his way through to join the Chief Inspector.

'Nix,' he said succinctly.

'Damn!' Finch said.

'So what's the theory?' Boyce added in a low voice so that Bradley could not overhear him.

In reply, Finch got to his feet and directed the beam of his torch to the left and right, illuminating short stretches of a narrow country lane on to which the opening led.

Boyce grunted in agreement. Someone could have come

Bradley turned to him with an air of relief as if glad to escape along the lane, gained access to Bradley's land and through it to the Hamiltons' back garden along the right of way. Which would tend to support the intruder theory, Finch thought. Anyone approaching the Hamiltons' house by this back route would have assumed, in the absence of lights, that the place was unoccupied. But he still wasn't convinced.

Scrambling back through the opening, he said to Bradley, 'Where does that lane lead to?'

'Nowhere much,' Bradley replied. 'It circles round the back of the village, starting on the far side of my land and joining the main road again opposite the church. It serves a farm, that's all. There used to be some cottages as well, I believe, but they were pulled down years ago.' He was silent for a moment, standing hunched up against the rain under the trees as Finch swung his torch round. Then he added, 'Well, have you seen enough?'

'For the time being,' Finch replied. 'I'd like another look at the place in daylight.'

'Suit yourself.' Bradley sounded resigned. He started off again towards the house, Finch and Boyce following, none of them speaking until they reached the paved area near the back door where Finch remarked, 'We won't come in again, Mr Bradley. We'll go back along the drive. But there's just a couple more questions I'd like to ask. When you were at the Hamiltons' party, did you happen to notice a shot-gun in the house?'

Bradley's answer was immediate. 'No, I didn't.'

'But you knew Mr Hamilton owned a gun?'

'I knew he went out rough-shooting from time to time with Napier,' Bradley said. 'But so did a lot of other people in the village.'

Finch nodded as if conceding this point before continuing, 'The other question is this: who were you phoning when you heard the shot?'

'What business is that of yours?' Bradley demanded. They had come to a halt outside the kitchen where it was possible to see his face in the light streaming out from the uncurtained window.

'I shall want to corroborate the time,' Finch pointed out.

'Yes, I understand.' Bradley seemed to accept this explanation although he looked embarrassed as he continued, 'It was Dr Livesey. I rang her up about a wing-mirror for her car I'd bought in Framden. It was her day off so she was out until this evening. That's why I phoned so late.'

'I see,' Finch replied although he understood a great deal more than this simple statement implied. Whatever Bradley's relationship was with Dr Livesey, it evidently caused the man some unease – a reaction Finch could understand when, shortly after he and Boyce had returned to the Hamiltons' house, he met Dr Livesey herself. She was in the hall with Felix Napier who was helping her on with her coat.

A plain woman, Finch decided, summing her up quickly. Although she was only in her late twenties or early thirties, she already had a spinsterish look about her. The clothes she was wearing were sensible rather than fashionable, a dark tweed skirt and plain black jumper, unrelieved by any jewellery, while her hair was cut like a boy's, very short all over her head.

Felix Napier was saying, 'I'm very grateful for all you've done for my daughter.'

She made no direct reference to his remark, merely saying, 'Try to keep her quiet, although she's over the worst of the shock. Either Dr Wade or I will call in to see her again tomorrow.' Picking up her medical bag, she crossed the hall, pausing in front of Finch to inquire, 'I take it you're in charge of the case? Detective Chief Inspector Finch, isn't it? I assume you'll want to question Mrs Hamilton. When you do, I must ask you to keep it as brief as possible at this stage. She's in no condition yet to make a lengthy statement.'

She seemed about to leave and Finch put out a hand to detain her. 'If you could spare a few minutes, Dr Livesey, there're a couple of questions I'd like to ask you.'

'Of course,' she replied.

Felix Napier hesitated for a moment and then put in. 'When you're ready, Chief Inspector, you'll find my daughter waiting in the drawing-room. As Dr Livesey said, she's still recovering from shock and I'm anxious to take her home with me. So I'd be grateful if any inquiries or tests you have to make are carried out as quickly as possible.'

And with that, he turned on his heel and re-entered the drawing-room, leaving Finch and Boyce alone in the hall with Dr Livesey.

Encountering her for the first time, Finch could understand Bradley's embarrassment when he spoke of her. There was a brusque directness about her which would not suffer fools gladly; not that Bradley was a fool but, if he cherished any hopes of a romantic relationship with her, as it seemed he did, he was wasting his time in the Chief Inspector's opinion, although Finch himself could understand the attraction. He, too, liked her type of woman – cool, intelligent, astringent, something of a challenge – although, at the same time, he had his reservations on a personal level. She reminded him too much of another woman doctor, Marion Greave, who had acted as locum some time before when Pardoe, the police surgeon who was normally called out on a case involving sudden death, had been on holiday. To his own surprise and chagrin, he had fallen in love with her, head over heels, like an adolescent, absurd though such behaviour seemed even to him. A middle-aged bachelor, cared for by his widowed sister, he had come to accept his way of life as settled. Besides, he was too private a person and too unsure of his own ability to sustain any deep relationship to want to commit himself. Ironically, when he had at last found the courage to propose to her, she had turned him down for exactly the same reasons.

He had not seen her for over a year, not since she had sold up her practice in Chelmsford to take up a hospital appointment in Leeds. They wrote to each other occasionally, friendly letters merely, which now formed the only link between them although Finch was grateful for even this tenuous connection. It was better than nothing.

Dr Livesey's similarity to Marion Greave had given him a sudden jolt of remembered pain and happiness, although the two women were not physically alike. All the same, they shared certain qualities in their directness of manner and air of brisk professionalism, common perhaps to all women doctors, which were enough to remind him of the ache of regret for what might have been; although no one, not even Boyce and his own sister, were aware of that sense of emptiness which he carried about inside him and which no other woman would ever be able to fill.

But there was no time to brood. Dr Livesey was saying briskly, 'If you want my medical opinion on Mr Hamilton's death, I'm afraid I'm not competent to give it, Chief Inspector. I know very little about gun-shot wounds.'

'No, it isn't that,' Finch explained. 'The pathologist's report will tell me all I need to know. I wanted to ask about another matter. I believe Mr Bradley phoned you earlier this evening.'

'That's right,' she replied. 'He rang just before a quarter-past ten; at ten-fourteen, if you want a precise time.'

'You're sure of that?' Boyce put in.

She turned on him the same cool regard. 'Yes. I'd only just returned home from a day in London and I was annoyed at getting a phone call so late in the evening.'

Although she did not say it in so many words, Finch suspected that some of her exasperation had been directed at the caller himself, Steven Bradley.

'And I understand,' Boyce continued, 'that he rang off suddenly?'

'No; in fact I rang off. He said he'd heard a noise like a gun going off somewhere outside, which had disturbed the dogs.'

As she spoke, she turned her head briefly towards the closed door of the study, then looked back at Finch, her very straight eyebrows raised. She had clearly made the connection between Bradley's statement and Hamilton's murder but, when Finch added no further comment, she continued, 'It was then I hung up.'

'You heard nothing yourself?' Boyce asked.

'On the other end of a telephone line?' Ruth livesey sounded amused and derisive.

Boyce looked embarrassed and Finch, to cover up the Sergeant's discomfiture, resumed the questioning. 'And later Mr Napier telephoned you?'

'Yes; he rang about twenty to eleven. As Dr Wade was already out on an emergency, the call was transferred to me. There was nothing I could do. When I arrived, David Hamilton was already dead. If that's all, Chief Inspector, I'd like to get home. It's been a long day.'

'Of course,' Finch agreed. She did indeed look tired, the cheekbones showing up sharply under the skin, making her face look pinched and taut.

Going over to the front door, he opened it for her, a small courtesy which she acknowledged with a brief nod of her head as, medical bag in hand, she walked with a determined, upright step out of the house.

Crikey!' Boyce remarked, as the door closed behind her. 'I wouldn't fancy her taking my pulse.'

'She's probably very competent,' Finch replied, feeling an absurd need to defend her for no better reason than that she was like Marion Greave, a woman doctor. He was quick to add, in order to change the subject, 'Come on, Tom, Mrs Hamilton's waiting in the drawing-room. It's about time we questioned her,' although, as he crossed the hall and tapped on the door, he realized he was not looking forward to interviewing the murdered man's widow. All the same, it had to be done.

9

Meeting Elizabeth Hamilton for the first time, Finch could understand Napier's concern over her. She looked pale and tired, although the Chief Inspector was struck not so much by her physical frailty as by her beauty. Despite the shock of her husband's death, she was still a very attractive woman, and as he crossed the room towards her he wondered if he need look any further for a motive for her husband's murder.

Other men would doubtless find her attractive. Had someone else fallen in love with her and killed her husband out of jealousy? It was a possibility he would have to bear in mind, although his expression betrayed nothing more than official sympathy which was not altogether feigned.

She was sitting in a chair close to the fire, wearing a sheepskin coat as if, despite the blaze, she were still cold. Her fair hair was tucked inside its collar which was drawn up close to her neck so that her face peeped out at him from the cocoon of fur like an exhausted child's.

'I'm sorry,' Finch began, intending the remark to be a general commiseration not only for the tragedy which had happened but also for his own part in having to question her. 'I'll be as quick as I can, Mrs Hamilton. If you wouldn't mind answering a few questions first, I'll send Detective Constable Wylie in afterwards to make the necessary tests. You understand why they have to be done?'

'Yes, of course,' she replied. 'I'll do anything you wish.'

She spoke with a quiet acceptance for which Finch was grateful although he noticed that Napier, who had opened the door to Boyce and himself, was quick to cross to her side and, seating himself on the arm of her chair, laid a protective hand on her shoulder, confirming the Chief Inspector's earlier impression that Napier and his daughter were very close.

In view of her state of shock, Finch began with those events closest to the time of her husband's murder, postponing a longer and more detailed examination to a later date.

'I believe you were out this evening, Mrs Hamilton?'

'Yes, I was in Framden,' she replied. 'In fact, I was there most of the day, shopping and going to the hairdresser's. This evening I went to my usual aerobics class with a woman friend – we go every Tuesday. On the way home, I had a puncture. I tried phoning David first but, as there was no reply, I rang daddy instead.'

It was said in a weary voice as if she lacked the strength to rouse any emotional response in herself other than exhausted resignation.

'What time was this?' Finch asked. He noticed that Boyce had seated himself unobtrusively on the far side of the room and was taking notes of the conversation, which was substantially the same as Napier's.

'I'm not sure. It was about quarter-past ten, I suppose, although I don't look at my watch. I had to leave the car and walk to a phone-box. Then I went back to the car and waited for daddy to pick me up. It was half-past ten when you got there, wasn't it?' She turned to her father in appeal.

'Exactly half-past,' Napier assured her. 'I remember you said I'd been quick and we both looked at the time.'

'And when would you have arrived at the house?' Finch continued.

'It's just under a ten-minute drive, so it would have been about twenty to eleven.'

It was Felix Napier who replied as if the matter of estimating times and distances were best left to a man.

'And the lights were out in the house, apart from the reading lamp in the study?' Finch asked, deliberately addressing Elizabeth Hamilton.

Again it was Napier who answered. 'Yes, as I've already told you, Chief Inspector.'

'I'd like to hear your daughter's account,' Finch said. 'The facts have to be confirmed.'

As if to ease the situation, Elizabeth Hamilton reached up to touch her father's hand as it lay on her shoulder before replying.

'Yes, the house was in darkness apart from the lamp in the study. But that wasn't unusual. I've got home before on a Tuesday and found most of the lights off. You see, once David got absorbed in his work, he'd be shut up in the study for hours. Unless he had to leave the room for some reason, it wouldn't occur to him to turn them on.' She paused to control her voice before continuing, 'I'd asked daddy in for a night-cap. I called David to come and join us, and when he didn't answer daddy opened the study door and found him. I don't really remember what happened after that, until Ruth Livesey arrived. She took me upstairs and made me have a hot bath and change out of my wet clothes.'

Damn! Finch thought, although he supposed that, in the circumstances, Dr Livesey could hardly have acted otherwise. All the same, it was unlikely that any powder stains would remain on Mrs Hamilton's skin; not that he necessarily suspected her of shooting her husband, but anyone closely connected with Hamilton would have to be checked on.

He made no comment, however, passing on to another aspect of the case – the question of motive, remembering the thought which had occurred to him as he had entered the room that jealousy could have been behind the murder.

'Do you know of anyone who might have had a reason for

killing your husband?' he asked, and saw her hand tighten on the collar which she was clutching to her throat.

'Oh, no!' she cried. 'No one could have wanted David dead. It's absurd! Everyone liked him . . .'

She broke off in tears to Finch's discomfiture, and he was almost relieved when Napier said in an authoritative voice, 'I think we'll leave it there, Chief Inspector.'

'For the time being,' Finch agreed, 'although I'll need to have longer statements from you both at some other time.' He rose awkwardly to his feet. 'I'll send in Wylie and another Detective Constable to take the hand swabs and fingerprints. I shall also need to have Mrs Hamilton's car taken to Divisional Headquarters to be examined, although I'll make sure it's returned tomorrow. You understand that all of this is part of the routine?'

'Yes, yes, you've already explained that,' Felix Napier said impatiently. 'Just get it over and done with. I want to take my daughter home.'

Outside in the hall, Finch sent Boyce to find Wylie and Marsh and, after the two men had gone into the drawing-room with their equipment, he signalled to the Sergeant to follow him into the kitchen where they held a brief conference.

There was little more that could be done that night. The house and part of the garden had been searched, the study and the container in which the gun might have been placed had been fingerprinted, the gun itself parcelled up for forensic examination. Wylie had been instructed to ask for the clothes that Elizabeth Hamilton had been wearing that evening so that they, too, could be tested for powder marks together with Felix Napier's which would have to be picked up the following day; all part of the routine of an investigation, as Finch had explained to Napier and his daughter. As for the body, that still had to be moved – although Finch was inclined to wait until Napier and Mrs Hamilton had left the house.

The rest, including a more detailed search of the Hamiltons' garden as well as Bradley's, would have to wait until daylight, although Elizabeth Hamilton's car could be towed away for examination at Divisional Headquarters that night as soon as Finch himself had taken a look at it.

'You can get on to that now, Tom,' Finch concluded, 'and, while you're at it, send in Gilmore, the local bobby. He should still be on duty at the front door.'

'What do you want to see him for?' Boyce demanded nosily.

'Just something I want to check on,' Finch replied with deliberate vagueness.

Boyce shrugged and went off to fetch Gilmore, returning in a few minutes with the young, fresh-faced constable in tow.

'Yes, sir?' he asked, coming to attention just inside the doorway. It was his first murder investigation and he was apprehensive at being summoned before a Detective Chief Inspector from Divisional Headquarters, assuming it was on account of some dereliction of duty on his part.

In the event, the Chief Inspector's question seemed innocuous enough. 'Is there a telephone kiosk in the village?'

'Yes, sir; it's outside the village shop, but it's out of order.'

His answer seemed to rouse the Chief Inspector's interest for he demanded sharply, 'Since when?'

'Since that storm this morning, sir.' Gilmore looked alarmed as if it were all his fault. 'A branch was brought down on the line. I know because someone from the village called at my house and asked me to report the fault as my phone was still working. I was told they'd send the engineers out as soon as they could but it'd probably not be until tomorrow. There's been quite a lot of damage done to lines and they were dealing with emergencies first.'

'So the phone-box in the village wasn't working this evening?'

'No, sir; it's still out of order.'

'Where's the next nearest kiosk?'

'A couple of miles along the Framden road; next to the filling station.'

Which seemed to be the same one which Elizabeth Hamilton had said she used to ring her father, Finch thought, although that fact would have to be checked.

'Just one more question,' he told Gilmore. 'You live in the village. You didn't happen to hear a sound like a gun being fired about quarter-past ten tonight?'

Gilmore shook his head.

'No, sir, I'm afraid I didn't. The police house is some distance from here. Besides it was too windy . . .'

His voice trailed away and Finch dismissed him with a nod of his head back to his post by the front door, adding, for Boyce's benefit as the door closed behind him, 'Just making a start on checking Mrs Hamilton's statement, Tom.'

Boyce's reaction was predictable, although that didn't prevent Finch from feeling exasperation rise as the Sergeant began, 'You don't think that . . . ?'

'Mrs Hamilton had anything to do with her husband's murder?' Finch completed the question for him. 'No, I don't; at least not at this stage. But her evidence has to be followed up. Now let's get things moving. I want a couple of men left here on duty overnight. If you'll organize that, I'll make arrangements for the ambulance to pick up the body once Napier and his daughter have left. I also want to make sure Marsh finger-printed that gun-safe in the study . . .'

Even so, it was another hour before they finally drove away, Boyce at the wheel, Finch in the passenger seat beside him. As they left, Finch glanced at his watch.

Seven minutes later, as he verified by a second glance at the time, they were drawing up at a gate opening where an MG was parked on the verge, the break-down van, sent for from Headquarters, already waiting in front of it to tow it away.

'Neat little job,' Boyce said admiringly, getting out to join Finch in the rain.

The Chief Inspector didn't bother to reply, merely squatting down to examine the near-side back wheel. Napier had been correct in his statement that it had taken under ten minutes to drive his daughter back to the house. The puncture, too, was obvious, the nail which had caused it sticking out between the treads.

On the way there, Finch had looked out for the telephone kiosk from which Elizabeth Hamilton had said she had telephoned her father and had seen it about a quarter of a mile further back along the road, next to a garage, approximately a five-minute walk from the gateway, although distances and timings would have to be checked later. It was now nearly three o'clock in the morning and he was wet through. Once the car had been towed away, it would be time to go home.

He would have preferred to be silent on the drive back to Chelmsford but Boyce was in a talkative mood. Finch had noticed before that tiredness tended to loosen his tongue, making him argumentative.

'I still think it could have been an intruder who shot Hamilton,' he began. 'That pen needn't be all that significant. Hamilton could have laid it down like that, thinking it was his wife coming in. We know, of course, that it couldn't have been; not if we assume that what Bradley heard just before quarter-past ten was the sound of the shot which killed Hamilton. She was phoning her father from that kiosk on the Framden road.'

'You're jumping to too many conclusions, Tom,' Finch pointed out, rousing himself from his contemplation of the road ahead of them, lit by the headlamps of the car as the wipers swept the rain from the windscreen. 'For a start, we don't know at what time Mrs Hamilton normally got home on a Tuesday. Come to that, until we've checked out her statement, we can't even be sure where she was at ten-fifteen. As for Bradley, how do we know he was speaking the truth? We only have his word for it. You remember what Dr Livesey said? She could hear nothing on the other end of the line. What was to stop Bradley from telling her he'd heard a noise like a shot?'

'So you think Bradley could have been lying? But why should he want to do that?'

'To give himself an alibi?' Finch suggested.

It was a mistake to voice such a speculation out loud. As Finch feared, Boyce seized on it immediately. 'An alibi? But that implies he was guilty of murder, and why should Bradley want to kill Hamilton? And if you're going to tell me it was over that right of way, then all I can say is – come off it! No one commits murder over a bloody path.'

'No?' Finch countered, stung into reaction despite himself. 'What about the case last year involving those two farmers? They nearly killed each other, and that was over a disputed field boundary. People can get very worked up over legal access and who owns a particular piece of land.'

'Bradley certainly lost his cool tonight over that right of way,' Boyce agreed reluctantly. 'But what about the letter we found on Hamilton's desk? If Bradley shot Hamilton, wouldn't he have taken it away with him? After all, it is evidence which could point to him.'

'If he knew it was there,' Finch replied. 'Look, Tom, I'm not putting this forward as a definite scenario of what happened tonight, only a possibility. All the same, it could hang together as a theory. We know that Bradley wrote to Hamilton about ten days ago, asking for a meeting to discuss the right of way. Bradley admitted that much himself. He also said he'd heard nothing from Hamilton apart from an acknowledgement that he'd received the letter. Now, supposing he rang Hamilton tonight to ask whether he'd come to a decision? Hamilton replied that he was going to refuse permission to close the path and rang off. But Bradley's call prompted Hamilton to write that letter which we found on his desk. As a solicitor, he'd realize the importance of sending off a written confirmation of a verbal statement as soon as possible. I know Hamilton made no reference in the letter to any telephone conversation he'd had with Bradley, but that doesn't rule out the possibility that one had taken place. Meanwhile, Bradley had had time to think over Hamilton's refusal and to work himself up into a state about it. If that's what happened – and I stress the word "if", Tom – he could have gone round to Hamilton's place to have it out with him face to face.'

'You mean, he let himself in at the back door, picking up the gun from that container in the hall on his way? I suppose he could have noticed it was there on Saturday evening at the Hamilton's party. I know he denied seeing it, but he'd hardly admit that if he'd killed Hamilton. In that case, it'd be a premeditated murder, wouldn't it?'

'Not necessarily. Supposing Hamilton let Bradley in by the front door, like any normal visitor, and took him into the study where a quarrel broke out? Bradley went storming out of the house, as Hamilton thought, but only got as far as the passage where he picked up the gun. He went back to the study, surprising Hamilton who'd sat down again at the desk. And if that's what happened, it was an unplanned killing, done on the spur of the moment. Either way, Bradley needn't have known about the letter Hamilton was writing to him. He may not have given Hamilton time to mention it, and in his panic he wouldn't have stopped to search the room, let alone the desk. He'd've cleared off as soon as possible, although he could have calmed down enough by the time he got home to make that phone call to Dr Livesey, pretending he'd just heard a noise outside like a gun going off. That way, he'd give himself an alibi, not a watertight one, but better than nothing. Later, when we turned up to start the inquiry, Bradley rang the house with the excuse he wanted to find out what was going on. But he could have had another motive – supposing, after he'd fired the gun, he hadn't waited around long enough to check Hamilton was in fact dead? If the hall lights were off, as Napier and Mrs Hamilton both stated they were when they got back to the house at twenty to eleven, then Bradley could well have fired from the darkened hall into a room only partly lit by the lamp on Hamilton's desk. Alternatively, he could have turned the lights off himself when he left in an attempt to establish the intruder theory. I'm not convinced, you see, that the house was in darkness, any more than I'm prepared to go along with Napier's statement that his son-in-law left the gun in that container in the hall.'

'But, hang on a minute!' Boyce protested. 'If the gun wasn't there, then the whole theory against Bradley falls to pieces!'

'That's right, Tom,' Finch replied, cheering up at the Sergeant's discomfiture. 'And if we assume that, we have to assume something else as well.'

'Which is what?' Boyce demanded suspiciously.

'That Bradley could be speaking the truth when he said he heard the sound of a shot at just before ten-fifteen tonight, in which case we can establish the time the murder was committed and we have to start looking at the evidence against other possible suspects.'

'Such as who?'

'Someone who was close to Hamilton – his wife, his father-in-law, any friends or colleagues. That's why I want to make a start tomorrow on checking out alibis, including Napier's and Mrs Hamilton's.'

'What about motive?' Boyce asked.

Finch closed his eyes wearily. 'Let's leave it for tonight, shall we, Tom? It's too late for any more speculation.'

They were approaching the outskirts of Chelmsford, and a few minutes later Boyce dropped the Chief Inspector off at his house in a quite suburban road which, at that hour of the morning and in the rain, looked like an abandoned film-set, unreal and ominously deserted.

As Boyce drove off, Finch let himself in by the front door, moving quietly in order not to disturb his sister, Dorothy. All the same, as he took off his wet shoes and coat and padded through into the kitchen to make tea, he heard her open her bedroom door and come out on to the landing where she switched on the light.

'It's only me,' he called out. 'Don't bother to get up. I can manage.'

She came downstairs nevertheless to join him in the kitchen, wearing her dressing-gown, her face full of concern for his sake and, as she took over from him the task of filling the kettle and getting the bottle of milk from the refrigerator, he was aware of a sudden surge of love, exasperation and guilt.

'I'm quite capable of making a cup of tea for myself,' he protested.

'You go and have a bath, Jack,' she told him. 'I'll have it ready for you when you come downstairs.'

It was sensible advice, typical of her, and he shrugged and smiled a little ruefully and he gave in. She was older than he was, in her mid-fifties, and so like their mother that even he was sometimes taken aback when, on glancing up suddenly or walking into a room, he saw the same pleasantly plain face, the grey hair smoothed back into a little coil at the nape of her neck, and, what was more, that familiar expression of affectionate concern or loving pride which only added to his own sense of guilty exasperation. As a child, he had longed to escape both from his mother and his boyhood home, irked by the restrictions they had placed on him, and yet there he was, reduplicating the relationship through his sister, concealing from her, as he had done from his mother, a large part of his life, including his own relationship with Marion Greave.

But that was over; or as good as over. There would be no

escape for him through her, however much he might yearn for it, into a different, freer life.

In his more objective moments, he was able to realize that both of them had lost out; Dorothy more than he had. Widowed at thirty when her husband had been killed in a farming accident, she had never remarried and yet she had seemed cut out for marriage and a house full of children. Instead, she had devoted all that care to him, willingly and without complaint. It seemed churlish on his part to feel, as he frequently did, stifled by so much unselfish devotion.

He paused in the doorway, stricken by a new cause for guilt. 'You got a lift home all right?'

She had gone out that evening to some social do or other run by the local church, from which he had promised to collect her in the car. Then he had been called out on the Hamilton case and, although he had telephoned the church hall and left a message explaining the circumstances, he had not given the matter another thought until now.

She had her back to him as she stretched up to get cups from the wall cabinet and did not look round.

'Yes,' she said, adding after a pause, 'Mr Goodall was kind enough to run me home.'

So that was all right, Finch thought, tramping up the stairs to the bathroom. Although he had noticed the slight hesitation, it did not strike him as particularly significant and he soon forgot it in his own relief and pleasure as, stripping off his wet clothes, he lowered himself gratefully into the hot water.

10

'So what about Napier and Mrs Hamilton?' Boyce asked, picking up the conversation from the night before as if it had only just been broken off. 'What evidence have we got against them?'

Finch suppressed a sigh. He had been hoping to avoid further speculation on the case but the Sergeant still seemed in an argumentative mood, made worse by the start of a head cold brought on by the previous day's soaking.

They were on their way back to Woodstone later than Finch had intended, part of the morning having been taken up by a conference at headquarters at which the Chief Inspector had been occupied with routine matters, all of them necessary but which had prevented him from getting on with the down-to-earth business of interviewing the suspects in the case. He felt fretted by the delay. All the same, some progress had been made. Arrangements had been started for a mobile headquarters to be set up in the village, a team of detectives and uniformed men had been sent out to make house to house inquiries, while Kyle, who had been given the task of checking on PC Gilmore's statement, had confirmed that the telephone kiosk in Woodstone had indeed been out of order most of the previous day. In fact, the line had only been repaired that morning.

The Chief Inspector referred to this point as he replied to Boyce's question.

'As far as Elizabeth Hamilton's concerned, I admit we haven't yet come up with much evidence against her, Tom. As I pointed out last night, if Bradley was speaking the truth about that shot he heard, then we're fairly safe in assuming that Hamilton was killed at roughly quarter-past ten last night. There was a slim chance that she might have had time to drive down to the village and make that call to her father a couple of minutes later but, as the phone-box in Woodstone was out of order, I can't see that she had enough opportunity to commit the murder. The next nearest kiosk is the one on the Framden road and that's too far away. It took us seven minutes to drive there so I can't see how he could have got to it in the time.'

'And Napier?' Boyce persisted.

'He was alone yesterday evening, so I suppose he could have had the opportunity to kill his son-in-law,' Finch admitted. 'But, if we accept Bradley's evidence, I can't see how he got back to his house, either, in time to take the phone call from his daughter so soon afterwards. We'll have to check on how long it would have taken him to drive home, of course, but . . .'

‘So it looks as if we can rule out both of them,’ the sergeant interrupted, in the tone of someone stating the obvious, and looked taken aback when Finch replied, ‘No, we can’t assume anything of the sort, not yet anyway. The case is still wide open. I simply said I couldn’t see how Napier or his daughter could have had the time to murder Hamilton. That doesn’t mean they’re innocent. For a start, they could have arranged the alibi of the phone call between them.’

He hadn’t intended the remark to be taken all that seriously. Even so, Boyce seemed outraged at the idea.

‘You mean they set up a conspiracy? But why the hell should they do that?’

‘I don’t know,’ Finch snapped, his exasperation getting the better of him. ‘I could give you any number of reasons. Supposing the Hamiltons weren’t happily married? Or that she was having an affair and wanted her husband out of the way? It’s not impossible. She’s a damned good-looking woman. Or, come to that, Hamilton himself could have had a mistress, and Napier and Mrs Hamilton decided to bump him off because of it. The point I’m trying to make is this, Tom – we haven’t yet got enough evidence to prove anyone’s guilt of innocence, and until we have we’re simply wasting our time going over the possibilities. Turn right at the church,’ he added as they approached the outskirts of Woodstone. ‘I want to have a look at the lane which runs behind Bradley’s place and the Hamiltons’. You can drop me off at the gate opening. I’ll meet you at the house later. In the meantime, you can get the men started on making a proper search of the Hamiltons’ garden.’

Which had the desired effect of shutting Boyce up, at least for the time being.

As soon as Dodie entered Frazer’s, Kate could tell something was wrong. It wasn’t just the fact that she was late. Dodie was rarely on time even at school, turning up late at staff meetings, apologetic and out of breath. She looked distraught, her hair bundled up anyhow and her mouth trembling.

Plumping herself down opposite Kate, who had already

drunk one cup of coffee while she waited, she said, 'Oh, Lord, Kate, I'm so sorry! I forgot we'd arranged to meet this morning until nearly a quarter to eleven. Something awful's happened which put it completely out of my mind.'

'To do with Mike?' Kate asked. Remembering the incident over the salad dressing, she wouldn't have put it past Mike to involve Dodie in some trivial domestic drama which had made her forget the appointment.

'No, it isn't about Mike,' Dodie replied, although she said it without much conviction. Mike was indeed on her mind as well. He had come home from the White Hart the precious evening in an even worse mood than when he had left and had hardly spoken to her since. But compared to the other events which had happened, this seemed of minor importance even to her. Besides, she wouldn't dream of confiding these problems to Kate, however much she might long for another woman's sympathy. So she hurried on, loosening her coat as she spoke and trying to fasten up her hair with the other hand. 'It's about the Hamiltons. David was killed last night. Isn't it dreadful? When I heard the news this morning, I could hardly believe it. God knows what Elizabeth must be feeling . . .'

'Killed?' Kate asked. 'You mean in a car accident?'

The news was a shock to her as well; not as much as it was to Dodie, of course, who knew the Hamiltons well and who was clearly still affected for she looked close to tears.

Dodie blinked rapidly and leaned across the table, lowering her voice. 'No, it wasn't an accident, Kate. Someone shot him.'

So it was murder, Kate thought. She hesitated to speak the word out loud, partly because of Dodie's reluctance to voice the same conclusion and partly because the very idea itself seemed absurd, especially in such a setting as Frazer's, among the cake trolleys and the white tablecloths, the discreet hum of conversation as other women like themselves chatted over the coffee cups.

David Hamilton murdered!

She recalled meeting him at the party only four days ago, although she remembered him less clearly than Elizabeth Hamilton, apart from a certain boyish charm, studious and, she felt, a little shy. And now he was murdered. Ridiculously, she thought of the Hamiltons' bedroom with its big, comfortable, chintz-draped bed which had seemed so safe and accommodating.

'They think someone must have broken into the house,' Dodie was continuing, although whether by 'they' she meant the police or local opinion, Kate couldn't tell. 'Thank God Elizabeth was out for the evening or he might have shot them both.'

'I'll ask for fresh coffee,' Kate put in quickly, summoning the waitress who had been hovering nearby, waiting to take their order and yet unsure whether to break in on what clearly was an intimate and distressing conversation.

The waitress's approach caused a small diversion, giving Kate time to collect her thoughts. It had been on the tip of her tongue to mention the fact that she had seen Elizabeth Hamilton in Framden only the previous afternoon, walking up Bruton Street in the rain, and then she remembered just in time that she had been on her way to Felix Napier's house for tea and to borrow his edition of the Jane Austen letters, an arrangement originally made by her to save the embarrassment of having to call on Dodie and explain her reason for being in Woodstone, Dodie and Mike having gone out for the day.

It had all become so complicated that it was best, she decided, to say nothing. Instead, as the waitress brought the fresh coffee, she asked, 'How is Felix Napier taking the news?'

As he was a near neighbour of Dodie's, it was possible that she might know. No doubt he'd be shocked, Kate thought, and wondered if she should write expressing her sympathy. Although she didn't know him all that well, she felt she ought not to ignore the situation. He had struck her as a lonely man, punctilious himself over such courtesies. He might appreciate a short letter, thanking him for tea and the loan of the book, with a few sentences of regret over his son-in-law's death.

Dodie was saying, 'I don't know. I haven't seen him, although I imagine he must be shattered. He was very fond of David. Elizabeth's with him, I gather. And the police are everywhere, of couse. I saw their cars parked outside the Hamiltons' house on my way here and it seems they're making inquiries in the village as well.' She broke off to dab at her eyes with a handkerchief and to drink a little coffee which Kate had poured for her before repeating, 'It's so dreadful. I can't believe it's really happened.'

'Stay with me for the rest of the day,' Kate urged. 'We could have lunch out together and then you could come back with me to the flat for the afternoon.'

'Oh, I'd love to, Kate, but I mustn't,' Dodie replied. 'I ought to get back. There's an order to pack up for the health-food wholesaler's and I promised I'd give Mike a hand with it. The police might want to question me as well; not that I can tell them much. I haven't seen either Elizabeth or David since their party on Saturday. And besides,' she hesitated before continuing, 'Mike's feeling a bit low and I don't like leaving him on his own when he's in that mood.'

'Why not?' Kate asked. It seemed to her absurd that Dodie should have to hurry home on that account.

'Oh, I don't know,' Dodie said vaguely, finishing her coffee so quickly that she slopped some of it into the saucer. 'We spent yesterday at my sister's and it wasn't exactly a success. The kids got on his nerves, I'm afraid. So . . .'

She left it there, wishing she had not raised the subject of Mike in the first place. After all, she couldn't expect Kate, who was unmarried, to understand. And Mike's moodiness wasn't just the result of the trip to her sister's. He had something else on his mind as well, although God alone knew what. Dodie couldn't get to the bottom of it herself, let alone voice it out loud to Kate.

'I must go,' she said again, getting up from the table. 'What about the bill?'

'My treat,' Kate replied.

On a sudden impulse, Dodie swooped down and kissed Kate on the cheek, to the astonishment of them both. Dodie herself wasn't sure why she did it. Part of the reason was pure affection. She was very fond of Kate. And she looked so neat and attractive sitting there in her well-cut coat, her hair drawn back into its smooth coil, like a beautifully made cottage-loaf Dodie thought absurdly, that she wanted to show how much she wished she could order her own image in the same fashion – controlled and intelligent, with no fuss and muddle.

Part of it was regret, too, that she couldn't say, as she longed to do, 'There are time when I almost wish I hadn't married Mike.'

But for all their sakes, that could never be said.

Finch got out of the car at the opening in the hedge behind Bradley's property, leaving Boyce to drive on along the lane to the front of the Hamiltons' house where he had arranged to meet him later. When the car had gone, he stood for a few moments, looking about him.

Bradley had been right when he had said this back lane was little used. It swung round in a rough semi-circle behind the village and seemed to serve one farm only, which stood well back from the road at the end of its own drive. As they had passed no other houses or cottages, the chances of finding any witnesses who had seen or heard a passer-by or a car were remote.

Nor did the covering of dead leaves and twigs lying in the opening carry any prints of shoes or tyres as Finch had suspected the night before, although he squatted down again to peer closely at them. He'd send Barney along to have a look, of course. He was the expert, but the Chief Inspector guessed that they would both be wasting their time.

Stepping sideways through the narrow gap left between the piles of broken branches and brambles with which Bradley had partially closed off the opening, Finch entered the spinnery where he paused again. The trees had been left standing but there were signs that the undergrowth had been cut back, leaving the pathway clear. That, too, seemed little used although its track could be traced to the edge of the spinney.

Here it divided, one branch leading off towards a gap in the tall fir hedge which separated Bradley's property from the Hamiltons', the other running straight ahead towards the kennels, thus giving the occupants of both houses access to the lane. And, Finch thought, to anyone else who chose to enter by this back way.

Once clear of the narrow belt of trees, he was able to get a clearer idea of the layout than he had been able to do the previous evening by torchlight.

Bradley's premises faced him, the larger of the two properties, its land extending to nearly a couple of acres, Finch estimated. Nearest to him was a wide expanse of rough grass. Then came the kennels, low, white-painted buildings, set out on both sides of the broad concrete path, each containing six separate boarding units with their own pens. About a third of them were occupied. He could see dogs moving about inside some of the yards, jumping up at the partitions or lying about on the concrete floors, either asleep or merely bored. A large area over to the left with a high chain-link fence round it was, he supposed, a special exercise pen. A girl in a white overall coat was trotting an Alsation on a lead round and round it, neither of them appearing to be getting much fun out of it.

Beyond the kennels, the back view of the house and its outbuildings was visible.

Finch was about to set off along the path which led towards the Hamiltons' property when he saw Bradley emerge from one of the kennel units. Bradley, too, seemed aware of his presence, for as he closed the door behind him he raised an arm, signalling to the Chief Inspector to wait before starting off at an awkward, loping stride across the grass. Something had evidently excited the man.

'I'm glad I've seen you, Chief Inspector,' Bradley announced as soon as he approached. 'I've got something to show you.'

'What's that?' Finch asked.

Bradley, who had set off again towards the house, explained over his shoulder. 'Some stuff of mine's been stolen from one of the outhouses. I only noticed it'd gone this morning.'

'What stuff?' Finch asked a little impatiently, wishing to God Bradley would get to the point. They were passing the kennels and he had to raise his voice above the barking of the dogs, excited by the presence of the two men. It made conversation difficult and, as Finch himself had to admit, if they'd made as much noise the previous evening, they would have effectively covered up the sound of Hamilton's murderer making a getaway, assuming that Bradley had been speaking the truth, a point which the Chief Inspector wasn't yet ready to concede.

'Sorry, I'm not making myself clear,' Bradley said. He smiled apologetically, his face taking on a more pleasant expression. 'It's only an old coat and a pair of gloves I wear when I'm clearing the spinney. But I thought that, as they must have been taken some time yesterday, they might be connected with Hamilton's murder.'

'What sort of gloves and coat?' Finch asked, his own expression blank, giving nothing away.

'The coat's one of those padded shooting jackets and the gloves are just an old pair of leather gauntlets. Both are thornproof, though. That's why I used them when I've been cutting down the brambles. I left them in here.'

They had reached the paved area at the back of the house which was surounded on two sides by outbuildings; storerooms mostly, by the look of them, although the one in front of which Bradley had halted was more of a shed, its door fastened by a padlock hanging loose on the hasp. Bradley removed it and swung the door open, revealing the interior which contained nothing more than a few garden tools and some lumber.

'The point is,' Bradley continued, 'they must have been stolen between ten and two o'clock yesterday.'

'How can you be so sure?' Finch demanded.

'Because I was wearing the damned things until about quarter to ten. Tuesdays are my day off, you see, Chief Inspector; the kennels are closed for business. I'd been clearing the spinney but I packed it in when it started to rain and came back to the house. I left the coat and gloves in here to dry off.'

'And you didn't lock up?' Finch asked. That much was obvious.

'No, I'm afraid I didn't. It was raining hard and I didn't bother. At about ten, I went into Framden, getting back here at about two o'clock. It wasn't till I heard that noise last night and went out to check the kennels that I remembered about the shed so I locked it up.'

'You didn't look inside?'

'No, I didn't. The padlock was on the hasp so I just turned the key in it.'

'And what made you go to the shed this morning?' The Chief Inspector put the question in a pleasant, casual voice.

'I wanted to get the fork out,' Bradley explained after a moment's hesitation. 'I was going to clear back some of the stuff I'd piled up near the gateway over there.' He jerked his head in the direction of the spinney.

'I'd rather you didn't touch that opening until my men have had a chance to examine and photograph it,' Finch said with the same pleasant air.

'Yes, of course,' Bradley agreed quickly. He seemed embarrassed and Finch could guess why. The right of way and Bradley's own attempt to close it off evidently caused the man some disquiet.

'And I'll send someone round to fingerprint the padlock and the door,' Finch went on. 'So I'd be grateful if you didn't touch either again until that's been done. The officer will have to take your own prints, I'm afraid, Mr Bradley, for purposes of elimination, of course.'

'Yes, I understand,' Bradley said although Finch noticed that he stuffed his hands into his pockets as he spoke. 'Is that the lot?'

'There's only one more question for the moment. If someone came up to the shed, the dogs would start barking, I assume?'

'Yes, as you must have noticed for yourself when we walked past the kennels just now,' Bradley replied. 'And there's no way anyone could have got on to my land except by the back route. That's one of the reasons I was keen to get that opening closed off. The rest of the property's secure.'

He jerked his head again, this time towards the front of the premises, screened off not only by the house and its outbuildings but by a high chain-link fence and a pair of tall double gates which would allow a van to have access to the yard. 'Those gates were locked,' he added. He had lost his apologetic air and spoke in a more belligerent manner which was largely defensive, Finch suspected.

'And anyone in the Hamiltons' house would have heard the dogs if they'd been disturbed?'

Bradley shrugged.

'I suppose so. The hedge cuts out a lot of the noise; that's why it was planted in the first place. The Hamiltons' place isn't in line with the kennels either. But, yes, I suppose they'd have heard something although at the time the jacket and gloves must have been stolen, it's likely only Elizabeth Hamilton was at home. David Hamilton would have been at his office.'

'Thank you, Mr Bradley. I'll check with her,' Finch said and strolled away, hands in his own pockets.

II

'So you were right after all. Hamilton couldn't have been murdered by an intruder,' Boyce said with a grudging air.

It was half an hour later. Finch had finished supervising the investigation team at the scene of the murder, despatching McCullum and Barney to photograph and examine the gate opening which led into Gade's Lane as well as Wylie to fingerprint the padlock and door of Bradley's shed, leaving the rest of the men to complete the search of the Hamilton's garden. He and the Sergeant were on their way to Felix Napier's house to obtain longer statements from both Napier and his daughter, even more essential in the light of Bradley's evidence.

'It certainly looks that way,' Finch agreed. 'Whoever killed Hamilton must have planned the murder beforehand. The gloves and jacket missing from Bradley's shed would suggest that.'

It indicated a lot more besides – that whoever had stolen them had not only known where to find them but had taken the clothing at some time between ten and two o'clock when Bradley was out of the house; assuming, of course, that Bradley was telling the truth. But before Finch could expand on these points, Boyce broke in to remark. 'They'd be a good protection against powder marks on the hands and clothing.'

'Which was why they were lifted in the first place. So we'll be wasting our time getting Wylie to take hand swabs from any suspects.'

'Who don't include Bradley any longer?' Boyce asked, glancing sideways at the Chief Inspector to gauge his reactions, anxious not to stick his neck out a second time.

He looked abashed when Finch replied, 'I don't think so, Tom. Who'd know better than Bradley himself about the clothing? We've only got his word for it that they've been stolen. He could have worn them himself and them dumped them somewhere afterwards.'

'Then why report they're missing? If he'd kept his mouth shut, we'd be none the wiser,' Boyce pointed out, not unreasonably.

'To throw us off the scent?' Finch suggested. 'If Bradley thought we were getting too close to him, it'd be a damn good red herring to drag across our path. As it is, we're going to have to extend the search beyond the Hamiltons' place unless we come up with some answers soon, although God alone knows where we start looking for a pair of gloves and a jacket in a place like this.'

As he spoke, he stared gloomily ahead of him at the scene through the windscreen of fields and hedgerows and woodland, bloody acres of potential hiding-places. Rousing himself, he added, 'On the other hand, if Bradley was telling us the truth, then we can start making a few more assumptions about Hamilton's murderer. It's likely to be someone close to Hamilton who knew where to find the gun and therefore must have had access to the house. We also know that he or she must have had the opportunity to steal Bradley's clothing as well as commit the murder, so we're looking for someone with no alibi to cover the time Bradley was out of the house between ten and two o'clock yesterday and around quarter-past ten last night. And even then we're making a hell of a lot of assumptions – that what Bradley heard *was* the sound of a shot and not a car back-firing, and that the gun *was* left in that container in the hall. As I said to you yesterday, I'm not yet convinced of either. Even so, I think we're safe in concentrating our inquiries on Hamilton's family and friends.'

'Including Felix Napier and Mrs Hamilton,' Boyce put in with assurance. At least, on this point, he was unlikely to be in the wrong. Finch himself had stated that their guilt or innocence had yet to be proved.

He seemed relieved when Finch replied, 'Yes, they're still in the running, along with anyone else who knew Hamilton well.'

He was thinking in particular of the party which the Hamiltons had given on the previous Saturday evening, only days before the crime and at which a potential murderer would have had the opportunity not only to get to know the layout of the house but also where the shot-gun was kept, although, as he had pointed out to Boyce, whether or not it was standing in the container in the hall was debatable. It was one of the aspects of the case he wanted to discuss further with Felix Napier as well as obtaining either from him or his daughter a list of the guests who had been present at the party and whose alibis would also have to be checked.

'What about motive?' Boyce was asking.

'God knows,' Finch admitted. 'So far we've turned up only one possibility – Bradley and that right of way. Someone else may have had a good reason for wanting Hamilton dead, although according to Byrne the Inspector from Framden, Hamilton was popular, at least as a solicitor. We'll have to check on what he was like as a husband, son-in-law or friend.'

They had reached the top of the long hill which led up from the village and had turned into the driveway of Felix Napier's place, a modern, detached house. Finch got out of the car and, crossing the gravelled forecourt, rang the bell, checking his watch as he did so. It had taken three minutes to drive there from the Hamiltons' house.

Felix Napier opened the door to them and showed them into a comfortable but nondescript room with patio doors overlooking a large garden bedraggled by the wind and rain.

'If you want to question my daughter, she's resting at the moment,' he told them.

He seemed tired and much older, less upright and brisk than he had been the previous evening as if the shock had begun to wear him down, sapping his vitality. Even the labrador dog which accompanied him seemed subdued, sinking down with a sigh in front of the fire as Napier indicated chair for the Chief Inspector and the Sergeant before sitting down opposite them.

Finch said, 'If you don't mind, I'll talk to her later, Mr Napier. There're a few more questions I'd like to ask you first. About the guests at your daughter's party on Saturday . . .'

'I really don't see why that's relevant,' Felix Napier started to protest.

'I'd like the names and addresses all the same,' Finch said with a bland persistence.

'Very well.' Felix Napier waited with a quiet but faintly disapproving courtesy until Boyce had produced his notebook and pen and then began at dictation speed.

Most of them had local addresses although a few were from Framden. Only two of the names were familiar to Finch – Steven Bradley and Ruth Livesey, the local woman doctor who had been called out after Hamilton's murder; and he interrupted Napier to ask, 'I take it Dr Livesey was your son-in-law's GP?'

The point was a minor one but he wanted it established and, having omitted to find it out from Dr Livesey the previous evening during his interview with her, it seemed a good opportunity to ask Napier.

'No, she wasn't,' Napier corrected him. 'David used to be one of Dr Wade's patients – he's the senior partner – but he'd transferred a few months ago to another doctor in Framden. Evidently this new man practises holistic medicine and, according to my daughter, David was keen to try it out. But, as he was so far away and I didn't know his name, I telephoned my own GP, Dr Wade. He was already out on a case, so Dr Livesey came in his place. Is that all? Do you want me to go on with the list?' As Finch nodded in confirmation, Napier resumed, 'And the Pagetts were at the party as well. They're close neighbours of mine who live a couple of hundred yards down the lane. They brought a friend with them, a Miss Denby, a colleague of Mrs Pagett. She lives in Framden but I don't know her address. You'll have to ask Dodie for it.'

Finch was aware of a slight change in tone and manner as Felix Napier mentioned this last guest, Miss Denby. He drew himself up more straight-backed and his voice had taken on a new animation.

'I believe that's all,' he concluded. 'I can't think of any other names, but you'll have to check with my daughter. Is there anything else?'

'Just a couple more points,' Finch said. 'You said last night that you thought your son-in-law put the shot-gun in the container in the hall on the previous Saturday after you and he had been out rough-shooting. Did you notice yourself if it was still there on the night of the party?'

'No, I didn't. If I had, I'd have made quite sure David unloaded it and returned it to the gun-safe.'

'Which was normally kept locked?'

'I assume so; and it's where the shot-gun should have been placed as soon as we got back from the shoot. I still blame myself about the damned thing being left there in the hall, still loaded. If only I'd reminded David about it . . .' His voice trailed away miserably.

Finch made sympathetic noises, although his attention was fixed mainly on the implications in Napier's statement. As it was unlikely that Hamilton's murderer could have gained access to the gun-safe immediately before the killing, because Hamilton himself appeared to have been sitting in the study at his desk shortly before he was shot, only two inferences could be drawn – that the murderer had got hold of the gun at some earlier time, which would reinforce the evidence that the crime had been premeditated; or that Napier was right in thinking that the gun was still standing in the container in the hall. In the former case, it narrowed down the list of possible suspects to two – Napier himself or Elizabeth Hamilton, the only likely people who could have gained access to the gun-safe before the murder was committed. In the latter, the field was more wide open; it could have been any one of the guests at the Hamiltons' party who, seeing the gun in the hall and on a quick examination discovering it was still loaded, could have picked it up on the way to the study and used it to kill Hamilton.

Or, come to that, Finch added to himself, the murderer could have arrived at the house ready equipped with a cartridge to put into the gun, unaware that there was still one left in the breach.

Marsh had fingerprinted the gun-safe, not that Finch held out much hope of the murderer's prints being discovered on it any more than on the gun or the padlock on Bradley's shed. Whoever had killed David Hamilton had planned the murder carefully and wasn't likely, in the Chief Inspector's opinion, to leave fingerprint evidence behind him. Or her, he corrected himself silently.

Which brought him back to the question of motive. He began circumspectly with a general query. 'Do you know of anyone who might have wanted to kill your son-in-law?'

Felix Napier's answer was immediate and emphatic. 'Certainly not! David was a quiet man, very steady and dependable; not the type who'd have any enemies.'

'No marital problems?' Finch continued, circling nearer. Although he was careful to hide behind the euphemism, this didn't prevent Napier from bristling up at once.

'I don't know what you're suggesting, Chief Inspector, but I want to make it absolutely clear that my daughter and son-in-law were very happily married. They were devoted to each other. If you don't believe me, ask anyone who knew them. Their friends will tell you exactly the same.'

Finch made no comment apart from making a slight inclination of his head, indicating that he bowed to Napier's judgement, at the same time making a mental note to do exactly what Napier had suggested and to ask the same question of the Hamiltons' neighbours and close acquaintances.

The next subject was just as tricky to introduce and Finch began with deliberate vagueness, letting the sentence dangle unfinished so that Napier could pick it up and make of it what he liked. 'About the right of way that crossed your son-in-law's land and Mr Bradley's . . .'

In view of his response the evening before the same topic, Napier's reaction was immediate and predictable, outwardly controlled but suggesting a depth of hidden hostility.

'Bradley wrote a letter to my son-in-law ten days ago; in fact, on the same say when David and I went out rough-shooting. In it, Bradley suggested a meeting with David to discuss the possibility of closing the right of way. I advised against it. Bradley knew about its existence when he bought the property from me and I didn't see he had any justification in trying to deny my daughter and her husband their legal rights of access into the lane. It's been there for years. But that's typical of the man . . .'

He broke off suddenly, aware of what he was saying and

conscious also that if he hadn't become so embroiled in the discussion over that damned letter, he might have remembered to remind David about the gun and the tragedy might never have occurred. Making an effort to control himself, he continued in a less clipped manner, 'But, of course, the decision was between Bradley and my daughter and son-in-law. At the time, David and Elizabeth seemed inclined to give their permission for the pathway to be closed off, but David must have changed his mind. He mentioned it briefly at the party on Saturday.'

'He didn't say why?' Finch asked.

'No; he merely said that circumstances had changed and he'd decided to turn down Bradley's suggestion after all.'

Which was roughly the same vague, unspecified reason which David Hamilton had given in the letter he had been writing to Bradley shortly before his murder, not that Finch had any intention of passing on this information to Napier. Nor was Napier's answer much help in clearing up the question of why Hamilton had changed his mind over the closure of the right of way. But as it seemed a small and relatively unimportant aspect of the case, Finch decided to leave it there.

'One last point, Mr Napier,' he continued, 'I'd like an account of your movements yesterday.'

'I've already told you. I was here in the evening until my daughter rang me.'

'I meant earlier in the day, from the morning onwards.'

'Has that any bearing on David's murder?' Napier demanded. 'I suppose it must have, otherwise you wouldn't have asked.' He looked inquiringly at Finch and, when he didn't answer, continued, 'I took the dog out for a walk soon after breakfast and got back here around quarter-past ten, about half an hour after it started raining. As I'd already got wet through once, I didn't go out again but spent the rest of the day indoors.'

Although Boyce made no overt movement, Finch was aware of the Sergeant's reaction. With head lowered, he went on taking notes but he stiffened as much as to say – *No alibi*; an unspoken response which matched the Chief Inspector's.

So it would seem that Napier could have had the opportunity to take the jacket and gloves from Bradley's outhouse. And what was more, Finch added to himself, Napier would not only know the layout of his son-in-law's house and have easy access to it, but he'd be familiar with Bradley's premises as well, having once owned the kennels.

He wondered if this was the reason behind Napier's insistence that Hamilton had left the shot-gun in the hall. If Napier were guilty of his son-in-law's murder, it would be to his advantage if the police believed the gun had been left lying so conveniently to hand for an intruder or some other suspect, such as Bradley, to pick it up.

'You were alone during the day?' Finch asked, anxious to have this point about Napier's lack of alibi confirmed.

Napier immediately appeared on the defensive.

'Yes, I was, until about three o'clock when I had a guest for tea.'

'And who was that, sir?'

It was Boyce who asked the question, raising his head from his notebook as if he, too, had sniffed out Napier's equivocation.

'A Miss Denby, Dodie Pagett's friend. I don't know her well, having only met her twice before – once when Dodie introduced us and a second time at my daughter's party when I offered to lend her a book. She came to pick it up yesterday afternoon and left, I suppose, about five o'clock.'

'Thank you, sir,' Finch said affably as if perfectly satisfied with this unnecessarily detailed explanation, at the same time making up his mind to interview Miss Denby at the first opportunity. 'And now if I might have a word with your daughter.'

Napier got to his feet, seeming relieved that the subject of Miss Denby and the tea-party had been passed over so quickly.

'I'd be grateful, Chief Inspector, if you didn't keep her too long. She's been prescribed tranquillizers and still isn't up to making a long statement.'

'I understand, sir,' Finch said sympathetically.

Within a few minutes, Napier returned to the room with his daughter, escorting her to the chair which he had just vacated, one hand cradled solicitously under her bebow, before taking up his position behind it.

As he observed the little scene, it occurred to Finch that, if he were looking for a motive for Felix Napier to murder his son-in-law, he need look no further than this relationship between father and daughter. If danger threatened, Napier would fight to the death to protect her. The only trouble with this theory, as with the other he had suggested to Boyce the previous evening of a possible conspiracy between them, was that he had no evidence to support it. It was mere supposition. What he needed was facts and so far he had uncovered too few.

'I won't keep you long, Mrs Hamilton,' Finch assured her as she sat down opposite him, hands clasped in the lap of the plain, dark dress she was wearing which, with its little white collar, gave her the appearance of a Victorian schoolgirl in mourning. 'All I want from you at this stage is an account of your movements yesterday. Shall we start from the morning, say about ten o'clock?'

Unlike her father, she didn't question the relevance of the inquiry but began immediately.

'I was in Framden most of the day. In fact, I left about ten o'clock or a little earlier.'

'Did you hear any disturbance next door at the kennels? Dogs barking, for example?'

'No,' she said simply. She accepted this, too, without any query although Finch saw Napier direct a puzzled glance in his direction and he hurried on without giving the man time to interrupt.

'What did you do in Framden?'

'What I usually do on a Tuesday. It's the one day of the week that my cleaning lady doesn't come, so I try to fit in as much as I can such as going to the bank or the library. Do you want me to give you the details?'

At Finch's request, she went through her itinerary, starting with coffee at Frazer's, where she had also had lunch, visits to various shops as well as the bank and the library, an afternoon appointment at the hairdresser's, after which she had met a woman friend, Cynthia fuller, for tea, returning to the friend's house by six o'clock.

It could all be checked, Finch assumed, listening as Boyce

took notes and only interrupting from time to time to ask for addresses which she gave with a simple directness.

'Cynthia and I had a sherry,' Mrs Hamilton continued, 'then I showered and changed into the clothes I'd brought with me for the aerobics class. We left, I suppose, at about quarter-past seven in my car. The class starts at half-past and ends at nine-thirty.'

Facts which could also be verified, Finch thought, breaking in to ask where the evening class was held.

'The Civic Centre,' Mrs Hamilton replied and waited while Boyce wrote it down before resuming her account. 'I dropped Cynthia off at her house at about quarter to ten, I suppose, although I didn't look at the time. We'd stayed talking to some of the other women for a few minutes after the class was over. Normally I'd've gone in with Cynthis and had a coffee with her, but as it was raining I decided to go straight home.'

'What time would you have arrived back if you had stayed for coffee?' Finch asked.

'About a quarter to eleven,' Mrs Hamilton replied. 'That was the usual time.'

Finch glanced across at Boyce as he noted down this fact although the Sergeant kept his head studiously lowered. All the same, her answer couldn't have been lost on him. So much for Boyce's theory that Hamilton, hearing someone enter the house, had mistaken his murderer for his wife returning from her evening class.

He turned back to Mrs Hamilton.

'Go on,' he said encouragingly.

She resumed her account, although it was clear she was finding it an ordeal. Her voice had grown more uncertain and Finch saw Felix Napier put one hand on her shoulder as if trying to give her the strength to continue.

'I started to drive home but somewhere along the road before the T-junction I must have got a puncture. I could feel the back tyre was flat from the way the car was handling so I drew off the road into a gateway. At first, I thought I'd try changing the wheel myself but the verge was rutted and I realized it wouldn't be safe to jack the car up. I knew roughly where I was and that there was a garage and a telephone-box a little further down the road, so I decided to walk there. The garage was shut, which I'd half expected anyway. But at least there was the kiosk. I tried ringing David first but there was no answer. He could have been out or in the bath . . . I really didn't give it much thought at the time, except to feel rather annoyed that there was no reply.' Her voice faltered but, as Felix Napier seemed about to interrupt, she looked up at him quickly. 'No, daddy, please let me go on. The Chief Inspector will need a statement and I'd rather get it over and done with. He's only doing his job, after all, although I think you know the rest,' she added, looking at Finch with quick appeal. 'I rang daddy instead and he came out to pick me up. Do you want me to go over it all again, about driving back to the house and finding David?'

'No; I don't think that's necessary,' Finch assured her. He had already taken statements from both her and Felix Napier the previous evening covering these events, although there were several details he wanted to confirm.

'You said yesterday that you had no idea at what time you rang your father?'

Mrs Hamilton looked apologetic. 'I'm afraid not. It was pitch-dark and raining. I didn't think to look at my watch.'

'I've already told you, Chief Inspector,' Felix Napier put in at this point, his voice severe, 'that it was just after ten-fifteen. *I* looked at the clock. If you want a more exact time, I would say that it was a couple of seconds off sixteen minutes past. I might add that all the clocks in the house are correct to the minute. I make a point of checking them with the Greenwich Mean Time signal on the radio at least once a week.'

Finch was prepared to take Napier's word that the clocks were correct. He certainly looked the type for whom such precision would be important, although whether or not either Napier's or Elizabeth Hamilton's story about the puncture and the subsequent phone call were equally as reliable was another matter altogether.

There remained only a few more questions to ask of Mrs Hamilton. She was visibly tiring, leaning back against her father's hand which still rested on her shoulder as if she gained comfort from the contact, and Finch hastened on with his next question.

'About your husband's movements yesterday, Mrs Hamilton. I take it he was in Framden at his office?'

Working on this assumption, it had crossed his mind to wonder if the Hamiltons had met in the town during the day, and had been a little surprised when Mrs Hamilton had made no reference during her account of her own activities in the town to such a meeting, not even a casual visit to him at the solicitor's.

Again, it was Felix Napier who replied on his daughter's behalf.

'David wasn't at the Framden office yesterday. For the past few months he's been going every Tuesday to Millbridge where the firm has a small branch. As the parnter who runs it is rather elderly, David used to help out with the more complicated cases or arrange for them to be transferred to the main office.' Addressing his daughter directly, he added, 'I take it that David's routine would have been much the same, though, as on any other day of the week?'

'He always left home a little earlier on a Tuesday morning,' Elizabeth Hamilton replied. 'It's a longer drive to Millbridge than to Framden. I can't tell you what time he'd leave Millbridge; you'd have to ask Wilfred Chitty that; and I can't tell you either what time he'd get home as I was always out myself at my evening class until quarter to eleven. I do know he used to stop somewhere on the way back for a snack supper, I assume at a pub, because he'd told me not to bother about leaving a meal ready for him – although we'd sometimes have a sandwich together when I got home.'

Her voice faltered and she seemed close to tears at the memory of this small, shared domestic intimacy and it was with relief that Finch turned to Boyce to complete the interview by checking with Mrs Hamilton the list of guests who had been at the party on the Saturday evening before the murder to which she added one more, Brian Mundy who ran an antique shop in Framden.

And that seemed to be that. Mrs Hamilton's movements while she had been in Framden would have to be checked on, although Finch intended handing that particular routine over to a couple of DCs, reserving for himself and Boyce the task of interviewing Wilfred Chitty at Millbridge about David Hamilton's activities on the day he was murdered.

As he rose to go, Felix Napier raised an aspect of the case which Finch had decided was better left to another time when he had had the chance of speaking to the Hamiltons' friends and when Mrs Hamilton herself had recovered from the immediate shock of her husband's death.

'The Chief Inspector asked me if David was happy,' Napier said to his daughter with an awkward gruffness.

It was an oblique way of referring to Finch's own inquiry into the Hamiltons' marriage, as if Napier were embarrassed to put the question more directly – although Finch suspected that he was anxious to forewarn his daughter that this was an aspect of the investigation for which she should be prepared. All the same, despite Napier's attempt to lessen the blow, Finch saw her eyes widen.

'Happy? Yes, of course he was. He'd been rather overworked recently and was feeling tired, but that was all. There was no other reason. Why shouldn't he be happy?'

She had jumped to her feet as she made the last remark, a note of hysteria in her voice and Finch, exchanging a glance with Boyce, also got up from his chair. It was time to go.

'We'll see ourselves out, Mr Napier,' he announced, although he doubted if Napier heard him.

When the door closed behind them, Felix Napier crossed the room to where Elizabeth was now standing by the patio windows, her back to him.

'Of course he was happy,' she repeated. 'I don't know why you ask.'

'Because Finch was going to put that question to you sooner or later,' Felix told her, 'and I wanted it to come from me, not him.'

He stood behind her, holding himself very still and erect, not knowing whether to touch her or not. In the days immediately following Helen's death he had shrunk from all physical contact, even from her, and he sensed that she, too, would want to keep her grief inviolate.

He saw her lift her head with the same proud resolve not to be broken which had sustained him.

'We loved each other,' she said. 'There was nothing and no one in the whole world who could have taken that away.'

'No, of course not,' he agreed quietly, adding silently to himself with a bitterness he was careful not to let her see: *except whoever murdered David*.

She was silent for a moment, looking out into the garden. Then she said, 'Oh, look at your poor roses, daddy! They're all ruined by the rain.'

She was close to tears and, knowing she would prefer to weep alone, Felix went out of the room, gesturing to the dog to follow and closing the door quietly behind them both.

12

For once Boyce had the sense to say nothing as they left Felix Napier's house except to ask, 'Where to now?' as he and the Chief Inspector got into the car.

'The Pagetts' house,' Finch told him. 'It can't be far. Napier said it was only a couple of hundred yards down the lane.' For Boyce's benefit, as the Sergeant remained uncharacteristically silent, he continued, 'I thought we'd drop in on them for a chat. As they knew the Hamiltons, I'm hoping that, if there's any local gossip, they'll be willing to pass it on. They were also at the party on Saturday, so one of them may have noticed the gun in the container in the hall.' He broke off to add, 'Slow up, Tom. That looks like their place on the left.'

The house, evidently two brick and slate-roofed cottages which had been knocked into one, was situated behind a narrow gravelled forecourt where a van was already parked. Boyce drew in behind it and the two men got out, Finch pausing to look about him with a quick, lively interest. About an acre of land extended behind the house with a range of outbuildings, including a small barn. A board announcing '*Pagett's Country Herbs*' was nailed up over its open door, through which a man and a woman emerged, curious, it seemed, to see who had arrived, the man tall and bearded, the woman small and plump. Both looked 'arty', as Finch mentally characterized anyone whose appearance was unconventional, the man's beard and corduroy jacket and the woman's thick brown hair, bundled up untidily, and loose, smock-like dress coming under this heading.

'Mr and Mrs Pagett?' Finch asked pleasantly, advancing to meet them. 'I'm Detective Inspector Finch and this is my Detective Sergeant, Boyce. We're making inquiries into the death of Mr Hamilton. I wonder if you'd mind answering a few questions?'

Their reactions were interesting. Pagett immediately scowled and said, 'Is it necessary to do it now? We're busy packing up an order . . .' But the woman broke in more sympathetically, 'Of course we don't mind, although there's not a lot we can tell you. Come into the house and I'll make coffee.' As she led the way into the house, she added over her shoulder to her husband, 'Come on, Mike. You were saying only a minute or two ago that you wanted a break.'

He gave in and followed them, although Finch noticed that he kicked the barn door shut behind him in a little outburst of pettishness at not getting his own way.

The sitting-room into which she showed them contained an extraordinary profusion of furniture and objects; floor cushions, armchairs with lengths of batik fabric thrown over them to serve as covers, handmade pots stuffed full of dried grasses and seed-heads, unframed paintings pinned to the walls; a lifetime's collection from junk-shops, art-rooms and hedgerows, lavishly and untidily on display and contrasting oddly with the unfinished state of the room itself with its incomplete fireplace and empty space where a door should have been, through which Dodie talked to them from the kitchen where she bustled about making coffee.

'I was so shocked to hear about David's death. It's such a dreadful thing to have happened. Poor Elizabeth! I can't imagine she'll ever get over it. Neither will Felix. They were such a close family.'

'You know them well?' Finch asked. He noticed that Mike

Pagett made no attempt to join in his wife's remarks but remained standing by the hearth in silence, looking aloof and disdainful as he filled his pipe and slowly lit it, drawing in the smoke, his eyes fixed on the bowl.

'Oh yes, we know all three of them, don't we, Mike?' Dodie said, coming in with the tray and handing round mugs of coffee and a bowl of brown sugar. When he didn't reply, she continued, 'Living in a village, you make friends with everyone sooner or later.'

'I believe you were at the Hamiltons' party on Saturday?' Finch asked. He had taken one of the armchairs at Dodie Pagett's invitation and sat back relaxed, holding his mug between both hands and looking for all the world like an old friend who had dropped in for a chat. 'It went off well, did it?'

'The Hamiltons' parties always do,' Dodie assured him. 'Elizabeth's marvellous at entertaining people. She always makes you feel so much at home.'

'No tensions?' Finch hinted gently. 'I ask because I understand Mr Bradley was there and there could have been some difficulties with the Hamiltons over a right of way . . .'

'I don't know anything about that,' Dodie broke in. 'And I certainly wasn't aware that anything was wrong between the Hamiltons and Steven Bradley. It's Felix and Steven who don't get on all that well. It's such a pity. I know Steven can be rather awkward at times but I don't think he means to be rude. No, it was a lovely party. I enjoyed it tremendously.'

'Felix Napier was telling me that you brought a friend with you,' Finch continued, dropping easily into first-name terms as if he knew all of them socially.

'That's right; Kate Denby. We teach at the same school in Framden.' Dodie Pagett laughed, the colour running up into her face. 'As a matter of fact, I'd asked her to lunch one Sunday and introduced her to Felix. I thought they might get on together. Anyway,' she hurried on, embarrassed at what Finch suspected had been an artless attempt at matchmaking on her part, 'Elizabeth met us in the lane and liked the look of Kate, so when she gave her party – Elizabeth, I mean – she asked me to bring Kate along as well. But Elizabeth's like that, so warm and friendly.'

'I believe Felix Napier asked Miss Denby to tea yesterday afternoon,' Finch remarked, and realized too late that he had made a gaffe.

Dodie's eyes widened in surprise. 'Felix asked Kate to tea! But she didn't say anything to me about it when I saw her this morning.' She seemed hurt by this omission, turning in appeal to her husband. 'Don't you think that it's odd she didn't mention it, Mike?'

His only response was to give a small, derisive smile, dismissing both her concern as well as her friendship with Kate Denby.

Finch hastened to repair the damage. 'I understand he wanted to lend her a book,' he explained. 'Perhaps it was one of those vague invitations to drop in some time.'

'Yes, it probably was,' Dodie agreed, mollified, it seemed, by this line of reasoning. 'I expect she intended to call in on us as well but found we weren't at home. We were in Ipswich all day yesterday.'

Which not only changed the subject, to Finch's relief, but led him on to the next part of the interview.

'What time di you set off?' he asked casually.

'About half-past ten,' Dodie replied. She seemed to accept the question as mere friendly interest, although Finch noticed Mike Pagett looked across at him with a sharper, more suspicious expression. 'We intended leaving earlier but Mike had to go down to the village for petrol.'

'You didn't go with him?'

Even Dodie seemed taken aback this time. 'No, Mike went on his own. But I don't see the point . . .'

'And what time did you get back from Ipswich?'

'About half-past eight,' she replied, 'although I still don't understand why . . .'

Mike Pagett at last contributed to the conversation. Removing the pipe from his mouth, he demanded abruptly, 'Just what are you getting at? I don't see what we were doing yesterday is any of your business.'

'Oh, Mike!' Dodie protested.

'No, it's all right, Mrs Pagett,' Finch assured her. Turning back to her husband, he continued, 'We're hoping to trace anyone who might have been out in the village between ten and half-past last night, and who might have seen someone acting suspiciously or noticed a car parked near the Hamiltons' house.'

He left it deliberately vague, hoping the explanation would satisfy the Pagetts.

Dodie Pagett seemed to accept it. Before her husband could answer, she put it eagerly, 'You were out about that time, weren't you, Mike? After we got back from Ipswich, you went down to the White Hart for a drink. You were back about half-past ten, so you might have seen something.'

'Did you, Mr Pagett?' Finch inquired, pressing home the point as Pagett seemed disinclined to answer. He had turned away and was looking for a box of matches on the mantelpiece, although and pipe was burning well and was dropping fragments of smouldering tobacco on to the rug in front of the hearth, which was scarred with other small black scorch marks.

'I didn't notice anything,' he said, his back still towards them.

'What time did you leave the White Hart?' Finch persisted.

Pagett shrugged. 'I don't know. I didn't look at the time.'

'But you were back here at about half-past ten. It must be – what? – a two- or three-minute drive from the village at the most, so you must have left at roughly twenty-five past, if you drove straight home?'

'If you say so,' Pagett replied. 'Unlike you, I don't make a habit of watching the clock.'

It was said in a supercilious voice as if Pagett's attitude to such mundane matters was superior to the Chief Inspector's, consequently making Finch something of a time-server.

He was also, Finch realized, on the defensive. Despite his contemptuous manner, Pagett was a poor liar and clearly had something to hide. His movements would have to be checked on.

'You must have passed the Hamiltons' house on your way back,' Finch persevered. 'Did you notice anything suspicious at the time?'

'I've already told you,' Pagett said, raising his voice, 'I saw nothing yesterday evening. Or do you want it spelled out for you in words of one syllable? I saw no one. No cars. No strangers. Not even a bloody dog. It was chucking it down with rain, and the place was deserted. And now, if you've finished asking your damn fool questions, I've got a living to earn.'

With that, he left the room abruptly, slamming the front door behind him.

Finch was amused rather than offended by his behaviour, although he felt sorry for Dodie Pagett who had sat very still during this outburst, her hands clasped tightly in the lap of her voluminous dress.

As the door crashed shut and the figure of her husband was seen striding past the window in the direction of the barn, she said in a subdued voice, 'I'm sorry, Chief Inspector. I'm afraid Mike isn't in a very good mood these days. He has a lot on his mind.'

'That's all right, Mrs Pagett,' Finch assured her cheerfully, at the same time wondering exactly what could be causing her husband such obvious stress. That, too, would be worth inquiring into. 'So you were here on your own yesterday evening?'

'Yes, until Mike came home,' she agreed simply, unaware, it seemed, of the significance of her reply.

'There're a couple more questions I have to ask you,' Finch continued. 'Firstly, when you were at the Hamiltons' party, did you happen to notice a shot-gun in the house?'

Her response was immediate. 'Heavens, no!' she exclaimed. 'Oh, you don't mean David was shot with his own gun?'

'And I'd also like the address of your friend, Miss Denby,' Finch went on blandly, ignoring her question. 'I'd like to check up one or two details with her.'

'Of course. I'll write it down for you.' Dodie accepted the explanation, vague thought it was, without query, crossing to the table and scribbling down an address on the back of an old envelope which she handed to the Chief Inspector. 'Is that all?' she added.

Finch hesitated before putting the next question. Although he was aware that there was a warm, naive quality about Dodie Pagett which would make her less likely to guard her tongue, he realized as well that she was not the type who would listen to or pass on harmful gossip about her friends. All the same, the question had to be asked and he decided that a frank appeal was probably the best approach.

'I'm sorry to have to ask you this, Mrs Pagett,' he began, his diffidence not entirely feigned, 'but in a murder investigation I'm afraid we sometimes have to carry out rather unpleasant inquiries.'

'Unpleasant?' Dodie asked, her eyes wide again with alarm this time.

'Into other people's private lives. Was there any gossip about either Mr or Mrs Hamilton?'

'Gossip?' she repeated. 'I don't understand.'

There was nothing for it but to come straight to the point.

'Have you ever heard any rumours to suggest that either David Hamilton or his wife was having an affair?'

'Certainly not!' she retorted, the colour high in her face. 'David and Elizabeth were devoted to each other, and if anyone tells you anything to the contrary they're lying. Now, if you've finished, I really ought to go and help my husband with packing up that order.'

Walking to the door, she held it open, giving them no option but to leave, although Finch paused on the threshold to ask one last question.

'Do you happen to own a bike, Mrs Pagett?'

'Yes, I do,' she replied and shut the door in their faces.

'*Bike?*' Boyce asked, as they got into the car. 'What the hell were you on about?'

'Just checking that she had some means of transport. It wouldn't have taken her more than ten minutes by bike to get down to Bradley's place while her husband was out at the garage, and pinch the clothing, hiding it somewhere handy to use later,' Finch explained. 'You noticed she didn't have an alibi, either, for last night?'

'Neither had Pagett,' Boyce pointed out. 'Come to that, he could just as easily have pinched Bradley's jacket and gloves while he was in the village. Getting petrol could have just been an excuse.'

'Exactly!' Finch seemed pleased with the Sergeant's perspicacity. 'And he was lying, too, Tom, about what he was up to last night. We'll check on that now. After that, we'll go into

Framden and have a word with Hamilton's partner at the firm's main branch and, while we're there, I think we'll drop in on Miss Denby, Mrs Pagett's friend.'

'Suits me,' Boyce said, turning the car into the lane. 'But why her?'

'Because she's not from the village and, as an outsider, she may have seen more of the game,' Finch explained, although this was only part of his reason. He was also curious to meet the woman who caused Felix Napier such obvious embarrassment.

Dodie watched the car drive away, but despite the excuse she had given the Chief Inspector and his Sergeant she made no attempt to join Mike in the packing-shed. Their inquiries, particularly about the Hamiltons, had distressed her and she didn't want to appear in front of Mike until she could put on the semblance, at least, of her usual cheerfulness.

Of course there was no question of either David or Elizabeth being unfaithful to each other. That was complete and utter nonsense. She had never seen two people who were happier together.

Lucky them! Dodie thought, although for the first time a doubt crossed her mind. It was as if Finch's questions had opened up a Pandora's box of meaner feelings which, until that moment, had been safely locked away.

After all, Elizabeth was very beautiful, Dodie told herself, remembering her at the party in that exquisite dress which had caught the light every time she moved, attracting to herself not only its radiance but the glances of admiration which seemed to be hers by right.

But not mine, Dodie added. Not even Mike has ever looked at me like that.

The thought of Mike distressed her too, but in a more generalized way. Something was worrying him. His moodiness and silences were getting worse, punctuated by outbursts of temper like his rudeness to the Chief Inspector who, after all, had only been doing his job in trying to find out who had killed David.

Oh, I can't bear to think of it any more! Dodie thought, but whether she meant Mike or Elizabeth or David's murder she herself wasn't sure.

Fred Walker, the landlord of the White Hart, was adamant; Mike Pagett hadn't been in his public house on Tuesday night.

'You're quite sure?' Finch asked him. Although he had been expecting it, he had to make certain that Walker's evidence was reliable. 'He couldn't have been served by someone else, and you missed seeing him?'

Walker put down the cloth on which he had been drying glasses and leaned across the counter. 'Look round for yourself, Chief Inspector,' he replied. 'There's only the one bar, and I can see it all from where I'm standing. I couldn't have missed him. Besides, the place was half-empty on Tuesday evening because of the rain. If Mike Pagett was in here, I would have noticed him.'

'Is there any other pub where he might have gone for a drink?'

Walker shrugged.

'Not in the village. There's the Boar out at Harston or the Three Bells on the Penfield road. They're the two nearest.'

Finch decided to leave it there. There was no point in asking him if he'd heard the sound of a gun-shot on Tuesday night. The White Hart was too far from the Hamiltons' house to make that likely. Besides, the same question would be asked by the detectives making the house-to-house investigation, and if Walker had heard anything it would be included in their report.

Instead, as if it was nearly one o'clock and he had eaten nothing since seven that morning, he ordered two ploughman's lunches and a couple of pints of bitter for himself and Boyce, carrying them over to a table on the far side of the bar where the Sergeant, who had been sent to make inquiries at Leverett's garage across the road, shortly joined him.

'Nothing much,' Boyce reported, lowering his voice so that he could not be heard by the other customers as he took his place opposite the Chief Inspector. 'Pagett called in for petrol all right yesterday morning, round about ten o'clock, according to Leverett, although he wasn't sure of the exact time.

The point is, Pagett could have had the opportunity to nick Bradley's clothing either on his way to the garage or on the drive home. It'd only take him a couple of minutes in the car to nip round by the back lane and help himself to the stuff. What did you find out?'

'Pagett wasn't in here Tuesday night,' Finch informed him. 'The landlord's positive he didn't see him all evening.'

Boyce, who had the opportunity to have a quick pull at his beer while Finch was speaking, put his glass down on the table.

'Then if Pagett was lying . . .'

He left the rest unsaid, the inference needing no explanation. Pagett not only had no alibi for the time of the murder but had lied about his movements, which in itself was suspicious.

'So what are we going to do?' Boyce continued. 'Go back and confront him?'

'No,' Finch replied. 'I think we'll let him stew for the time being. We'll keep to our original plan and go into Framden to see Hamilton's partner and also Mrs Pagett's friend, Miss Denby. If we're not too late, I'd also like to drive into Millbridge afterwards and interview Hamilton's other colleague, Chitty. It's about time we began checking on what Hamilton was doing on Tuesday. So far we've not even made a start on finding out his movements.'

'It's early days,' Boyce remarked with an off-hand air. 'We haven't been on the case for more than a few hours.'

Which was true enough but which didn't stop the Chief Inspector from feeling restive at any delay, prompting him to remark, 'I know, Tom, but there's a hell of a lot to do. So eat up and let's get a move on.'

All the same, it was Finch who kept the Sergeant waiting when, shortly afterwards, having bolted down their beer and bread and cheese, they emerged from the White Hart and crossed the forecourt to where their car was parked, its back to the road.

As Boyce got in behind the wheel, Finch paused in the act of climbing in beside him, his attention fixed on Leverett's garage on the opposite side of the road.

Ruth Livesey was at that moment coming out of the office, where presumably she had been paying for petrol, and was starting to walk towards a Renault car which was drawn up in front of the pumps.

At the same time, a white van with the words '*Woodstone Boarding Kennels*' emblazoned on the side in black lettering, approached from the direction of Paddocks and drew up suddenly alongside the Renault, its tyres sending the gravel flying.

As it did so, Finch scrambled into the passenger seat beside Boyce who was craning his neck round to see what was causing the delay.

'I thought you were in a hurry,' he began in an aggrieved voice.

'Hang on for a minute or two,' Finch told him, stretching up to adjust the driving-mirror so that he had the rear window in view. 'I'd like to see what happens between Bradley and Dr Livesey before we start chasing off to Framden.'

Steven Bradley's decision to stop and speak to Ruth Livesey was made almost without thinking. He was on his way to collect a dog for boarding from a client who couldn't deliver it himself to the kennels, and he was already late for that appointment. But, at the sight of Ruth Livesey emerging from the garage, he slammed on the brakes and brought the van to a halt.

He had neither seen nor spoken to her since David Hamilton's murder although he had been tempted to ring her up several times. It was only his inability to think of an excuse which had prevented him from doing so. He could hardly say to her that he wanted her reassurance but that was exactly what he was looking for, not just about their relationship, if indeed they had one, but about Hamilton's murder as well.

The two interviews with Finch, one over the shot he thought he had heard, the other over the missing loves and jacket, had shaken him badly. So, too, had the arrival that morning of a plain-clothes detective who had fingerprinted him and the shed door, as well as several uniformed men who had spent almost an hour examining the gateway and path leading into Gade's Lane.

All this official interest and activity had left him feeling oddly isolated and friendless, a new and uncomfortable sensation. Normally it did not bother him that he had few close relationships. He preferred his own company. But the suspicion which seemed to hang over him, even the quarrel with Napier, made him more eager than ever to assure himself that Ruth Livesey regarded him at least as a friend, if nothing more. But her expression as he walked towards her across the garage forecourt was hardly welcoming.

'Oh, it's you, Steven,' she said.

She had stopped by her car, one hand on the driver's door, indicating that she was in a hurry.

'I was hoping I might run across you in the village,' Bradley replied and then hesitated, wondering what to say next.

'Yes?' she said which was no help at all.

'It's a terrible business about David Hamilton,' Steven Bradley continued awkwardly. 'The police have been round to my place twice, checking up on that noise I heard when I was phoning you yesterday. And then some of my stuff's gone missing . . . '

It wasn't at all how he had intended to express himself. It sounded as if he was merely concerned about how Hamilton's death and the subsequent investigation had discommoded him personally, whereas he had wanted her to understand and sympathize with the dilemma in which he found himself.

Look, he was trying to say, *I'm worried that the police may think I had something to do with it.*

And then she would reply, perhaps putting out a hand to touch his arm: *But that's nonsense, Steven.* I *know you're innocent. There's no need to be afraid.*

It was soap-opera stuff of course and on one level he was aware of it himself.

Instead, she opened the car door and got in behind the wheel before saying, without even looking up at him, 'The police are bound to ask questions in a murder inquiry.'

It was in the nature of a rebuke.

'Yes, I realize that,' he said quickly, adding almost in the same breath, 'If you'd like to call at the kennels some time for coffee or a drink . . .'

As he spoke, she raised her eyes to his and he saw that he was wasting his time. 'I'm sorry,' she said and started the engine, forcing him to step back as she drove away.

Bradley remained standing for a few seconds where she had left him before, walking back to his van, he, too, drove away in the opposite direction.

From his vantage point outside the White Hart, Finch watched this exchange in the rear view-mirror with close attention.

'I think we've just seen Dr Livesey give Bradley the brush-off,' he remarked to Boyce.

'Go on,' the Sergeant replied without much interest as he straightened the mirror, adding in the tone of someone kept waiting far too long by such tomfoolery, 'Well, if you're ready, we'll get going into Framden, shall we?'

13

They called on Ralph Dunbar first; not that he had much to tell them, a point he made several times at some length during the interview, as if by expanding on this lack of information he hoped to give it more substance.

He was a large, genial, middle-aged man who, as senior partner in Dunbar and Hamilton, occupied the front office overlooking the High Street which he seemed to find a distraction, for as he talked he kept glancing out of the window at the street below, crowded with cars and shoppers.

But no, he hadn't been at the Hamiltons' party although he had been invited.

'Couldn't make it on Saturday,' he explained. 'I'd already booked something else up weeks ago which I couldn't cancel – a Rotary Club dinner. Rather a bore, actually, because David and Elizabeth's get-togethers are usually fun. I was sorry to miss it.'

He knew nothing either about the discussion between Hamilton and Bradley over the right of way nor of anyone who might have borne Hamilton a grudge, either professionally or personally. 'He was the last man on earth to have any enemies, I should have thought. Thoroughly reliable and trustworthy.

Everyone liked him. God know how I'll manage here without him. I can't tell you how shocked I was to hear of his death. Felix rang me; seemed to think it was some intruder who'd broken into the house. Dreadful business. Quite dreadful.'

As for the Hamiltons' marriage, his only comment was, 'Ideal, as far as I could see. You've met Elizabeth, of course? Lovely girl. David was devoted to her and she adored him. Perfect couple. She must be absolutely shattered.'

'I understand Mr Hamilton had been taking a lot of work home recently,' Finch put in a little wickedly. Dunbar's wordy geniality was beginning to get on his nerves.

'Ah,' said Dunbar and his eyes swivelled again to the scene outside the window. 'That was my fault, I'm afraid. I've been having a few domestic problems recently and I may have relied a little too heavily on David's good nature. Not that he complained, and you could say I was doing him a good turn introducing him to more clients.'

Even Dunbar seemed unconvinced by this argument for, after a small silence in which he kept his eyes fixed on the window, he added, 'Perhaps I did overburden him. He had enough work of his own to keep him busy.'

'Including the branch office at Millbridge, which I understand he helped run,' Finch pointed out.

Dunbar got up and held out a plump, warm hand for Finch to shake. 'You'll have to ask Wilfred Chitty about that, Chief Inspector. I don't know much about that side of the business. And now, if you'll excuse me, I have a heavy work-load to get through this afternoon.'

Which included tea and biscuits, Finch commented silently to himself, meeting Dunbar's secretary in the doorway, carrying a tray, as he and Boyce came out of the office.

Hamilton's secretary hadn't much to add either. She was a pleasant woman in her forties, clearly still distressed by Hamilton's death, but as much in the dark as Dunbar about the motive behind it.

'He was such a quietly spoken, considerate, *nice* young man,' she concluded, stressing the last epithet as if it summed Hamilton up. 'Why should anyone want to kill him?'

'But somebody did,' Finch remarked sourly as he and Boyce emerged into Framden High Street.

'Perhaps he was too bloody nice,' Boyce replied.

'What do you mean by that?' Finch demanded. It struck him as a new and startling approach to the question of motive, and he wondered if the Sergeant had some specific theory in mind. But it seemed he hadn't, for he replied vaguely, 'Oh, I don't know. It just seemed to me that nice people can be damned infuriating at times. I've got a brother-in-law like that. He'll do anything for you – help fix things round the house, lend you a fiver if you're short. It's when people like that let you down that you get angry.'

'Go on,' Finch said, intrigued.

Boyce looked embarrassed.

'Well, that's it really,' he said awkwardly. 'You come to rely on them always saying yes, so that when they don't it comes as a bit of a shock.'

'And what did your brother-in-law say no to?'

Boyce grinned a little ruefully.

'Giving me a hand to tune the car a couple of Sundays ago. I'd counted on him. Like I said, you don't expect to be turned down. But he'd promised my sister and the kids a day out and he didn't like to disappoint them, blah, blah. He was quite right, too, but that didn't stop me from feeling bloody peeved at the time.'

'Yes, I know,' Finch said. He was thinking of his own sister. She, too, rarely said no and, on the few occasions when she did, Finch had also experienced that sense of aggrieved amazement.

He wondered if the same motivation could be applied in Hamilton's case. Had he been, as Boyce put it, too bloody nice and been murdered because of it?

But there was no time to follow the idea further. Boyce was saying, 'If you've got Miss Denby's address, we'll get round there, shall we?'

Kate Denby also warned them that there was not much she could tell them, although she made the point far more succinctly than Dunbar. 'I don't know the Hamiltons at all well,' she explained before the interview began. 'I only met them once at their party last Saturday so I'm something of an outsider.'

She had been surprised to find the two plain-clothes policemen at the door of her flat making inquiries into David Hamilton's death, although she had asked them into her sitting-room where she noticed the short, stocky one, Detective Chief Inspector Finch, had looked about him with quick, little glances, taking in the details of his surroundings with an alertness that warned her that there wasn't much he would miss. The other one, the Detective Sergeant, was much more stolid.

'But it's as an outsider that your opinion will be useful,' Finch replied artfully.

He had already taken her measure on the doorstep. She was an intelligent woman, efficient and used to running her own life, an impression which her sitting-room with its well-organized tidiness, its shelves full of books and its neat desk tended to confirm. Here was someone in control of both herself and her surroundings, unlikely therefore to be inveigled into a gossipy chat about her friends and acquaintances. He'd get more out of her, he decided, by appealing to her good sense.

'You see,' he went on, 'the people close to David Hamilton knew him almost too well. I'd welcome another point of view. First impressions are often revealing, aren't they?'

Kate Denby didn't seem convinced of this.

'They're often wrong,' she pointed out. 'But, for what it's worth, I thought he was a pleasant man, rather quiet and serious.'

'Not the type to have any enemies?'

'I shouldn't have thought so.'

'And Mrs Hamilton?'

'Very attractive; charming, vivacious; the perfect hostess.'

She spoke reluctantly, choosing her words with care, which suggested to Finch a certain reservation about Elizabeth Hamilton that Kate Denby herself seemed aware of, for she added, 'I'm sorry, Chief Inspector. I find it difficult to describe other women, especially those like Elizabeth Hamilton. We have so little in common. You'd do better to ask someone else. To be frank, my opinion would be biased.'

'By what?'

Kate Denby looked both amused and annoyed.

'How persistent you are, Chief Inspector! All right; I'll try to explain. Elizabeth Hamilton struck me as the type of woman who is born to be cherished, and I don't believe life should be made as easy and as comfortable as that.' She stopped suddenly, aware of what she had said, before resuming, 'I shouldn't have spoken of her like that. After all, she can't be very happy now, can she? And I'm genuinely sorry that her husband is dead. No one would have wished that on her. Yesterday when I saw her . . .'

'You saw her yesterday?' Finch broke in. 'Where?'

'Here in Framden.'

Kate had been about to describe the image that the unexpected glimpse of Elizabeth Hamilton walking in the rain under her yellow umbrella had evoked in her, as being a symbol of that special protection which women like her seemed to carry about with them, in order to explain her feelings a little better to the Chief Inspector. She regretted having spoken so frankly about Elizabeth Hamilton but Dodie's news that morning over coffee about David Hamilton's murder and her own attempt to compose a letter to Felix Napier had unsettled her.

It still lay unfinished on her desk, broken off at the point where she had been writing, '*Please convey my sympathy to your daughter* . . .' The words had an insincere ring to them, not only because she did not know Elizabeth Hamilton intimately enough but because of the ambiguity of her own feelings towards the woman. Finch's arrival had caught her at a sensitive moment when her guard was down, and she realized that she had been trapped into using him as a sounding-board against which to test out her own reactions. It had been a mistake and she was relieved that he had turned his attention to this other aspect of the subject.

'It seems dreadful to think now that only a few hours later her husband was murdered,' she concluded a little awkwardly.

'What time was this?' Finch asked. Elizabeth Hamilton's

movements had yet to be checked on, and any sighting of her could be useful in establishing her timetable.

'About half-past two.'

'Did you speak to her?'

'No; I only caught a glimpse of her walking up Bruton Street. I was in the car at the traffic lights.'

'On your way to visit her father, Felix Napier?'

'Who told you that?' Kate demanded. She was angry and disconcerted that the Chief Inspector had such knowledge of her own activities, although his answer seemed reasonable enough.

'Mr Napier mentioned it himself,' he replied. 'You must understand, Miss Denby, that in an investigation like this we have to make inquiries into what possible witnesses were doing at certain times of the day.'

All the same, she saw the flaw in his argument.

'At half-past two in the afternoon?' she asked. 'I thought David Hamilton was murdered much later in the evening. At least, that's what Dodie Pagett told me.'

Finch, who had no intention of explaining to her the reason behind this particular line of inquiry, made a vague gesture with one hand. 'It's sometimes necessary. To get back to the subject of Mrs Hamilton, I'd be grateful for your opinion on another matter. Was it your impression that she and her husband were happily married?'

'Yes; I should have thought so.'

'No suggestion of any tension between them?'

'What are you implying?' she asked, looking him straight in the eyes and was gratified to see that, for a moment, Finch himself looked disconcerted although he quickly recovered that open, guileless expression which she realized was an effective cover for a much more subtle and ingenious mind than she had at first imagined.

'An affair?' he hinted gently. 'You were frank with me, Miss Denby, and so I'll put my own cards on the table. We're looking for a motive. Mrs Hamilton is a very attractive woman, as you quite rightly pointed out. It is possible she might have had a lover? You were at their party. What was your impression?'

Kate hesitated, remembering Mike's face as he had looked at Elizabeth Hamilton, his expression full of hungry desire.

'Men certainly found her attractive,' she said, reluctant to be trapped again into an unguarded reply.

Finch, noticing both her hesitation and caution, pressed home the point. 'Any man in particular?'

'No,' she replied more positively than she had intended and she hurried on to cover up her mistake. 'Most men were under her spell, although I think she was simply being the perfect hostess, very charming and attentive. It was nothing more than that.'

'On her part?'

'Yes; I should have thought so.'

'And on theirs?'

'I really can't give an opinion on that, Chief Inspector. You'll have to ask them yourself. Is that all?' She was anxious to end the interview, aware that she had said more than she had intended. Indicating the desk where a pile of essays had been set on one side while she tried to write the letter to Felix Napier, she added, 'Although it's half-term, I still have a lot of school-work to do.'

'Yes, of course,' Finch agreed. 'I shan't keep you much longer. There are only a couple more points I'd like to ask you about. I believe you're friendly with the Pagetts?'

The question seemed ominous in view of Finch's earlier inquiry regarding the men who had been attracted to Elizabeth Hamilton, and Kate hoped to God that the Chief Inspector hadn't picked up her reaction to it and connected it with Mike Pagett. Trying to keep her voice and expression neutral, she replied, 'I know Dodie Pagett well; we work together. As for her husband, I've only met him twice and it wouldn't be fair of me to express an opinion on him, either.' Not giving Finch time to press on with the subject of the Pagetts, she continued with deliberate briskness, 'And your other question?'

Left with no option, Finch asked it. 'Did you happen to see a shot-gun in the Hamiltons' house on Saturday?'

'No, I didn't,' she replied.

Finch thanked her and got to his feet. So that was that. There was a lot more he would have liked to ask her, not only about the

Pagetts but Felix Napier as well, but he knew he would get nothing more out of her. Her defences were up. From now on she would be on her guard and he'd be wasting his time.

It was with relief that Kate showed them to the door and watched as they retreated down the stairs towards the entrance, aware that she had handled the interview badly. Well, it was too late, she told herself, although it was small comfort.

Despite all her intentions, she was being drawn deeper and deeper into an unwilling involvement, first with Felix Napier and his daughter and now, it seemed, in his son-in-law's murder.

Returning to the sitting-room, she sat down at the desk and stared at the unfinished letter she had been writing to Felix Napier. The words '*Please convey my sympathy to your daughter*' appeared to stand out from the page like a reproach. All the same, it would have to be completed and sent. She felt she owed him at least that much and, picking up her pen, she added with sudden resolution, writing quickly before the impulse faded, '*I remember her warmth and kindness in welcoming me to her house last Saturday, which made me feel more like a friend of the family than a stranger.*'

And that also was true, she thought, and a more generous judgement on Elizabeth Hamilton than her comments to the Chief Inspector had been.

Outside the block of flats, the Chief Inspector and the Sergeant walked towards their car.

'Well, you didn't get much out of that,' Boyce commented, getting in and slamming the driver's door.

'No?' Finch sounded less certain of this fact than the Sergeant. 'I think we can assume that one of the men who came under Elizabeth Hamilton's spell, as Miss Denby put it, was Mike Pagett.'

'What makes you say that?'

'She was too quick to deny that she'd noticed any one individual who was attracted to Elizabeth Hamilton. Now Miss Denby knew only two men at that party – Felix Napier, who doesn't count in this particular situation, and Mike Pagett, the husband of her friend and colleague. And you remember what his wife said about him this morning? That he'd had a lot on his mind recently? It could be that he'd fallen for Elizabeth Hamilton.'

'And shot her husband?' Boyce suggested looking interested. 'Perhaps that's why he lied about being at the White Hart yesterday evening. He could have been trying to give himself an alibi, but we'll find that out when we interview him. Where to now?'

'Back to Woodstone,' Finch told him. 'But not to see Mike Pagett. I want to time the walk from the gateway where Mrs Hamilton left her car to the phone-box. On the way, drive down Bruton Street if you can.'

'Bruton Street? Why, for God's sake? Oh, that's where Miss Denby said she'd seen Mrs Hamilton yesterday afternoon. It's all right by me, but what are you hoping to find?'

'Just checking,' Finch said vaguely.

In the event, there wasn't much to see. Bruton Street was part of the one-way system, a short, unremarkable road of terraced houses and a small parade of shops – a launderette, a sub post-office, an Indian grocer's and a tobacconists's. At the end of it, they had to turn left into Market Street which led into the main shopping centre by the side of the library which Finch remembered Mrs Hamilton saying she had visited the day before.

Boyce's comment that it had been a waste of time seemed justified, especially as they were now heading down the High Street in the wrong direction and had to double back through the side turnings in order to get on to the Woodstone road.

On the way they passed the end of Furzeden Avenue, Miss Denby's address, so they had driven round in a bloody great circle, as Boyce took the opportunity to point out. The block of flats where she lived was visible, neat and white among the trees of the communal gardens which surrounded it, although they were too late to catch a glimpse of Kate Denby herself who, about quarter of an hour earlier, having finished her letter to Felix Napier, had put on her coat and, before she could change her mind over its wording, had walked to the pillar-box on the corner where she had posted it.

The detour round the centre of Framden and the delay while they waited in the queue of home-going traffic to filter into the roundabout on the outskirts of the town, had taken more time than Finch had bargained for and it was nearly five to six when Boyce dropped Finch off at the gateway, too late to fit in an interview with Walter Chitty at Millbridge whom Finch had been hoping also to question that afternoon.

Well, it couldn't be helped. It would have to wait although, as Finch set off along the road, following the same route as Elizabeth Hamilton said she had taken, he made up his mind that, whatever else turned up, he'd make damned sure he found time the following day to see Chitty and check on Hamilton's movements.

The sky was still overcast and dusk was already beginning to settle down over the countryside, although there was enough light for Finch to pick out the features of the place as he set out to walk towards the telephone-box and the little, anonymous hamlet.

It was the first time he had examined the area at such close quarters, having stopped only briefly there in the darkness in the early hours immediately after Hamilton's murder, and driven past it on the way to and from Woodstone that morning with Boyce in the car. On foot, he saw that it was an undistinguished landscape of farmland, fields of winter wheat mostly, although he passed one pasture, its gateway tramped into mud by the cows that would normally occupy it, with a small pond in one corner surrounded by stunted willows.

As he walked, trying to imagine what the place had looked like in the darkness and the rain of the previous evening, and matching his pace to what he thought would be Mrs Hamilton's, he became more and more convinced that the theory he had put forward to Boyce about a conspiracy between Felix Napier and his daughter was unlikely. At the time, he had not meant it to be taken too seriously; it had been more in the nature of a diversion to draw Boyce's attention from the other theory that Hamilton had been murdered by an intruder. Nevertheless, there had been the possibility that Napier and Elizabeth Hamilton could have arranged the alibi between them.

Now, seeing the place at close quarters, he was inclined to dismiss it. Mrs Hamilton's car had been left in the gateway; he had seen that for himself. He had also seen her clothes which Wylie had collected from her for forensic examination and there was no doubt that they had been wet through, and not just her outer clothing either. The collar and the sleeves of the blouse she had been wearing had also been wet, all of which substantiated her story that she had walked some distance in the rain to the telephone-box and back to the car. It could, of course, all be part of the alibi she and Napier had cooked up between them but, having seen Napier's protective concern towards his daughter, Finch doubted if he would have allowed her to take part in such an elaborate and uncomfortable charade which necessitated her getting soaked to the skin. They would have concocted a simpler and easier method.

Which suggested that she had been speaking the truth about the puncture and the subsequent phone-call and, in that case, Finch added, as he reached the kiosk and checked his watch again, there was no way he could see that she could have murdered her husband.

It had taken him nearly five minutes to walk from the gateway where she had parked the car. And, if Bradley's evidence could be relied on and he had heard the sound of the gun-shot only one or two minutes before Elizabeth Hamilton rang her father, then she certainly wouldn't have had time to get from the scene of the murder to this particular phone-box which, as the kiosk in the village had been out of order, was the only one she could have used.

If, if, if, Finch thought gloomily. The whole bloody case was bedevilled with supposition.

As arranged, Boyce was waiting for him in the car by the garage and Finch was about to walk on the few yards to join him when, on a sudden impulse, he signalled to Boyce to wait and, pulling open the door of the telephone-box, he stepped inside.

He would phone his sister, he decided, and warn her that he would most probably be late home for supper. He rarely bothered to do so when he was on a case, but Boyce's remarks earlier about his own sister and brother-in-law had jolted the Chief Inspector's conscience. And, after all, the phone-box was there; it would only take a few minutes to ring her.

Fumbling in his pocket for change in the dim light of the bulb obscured by dirt, he found a ten-pence piece and dialled his home number.

There was no answer. Finch let the telephone ring for almost a minute, disconcerted and also a little exasperated that she was not at home. She ought to be. It was now nearly five past six, so she couldn't be out shopping. It was too late.

Banging down the receiver, he joined Boyce in the car.

'Where to now?' the Sergeant demanded.

'Back to headquarters,' Finch said snappily, still irrationally annoyed that Dorothy had not been there to take his call when he made a special effort to ring her.

'You don't want to interview Pagett?' Boyce asked. 'We're only a couple of miles from Woodstone.'

'No; he can wait until tomorrow,' Finch replied. 'The men should be reporting back from the house-to-house inquiries. I'd like to hear what they've found out.'

'Suits me,' Boyce said, shrugging and starting the engine. Whatever had peeved the Chief Inspector was none of his business.

Dorothy's absence still rankled when, having listened to the verbal reports of the detectives who had turned up damn-all, and made a start on typing up his own accounts of the interviews he and Boyce had carried out, Finch eventually drove home.

He had made no further attempt to phone his sister and he made no reference to her absence from the house, until nearly bed-time when, having eaten his supper which had been kept warm for him in the oven, Finch joined her in the sitting-room.

She was seated by the fireplace, knitting a small, white, baby's jacket which he assumed was for some church bazaar. As both of them were childless, the possibility of a grandchild was out of the question.

It was at times like this in the late evening, with the curtains drawn and work over for the day that Finch missed Marion

Greave the most and felt most deeply that sense of loss for what might have been.

Had she accepted him, it might have been she, not Dorothy, who was sitting opposite him, her head tilted, her face full of that amused interest which he had at first resented and had then come so desperately to need.

They would have talked together about the case, he thought, discussing it with a professional objectivity which he was not able to achieve even with Boyce and certainly not with Dorothy in whom he never confided anything other than the most trivial details about himself.

It was a form of betrayal, of course, as he realized, and to ease his conscience, not only on that account but for his earlier exasperation with her, he roused himself and made an effort at conversation.

'I'm sorry I was late tonight,' he said. 'I tried ringing you, but you were out.'

'When was this?' she asked, looking up from her knitting.

'About five past six.'

'Oh, I see.'

The reply told him nothing and, curious to find out what exactly she had been doing for she was not normally evasive, he continued, 'Where are you, by the way?'

'Having tea with a friend,' she said. At the same time, she began to roll up the knitting, putting it away in its plastic bag to keep it clean. 'Do you want any more coffee, Jack?'

'No, thanks. It'll keep me awake.'

'Then, in that case, I think I'll go to bed,' she said, getting to her feet.

It was the same exchange of banal remarks which they made to each other every evening and yet, as Dorothy left the room, Finch had the uncomfortable and quite unfamiliar feeling that for once it was his sister and not himself who had something to hide.

14

Felix had already decided that he would have to go into Framden to cash a cheque at the bank on Thursday, even before Kate Denby's letter arrived by the morning post. Reading it, he was touched not only by her good manners in sending it – so few people nowadays bothered to write thank-you letters – but also by the sentiments she expressed about Elizabeth which struck him as genuinely sincere.

A thoroughly nice woman, he thought. It would be very pleasant to see her again. And why not that morning? he surprised himself by adding. Her telephone number was included in the printed address at the top of the letter. He only had to ring her and suggest that they meet for coffee at Frazer's while he was in Framden.

The idea filled him with guilty relief and pleasure. Much as he loved Elizabeth and mourned himself for David's death, he realized how great was his own need to escape from the house, which seemed permeated with grief, into the normal, everyday world again, if only for a few hours.

Yes, he would ring her, he decided. He'd also telephone Dodie and ask her to come and stay with Elizabeth while he was out. It would be company for his daughter and would set his own mind at rest. He did not like leaving her alone.

He rang Dodie first, using the study extension so that Elizabeth could not overhear the arrangements he was making on her behalf.

'I shall only be away for a couple of hours,' he added when Dodie had agreed to come. He said nothing to her about the possibility of meeting Kate whom he hadn't yet telephoned; nor did he intend saying anything either to her or Elizabeth. It was deceitful, of course; he was well aware of that. All the same, the sense of guilt added to the anticipation of seeing Kate Denby again. It was like making a secret assignation.

'There's no need to hurry back on my account,' Dodie assured him.

She, too, felt relieved, as well as gratified, by the invitation to keep Elizabeth company, seeing it as something of an hour to be asked. It would also be an excuse to get away from Mike whose mood had not improved and who still wasn't speaking to her properly.

Kate's initial reaction was one of surprise when, having given himself a few moments to think about what to say to her, Felix Napier rang her number. She had not expected to hear from him so quickly, certainly not on the same day that he had received her letter, and listening to his opening remarks, which she suspected had been rehearsed, she was herself touched by what she saw as his lack of guile. He would be in Framden that morning, visiting the bank. Could she possibly meet him for coffee?

It was partly this naivety which prompted her to agree; that, and the impossibility of refusing someone so recently bereaved.

Other people's grief, she thought wryly, was a powerful persuader, although she realized, as she rang off having confirmed the arrangements to meet at Frazer's at eleven o'clock, that she had not said 'yes' entirely for his sake.

Elizabeth was the only person who demurred, not on Felix's account but because of Dodie.

'Of course you must go, darling,' she told him when Felix explained the situation to her, mentioning only his proposed visit to the bank. 'It'll do you good to get out of the house. But there was really no need to send for Dodie. I should have been quite all right on my own.'

She had only just got up, the sedatives which Dr Livesey had prescribed for her making her sleep long and heavily as well as giving her, even during the day, the numbed, dulled air of someone only partially awake. All her light was quenched. Seeing her like this, Felix felt guilt overwhelm him.

'I won't go,' he said quickly. 'I'll phone Dodie and tell her not to come.'

'I shall be cross if you do,' she replied, trying to speak in her old, teasing manner. 'You need a change and I'm sure I can put up with Dodie for an hour or two. She's a darling, but she does chat on so.'

'I'll make sure that she doesn't,' Felix assured her.

He was careful, when Dodie arrived at ten o'clock, to detain her just inside the front door in order to make this very point, although he tried to express it diplomatically.

'Elizabeth's still shocked,' he explained, 'and she finds it tiring to talk too much.'

'Oh, I do understand, Felix!' Dodie exclaimed, her eyes big with sympathy. 'I shall be very, very careful what I say and I shan't mention a word about what's going on.'

'What *is* happening?' Felix asked on an impulse. Opening the study door, he ushered Dodie inside, partially closing it behind them. Elizabeth was in her room, getting dressed, and he wanted to hear when she came downstairs so that he could break off his conversation with Dodie.

Despite himself, he was curious to find out how the investigation was progressing. Apart from the interview with Finch the previous day and two subsequent visits by the police, once by a plain-clothes detective who had taken away the clothes he had been wearing on the night David was murdered and, on the second occasion, when uniformed men had returned Elizabeth's car, he was totally in the dark about the official inquiry, not having been down to the village.

'Well,' Dodie began, taking a breath and speaking, as he had done, in a hurried undertone, 'they've set up a mobile headquarters outside the village hall and they've been making house-to-house inquiries.' She passed over this part of the account quickly, reluctant to tell Felix about Finch's interview with her in which he had asked about Elizabeth and David's marriage, the thought of which still angered her. The nerve of the man to suggest that either of them might have been having an affair! 'And I gather they've been questioning Steven Bradley,' she concluded.

'Bradley?' Felix asked sharply. 'What's he got to do with it?' He couldn't see the point of it. If David had been shot by an intruder, why should Finch be interested in Bradley?

'I don't know exactly,' Dodie confessed. 'But it seems some clothes of his were stolen from an outhouse and the police have been round to the kennels checking up on him and taking his fingerprints.'

She had heard the story the previous afternoon in the village shop where she had gone to buy bread, her own baking routine having been disrupted by meeting Kate in the morning as well as by the interview with Finch which had followed. Besides, the shock of the tragedy, David's murder, Felix and Elizabeth's loss, had made it impossible for her to put her mind to anything.

'What clothes?' Felix was demanding.

'A coat and a pair of gloves, although I'm not sure if anything else was taken,' Dodie admitted. The gossip had been fragmentary and she wished now that she had not mentioned it in the first place. 'Anyway,' she added, 'it seems the police are keen to find them. They've put up notices asking people to report it if they do and they've started looking themselves. At least, someone said they're going to begin searching the woods and dragging the ponds if the clothing doesn't turn up soon.'

This last piece of information was pure supposition, the gossipers in the shop merely speculating on the likelihood of the police frogmen being called in to add to the drama. Not that Felix seemed interested. His attention was still on Bradley.

'You said they've taken Bradley's fingerprints?' he asked.

'Yes, according to what I heard,' Dodie replied. How extraordinary! Felix thought. Why on earth should the police bother to do that? He could understand it in the case of Elizabeth and himself. As Finch had explained, he needed to check on the prints in the house for the purpose of elimination. But surely Bradley's weren't necessary?

Unless, of course, Finch had other reasons to suspect the man. But of what? he asked himself.

The answer was too terrible to contemplate. Much as he disliked Bradley, even he could not find the words to express it, and it was with relief that he heard his daughter cross the landing and start to come down the stairs. Ushering Dodie hurriedly out of the study in time to meet Elizabeth in the hall, he thrust the unanswered question to the back of his mind, almost forgetting it in the flurry of escorting the two women into the drawing-room and making his own preparations for the drive into Framden.

Percy followed him to the front door, thumping his tail on the carpet and turning up his eyes in appeal. At first Felix was inclined to send the dog away and then changed his mind. The poor old chap hadn't had any proper exercise since Tuesday morning. If he took Percy with him, he could give him a quick run on the way back from Framden. Besides, the dog was unhappy and subdued, sensing the grief in the house, and the change would be as much to Percy's benefit as it was to his own.

'Come on then, old boy,' he said. 'But you'll have to wait in the car until I can let you out for a run.'

Calling to Eizabeth that he was taking the dog with him, he went out to the Range Rover where he shut it in the back.

As he turned out of the drive into the lane, he heard Percy give several small whimpers of excitement at the sudden and unexpected outing which Felix himself could understand, and he felt his own spirits rise a little at the prospect of the morning's treat ahead of him.

Knowing Felix Napier's punctiliousness, Kate was careful to be exactly on time, entering Frazer's as the Market Hall clock struck eleven.

Felix was already there, the only man in the restaurant, occupying a corner table for two. As soon as she appeared, he rose to his feet to draw out her chair, causing a little rustle of interest among the women shoppers at the other tables and the immediate attention of the waitress who came for their order.

They probably think he's in love with me, Kate thought, aware that their curiosity was touched by a little envy as well. Few husbands would behave so gallantly.

For the first time, she considered Felix in the role of a potential lover, realizing that she should have been warned by his alacrity in telephoning her so soon after receiving her letter, and she looked at him with a new alertness across the little table as he ordered coffee and cakes for two.

The death of his son-in-law had obviously affected him. He seemed tired and a little older although he carried his grief well. But, by his code, it would be bad manners to make a public parade of his feelings. She knew that as a lover he would be kind, considerate, thoughtful.

But was it enough? she wondered, although God alone knew what else she was expecting. Hardly a grand passion. And anyway, wasn't such speculation premature? All the same, she realized that at some point during their relationship she would have to come to a decision as to whether or not she saw him again, for his sake if not for hers. As she poured the coffee and passed him his cup she was aware that there was a different quality in his manner towards her as well, which she could only describe as a form of gentle and hesitant intimacy, as courteous as ever for, after all, he was nothing if not a gentleman, but suggesting that, at least as far as he was concerned, their relationship had passed beyond the stage of mere acquaintances.

For his part, Felix had to steel himself not to confide in her. Looking at her across the little posy of flowers which decorated the centre of the table, he thought how much he needed her – for her dark, sensible good looks, for her air of quiet self-confidence and, more than any of these qualities, for that common sense and good humour which he prized above all else in a woman.

He was tempted to unburden himself of his grief – David's death, Elizabeth's bereavement, even his concern over Bradley, placing himself in her firm and competent hands. It would have been like coming home at last and finding peace and solace.

But he hesitated to confide in her; at least, not yet. There would be time later for more intimate and personal conversations. This occasion, he felt, was too premature, and he feared that by referring to the dark shadow of tragedy which hung over his own spirits he might despoil the young, tender bloom of their relationship, like a delicate fruit which is bruised by handling too soon and too roughly in the picking.

And so he held back, steering the conversation towards the subject of Jane Austen and the edition of her letters which Kate had begun reading but hadn't yet finished, trying to speak with the same enthusiasm with which he had done when he had first lent her the book, as if, Kate thought, he were trying to recapture that occasion and to establish that it was here, in their mutual interests, that any further development in their relationship would be founded.

It was only when he called for the bill that he mentioned his daughter, the remark also containing an oblique reference to a further meeting between himself and Kate.

'You'll forgive me, I hope, if I have to hurry away this time. I would have liked to stay longer, but I feel I mustn't leave Elizabeth alone for too long. Dodie's with her but I can't expect her to give up too much of her time.'

'Of course I understand,' Kate replied, gathering up her gloves and bag.

The words 'this time' had not escaped her. He obviously intended that they would see each other again. But her own mind was made up, not through any shortcomings on his part but on account of Elizabeth.

I could not share him, she thought; not with her. I would always be an interloper in a relationship which was too long-standing and exclusive to allow me to be anything more than a newcomer. As a late arrival at a feast, room would be made for me at their table but it would not be enough. I have lived alone for too long and grown too selfish to play a secondary role with any grace or sincerity.

The book would be returned by post, she decided, as they shook hands outside the restaurant and, although she smiled, she avoided looking directly into his blue eyes before walking away without a backward glance.

On the journey back to Woodstone, Felix tried not to think of either Kate or Bradley, concentrating on driving and on the other traffic which was heavy along the main road. Kate was a new concern, although Bradley had been at the back of his mind all morning, kept at bay by the visit to Framden and the pleasure of seeing Kate again. Now both of them crowded into his thoughts, each demanding the concentration which he knew he would have to give them before returning to Elizabeth. As soon as he arrived home, she would absorb all his care and attention.

Once he had turned off at the T-junction, the traffic eased. He was on the miror road which led to Woodstone and, as he reached its outskirts, he turned again opposite the church into Gade's Lane, drawing the car on to the verge alongside the path which led towards the wood, Helen's favourite walk and the same route by which he and David had returned from their afternoon shoot less than three weeks before. It now seemed another lifetime away.

Releasing Percy from the back of the Range Rover, he flung a stick for the dog to retrieve, not that Percy needed any encouragement. Let loose from the confines of the car, he bounded eagerly ahead of him, tail high, muzzle straining forward, excited by the freedom.

Felix followed more slowly, intent on his thoughts. Kate came first. Compared to her, Bradley was of secondary importance. He had lost her; he wasn't quite sure how or why, but that fact was indisputable. The handshake as they parted, the expression in her eyes, not quite meeting his, the sudden manner in which she had turned and walked away, all seemed to confirm the end of the relationship. Remembering her face across the table, the absurd details of her hand lifting the coffee pot, the way her wrist had turned, he was overwhelmed with a sense of loss.

The word began to assume obsessive proportions in his mind. Loss. Loss. Loss. First Helen's, and then David's. Now Kate's. It was all around him, too, in the hedges stripped of their leaves, the wet grass along the verges sinking back into the tangled litter of winter, the brown fields stretching away to meet the grey sky.

Reaching the end of the path, he went forward a few paces into Gade's Wood where he stood under the trees, listening to the wind stirring the branches before, calling to Percy, he turned and began to walk back to the car.

The dog ran a little in front of him, less joyfully now, aware of Felix's mood and subdued by it, busying himself with nosing along the ditch at the side of the path among the dying grass and the wet leaves which had been swept into it by Tuesday's storm. One heap in particular, close to the road, seemed to excite his attention, for as Felix felt in his pocket for the car keys the dog remained behind, scratching at the heaped leaves and scattering them with his paws.

His eagerness attracted Felix's notice and, walking back, he bent down to see what the dog had found, pulling Percy away by the collar.

A man's jacket and a pair of leather gauntlets, sodden with rain, were lying in the ditch under the autumn debris, wet leaves still clinging to them. Thinking at first they were rubbish, Felix was about to turn them over with the toe of his shoe when he recalled Dodie telling him about Bradley's stolen clothing, also a coat and gloves. The kennels were only a couple of hundred yards down the lane. If they were Bradley's, as seemed likely, it would have been easy for someone to dump them here just beside the pathway.

Shutting Percy up in the back of the Range Rover, Felix returned to examine them more closely, remembering Dodie had also said that the police were eager to find them.

But what had Bradley's jacket and gloves to do with David's death? Felix wondered, their full significance escaping him although their theft suggested to him that the intruder theory was no longer tenable. His son-in-law's murder had been no random killing. Someone had planned it and had taken Bradley's clothing as part of that plan. But what part was Bradley himself playing in the investigation? It was the unanswered question which so far he had managed to keep at the back of his mind. If the police had questioned Bradley and taken his fingerprints, didn't this imply they had some reason to suspect him?

But why? Bradley could have no possible reason for wanting to kill David unless . . .

The solution came to him without any conscious effort on his part.

Of course, that confounded right of way! David had intended refusing Bradley permission to close it.

At the same time, as he straightened up, another thought struck him with as much clarity and force.

It was absurd.

He turned away and walked back to the car, his mind made up. He would report his finding of the clothes at the mobile headquarters which Dodie had mentioned and which he himself had seen outside the village hall on his way through the village that morning. That much was his plain duty. It was also his duty to inform Finch that any suspicions he might have against Bradley were totally unfounded although, as he climbed into the driver's seat and started the engine, he was aware that the whole controversy over the right of way was largely his responsibility. It was he himself who had magnified it out of all proportion, an unpleasant truth which nevertheless had to be faced.

There was nothing he could do about David's death, Elizabeth's grief or his own sense of loss over the end to the gentle, burgeoning relationship with Kate Denby. But there was one wrong which he could put right – by making damned sure that Bradley's name was cleared of any taint of murder.

15

There was no sign of Dodie Pagett to Finch's relief when, on Thursday morning, he and Boyce arrived to interview her husband.

Instead, they found Mike Pagett alone in the barn, standing at a long bench where he was packing sprigs of herbs into shallow plastic trays which he then covered with squares of cling-film, a task in which he appeared not to be finding much satisfaction for he was muttering angrily to himself and shifting impatiently from one foot to the other, crushing the discarded leaves which lay on the floor so that the whole barn was permeated with the aromatic scent of mint and thyme.

Aware of the presence of the two men in the doorway, he turned to face them, his scowl deepening.

'Dodie's not here,' he informed them. 'She's gone to Felix Napier's. It seems Elizabeth Hamilton can't be left on her own while her father's out for a couple of hours.'

His expression and the sarcastic note in his voice suggested that he disapproved of these arrangements, largely, Finch suspected, because he had been deprived of his wife's assistance, an impression which seemed confirmed when, as Pagett was struggling to cover one of the trays, the thin film buckled and, with an impatient gesture, he crumpled it up and flung it along the bench.

'It's you we've come to see,' Finch said pleasantly, stepping into the barn with Boyce at his heels.

'Oh?' Pagett replied belligerently, trying to brazen it out. 'What about?'

But he knew all right. As Boyce took a pace forward to assume the questioning, Pagett backed uneasily away.

'It's about your movements on Tuesday evening, sir,' Boyce said, getting out his notebook. 'We've checked with the landlord at the White Hart and it seems you weren't there. So we'd like to find out exactly where you were and what you were doing.'

He used his official voice, politely non-committal, into which he nevertheless managed to introduce, to Finch's secret amusement, a tone of controlled menace – which was why Finch had left the Sergeant to open the questioning. It had broken better men that Pagett whose aggression was, in Finch's estimation, nothing more than a defensive pose.

All the same, Pagett had one last try. 'I don't see that it's any of your business,' he retorted.

Boyce waited, massively patient, notebook in hand, as the man turned to the Chief Inspector in appeal.

'Is this necessary?' I don't see that what I was doing on Tuesday has any bearing on Hamilton's murder.'

'It's up to you, Mr Pagett,' Finch replied. 'You can either answer the questions now or, if you prefer, you can come with us to Divisional Headquarters in Chelmsford and make a statement in the presence of your solicitor.'

He spoke with cheerful indifferent as if Pagett's decision was of little importance to him one way or the other.

Pagett gave up. 'I was with somebody over at Loxleigh,' he muttered.

'The name, sir?' Boyce asked, resuming the questioning.

'Linda Wade.'

As he spoke, Pagett looked quickly from the Sergeant to Finch, trying to gauge their reactions, but they remained impassive, their expressions giving nothing away although Boyce asked, with the air of someone interested merely in getting the facts right, 'Is that "Miss" or "Mrs", sir?'

'"Mrs",' Pagett replied. 'She's divorced. I haven't known her all that long. I met her three or four weeks ago in Loxleigh. I'd dropped in at the Bell there for a drink on the way back from the wholesaler's and she happened to be in the bar. We got talking – you know how it is?'

Now that he had started, Pagett was anxious not just to explain and to justify himself but also to obtain their approval, as if their good opinion mattered in maintaining his self-esteem; and in order to encourage him Finch gave the man the benefit of a quick nod which was enough to keep him going.

'I've seen her a few times since,' Pagett continued. 'We usually meet at the Bell and then go to her house. It's not a serious relationship. I mean, she knows I'm married and . . .'

She's a bit on the side, Finch added to himself as Boyce broke into Pagett's account to ask, 'What time did you arrive there on Tuesday?'

'Tuesday?' In his eagerness to explain, Pagett seemed to have forgotten the purpose behind the interview. 'Oh, yes, of course. I got there about a quarter to nine. We had a quick drink as usual and then she took me back to her place.'

He glanced down at his feet, shuffling the toe of one shoe uneasily among the scattered leaves of the herbs as if aware himself that, rather than being taken, as he had put it, he had accompanied the woman only too willingly.

Boyce passed over the equivocation without so much as a flicker of an eyelid. 'What time did you leave Mrs Wade's house, sir?'

'About ten o'clock.'

'You're sure of that?' Finch broke in to ask.

Pagett looked at him, hesitated and then admitted, 'It could have been a little earlier, I suppose.'

'And you arrived home at about half-past ten,' Finch pointed out. That fact had already been established in the first interview with the Pagetts. 'How long does it take you to drive from Loxleigh to Woodstone?'

'About a quarter of an hour; in good driving conditions, that is. It was pouring with rain on Tuesday evening so it could have taken a bit longer. I wasn't in any great hurry to get back anyway. I'd told Dodie I'd gone for a drink at the White Hart so I didn't want to arrive home too soon after closing time. The Hart's only a few minutes' drive away.'

Despite the position he found himself in, Pagett couldn't resist making these last remarks with a self-satisfied air, evidently pleased with his manipulation of the timing, contrived to deceive his wife; and Finch took some pleasure of his own in asking with pretended casualness, 'So you'd have driven past the Hamiltons' house on your way back from Loxleigh?'

The point of the question wasn't lost on Pagett, who replied with some of his former belligerence, 'I told you yesterday that I saw nothing. And if you're trying to insinuate . . .'

'I think that's all, Mr Pagett,' Finch broke in, pausing deliberately before adding, 'for the moment, anyway.' Turning to Boyce, he inquired, 'Are there any further questions you wanted to ask Mr Pagett, Sergeant?'

'Only for Mrs Wade's address,' Boyce replied.

If the subtleties of the exchange, practised between them over years of collaboration, had amused him, there was no sign of it on his face which maintained its polite, official expression.

Finch cocked an eyebrow at Pagett who replied with a sulky air, 'Number 15, Branch Road. That's a turning two doors down from the Bell.'

'I expect we'll find it without too much difficulty,' Finch assured him as, nodding pleasantly at Pagett, he and Boyce walked out of the barn towards their car, leaving the man standing at the bench. It was only after they had gone that, in a sudden outburst of angry frustration, he swept the trays of herbs on to the floor.

'That wasn't very sensible of you,' Dodie remarked from the doorway.

Walking forward, she began to pick up the scattered packets, putting them back on to the bench in a tidy pile.

Mike watched her warily for a few moments. 'How long had you been outside?' he asked at last.

'Long enough,' Dodie replied. Retrieving the last tray, she straightened up and faced him, 'I got back just after Finch and his Sergeant started asking you about that woman in Loxleigh. Elizabeth was tired so I didn't stay long.'

It was the only explanation for her unexpected and early return that she was prepared to give him. The rest of it, which she might have described to him in some detail in other circumstances, was better left unsaid.

The morning had not turned out as she had expected. When Felix had first asked her to keep Elizabeth company, Dodie had imagined herself in the role of surrogate mother, offering solace and understanding, woman to woman.

It had been, as she saw now, an absurd conception.

Instead, Dodie had found Elizabeth remote and unapproachable. It was as if she had retreated, Dodie had thought, behind a sheet of plate glass; still beautiful with that pale, exquisite fragility which seemed a reproach to Dodie's own plump untidiness but, like a dummy in a shop window, lacking any life or real animation.

They had talked; or rather it was Dodie who had chatted on about trivial, non-controversial topics – school, village affairs, the cushion covers she was printing for the church bazaar – conscious all the time that Felix had asked her not to tire Elizabeth too much and yet unable to keep silent.

At quarter-past eleven, after Dodie had made coffee for them both, Elizabeth had more or less asked her to go, pleading a headache.

But what could she do? Dodie had asked herself. Although Felix had not yet returned, she could hardly force her company on Elizabeth. So she had reluctantly taken her leave and walked home, where she had found Finch's car parked outside the house and the sound of men's voices, including Mike's, coming from inside the barn.

She had, of course, no business to eavesdrop but, catching the name Linda Wade and the word 'divorced', she had waited out of sight round the corner of the barn where it was possible to continue listening without being seen.

To her surprise, Mike's account of his infidelity came as no real shock to her. She had been a fool, she realized, not to have suspected something of the sort all along and it was as much this awareness of her own stupidity as Mike's betrayal which made it possible for her to confront him with a hard, dry-eyed control which, judging by his expression, was more effective than tears or accusations would have been.

'What are you going to do, Dodie?' he was asking.

He looked not so much guilty, she thought, or even ashamed, but alarmed and shifty at having been found out, backing away from her and trying at the same time to smile as if that alone would make up for everything.

Instead of answering directly, she held out her hand. 'Give me the keys to the van,' she told him.

Surprised by her reaction, he felt in his pocket and handed them over before he had the sense to ask, 'What do you want them for?'

'Because I'm leaving you,' she said and began to walk away towards the door.

He called out after her in protest. 'That woman doesn't really mean anything to me, Dodie! I'll give you my word I'll never see her again.' When she took no notice, not even bothering to turn her head, he added, 'But what am I going to do without you? I can't manage here on my own.'

Pausing in the doorway, Dodie said over her shoulder, 'That's not my problem any more. It's yours.'

Getting into the van and starting the engine, she congratulated herself on her exit line. It had been brief and to the point. Moreover, she realized, it expressed what she had been longing to say to him for months.

She would go to her sister's for a few days until she had time to think about what to do next, she decided. Besides, her lack of luggage wouldn't matter at Fran's, unlike a hotel. She could borrow from her sister whatever she might need for the time being.

Turning the van into the lane, she caught a last glimpse of Mike. He was standing in the open doorway of the barn, shoulders bowed, looking self-pitying and, it had to be admitted, also a little lost and foolish.

Boyce was saying, 'What do you reckon? Could Pagett have had the time to murder Hamilton?'

'It's possible,' Finch replied. 'If he left Loxleigh at around five to ten, he'd just about have made it back to Woodstone by quarter-past, the time Bradley said he heard the shot. That is,' he added as a proviso, 'if we can rely on Bradley's evidence. We'll have to check with Mrs Wade the time Pagett left, of course.'

They were on their way down Brookhouse Lane towards the village, making for the main road in order to drive to Millbridge to question Chitty, an interview which came next after Pagett's on the Chief Inspector's agenda for the day.

The rest, including a check on Mrs Hamilton's movements in Framden on the day her husband had been murdered, had been left to subordinates like Kyle and Marsh to whom Finch had consigned the task of following through her itinerary before setting out from Divisional Headquarters that morning. A team of uniformed men under Inspector Stapleton had also been despatched to search the hedges and ditches in the immediate vicinity of the Hamiltons' house for Bradley's missing coat and gloves; not that Finch expected them to be found. They could have been dumped anywhere.

'But if Pagett had found himself a girl-friend,' Boyce continued, 'wouldn't that knock on the head your theory that he fancied Mrs Hamilton?'

'Not necessarily, Tom,' Finch replied. 'Mrs Wade might be second best.'

'I don't get you,' Boyce replied.

His lack of perception could, at times, be exasperating although Finch tried to control his impatience as he roused himself to spell out his thoughts for the Sergeant's benefit.

'Pagett was clearly on the look-out for a bit on the side. Supposing he cast his net first in the direction of Elizabeth Hamilton; perhaps even thought she was encouraging him? You heard what Miss Denby said yesterday: Mrs Hamilton could make herself very charming and attentive when she wanted to. So Pagett, who I imagine is the type to have too high an opinion of himself, misread the signals and thought she fancied him as well. It's ludicrous, of course, but Pagett wouldn't see it that way. So he made his feelings known but Mrs Hamilton rejected him in no uncertain terms. Pagett then took his wounded ego off and found solace with someone else who would accept him – the young lady from Loxleigh; second best, in other words. But supposing that wasn't enough to heal the wound? He could very well have wanted to hit back at the Hamiltons, David Hamilton in particular.'

'But why him?' Boyce demanded. He still hadn't grasped the point.

'Because he was the lucky possessor, as Pagett would see it, of the lovely and desirable Elizabeth Hamilton,' Finch replied. 'That's one possibility. The other is that Hamilton knew what was going on and warned Pagett off from pestering his wife. Either way you could have a motive for murder. Envy. Injured pride. The need for revenge. Take your pick. By my reckoning, Pagett's capable of any of them.'

'So you'll get Wylie to run the swab test on him?'

'Later,' Finch told him. 'I want to get that interview with Chitty over and done with first.'

'And what about Mrs Pagett?'

'I'm not sure, Tom,' Finch confessed. 'As I said to you yesterday, she could have had the opportunity not only to kill Hamilton but also to pinch Bradley's clothing. As for motive, I suppose if she thought her husband's interest was straying towards Elizabeth Hamilton, she might have wanted to get her own back, although it seems a bit far-fetched, I admit. There could, of course, be another reason which we haven't so far turned up . . .'

He paused as the car radio broke in, giving their call sign. The message, received by telephone at Divisional Headquarters from the mobile unit in Woodstone and relayed from there, was reported in the flat, unemotional voice of one of the women operators.

Certain articles of clothing, a jacket and a pair of gloves, had been discovered in the vicinity of Woodstone. Would Detective Chief Inspector Finch report as soon as possible to the mobile unit in the village centre?

'Well, there's a turn-up for the books!' Boyce commented as

Finch acknowledged the message. 'So what do you want to do now? Shall I go back or drive on to Millbridge?'

They had, in fact, passed the caravan, which served as the mobile headquarters and which was parked outside the village hall, only minutes before and were now heading towards the T-junction and the main road.

Finch hesitated.

The information about the discovery of the clothing was good news indeed; the first piece of real luck they had so far encountered on the case. Only half an hour earlier, on their way to interview Pagett, Finch and the Sergeant had stopped at the caravan to inquire if anyone from the village had reported in with any useful information, but had drawn a blank.

The officer in charge, Sergeant Benson, had told them that so far no one had come forward apart from an elderly woman who seemed to have a grudge against her neighbours and had told a long and rambling story about damage to her fence. Apart from that, there had been nothing, although Benson, who seemed to think this lack of evidence somehow reflected on his own professional competence, had pointed out that, considering the weather on Tuesday evening, it wasn't surprising that most people had been indoors and had seen and heard nothing.

On the other hand, the interview with Chitty had already been postponed and it was vital that Hamilton's movements were checked on as soon as possible.

'Well?' Boyce demanded.

He had slowed down and was idling the car along the side of the road.

'Turn back,' Finch said, coming to a decision. After all, with a little more luck, it might still be possible to inverview Chitty later in the day.

Making a smart three-point turn, Boyce headed the car back towards Woodstone.

Five minutes later, Finch was squatting down over a ditch a few yards along a pathway which led off Gade's Lane, Benson having given him directions to find the place when he and Boyce had called at the mobile unit.

'Potter's keeping an eye on them,' Benson had added, Potter being the young uniformed constable who, together with Benson, was manning the caravan.

Finch, who had merely stuck his head round the door, had waved an acknowledgement and gone back to the car. He could probably find out whatever else he needed to know from Potter. Like Dunbar, Benson was the type who, given half a chance, tended to make the most of even the scantiest information. It had taken him nearly five minutes to report on the old lady and her fence when Finch had called earlier.

Potter kept both his distance and a respectful silence once he had shown the Chief Inspector and the Sergeant where the clothing was to be found.

Seeing it, there was no doubt in Finch's mind that it was Bradley's. It answered the description which Bradley had given him and the chances of one pair of leather gauntlets and a jacket going missing and another set turning up was too much of a coincidence. Besides, the place where they had been hidden was only a couple of hundred yards from the kennels. If it weren't for the slight bend in the lane, Finch could have seen the opening in the hedge which led on to Bradley's land.

'When were they found?' he asked Potter, straightening up and walking across to where the young PC was standing.

'About half an hour ago, sir.'

'Who by?' It was Boyce who asked the question.

'A Mr Napier.'

'Napier!'

'That's right, Sergeant,' Potter explained. 'He was evidently out walking his dog. On his way back, he called in at the mobile unit to report finding the stuff. Sergeant Benson sent me back here with Mr Napier so's he could show me the exact spot, while the Sergeant phoned through to Divisional headquarters.' He seemed interested in Boyce's reaction to Napier's name for he kept a bright-eyed watch on both the Serveant and the Chief Inspector as he added, 'He's gone home, by the way, sir. Mr Napier, I mean.'

'Thank you, Constable,' Finch said in his official voice and, jerking his head at Boyce, walked back to where the jacket and gloves lay in the ditch, still partly covered by wet leaves.

'Napier!' Boyce repeated but taking care to lower his voice this time.

'I know, Tom,' Finch agreed. 'On the face of it, it looks too much of a damned coincidence. But in Napier dumped them, and I assume that's what you're thinking, why the hell should he go to the trouble of pretending to find them?'

'He might,' Boyce pointed out, 'if he thought we'd got good reason to suspect him of his son-in-law's murder. He could have been trying to shift suspicion off himself.'

It was a reasonable point which Finch acknowledged with a nod of his head before continuing, 'We'll have to get Bradley to identify them, although I'm quite sure in my own mind they're his. Take the car and pick him up. After that, if it's a positive ID, we'll need to call in McCullum to photograph them and Wylie to make a search of the area.' As he spoke, he glanced at his watch. It was now nearly a quarter to one. 'And tell Bradley not to hang about,' he added, raising his voice as Boyce walked away to the car. 'I want to get over to Millbridge this afternoon if there's still time.'

Boyce was back within minutes, accompanied by Bradley who merely glanced down at the clothing before saying abruptly, 'Yes, they're mine.'

'You're sure?' Finch asked.

Bradley turned to look at him with a morose, sarcastic expression. Since his encounter the day before with Ruth Livesey outside Leverett's garage, at which she had made it quite clear that she wanted nothing more to do with him, he had been nursing a deep sense of grievance and was in no mood to make himself agreeable to Finch or anybody else. 'I told you, they're mine,' he repeated. 'And if you don't believe me, you'll find my name on the tab inside the jacket. Who found them, by the way?'

'Thank you, Mr Bradley,' Finch said cheerfully, ignoring the man's question. 'Can my Sergeant give you a lift home?'

Bradley seemed amused by the offer.

'I reckon I can manage the walk back to my place,' he replied and, hunching his shoulders, he set off along the lane in the direction of the kennels, an awkward, disconsolate figure, his head bowed and his hands stuffed deep into his pockets.

Finch watched him go. But there was no time to waste on feeling sorry for the man, and as soon as Bradley had disappeared out of sight round the bend in the lane the Chief Inspector turned back to Boyce.

'Right!' he said. 'Get Headquarters on the radio, Tom, and tell them I want McCullum and Wylie over here straight away.'

'And then we question Napier?' Boyce asked.

'No, we don't,' Finch retorted. 'Napier can wait till later. As soon as McCullum and Wylie have finished, we go over to Millbridge.'

He was damned if he was going to postpone the interview with Chitty for a second time.

16

Even then it was mid-afternoon before McCullum and Wylie had finished and the clothing could be parcelled up for forensic examination, although Finch had no doubt about the outcome of the tests. Powder marks would be found on the front of the jacket and on at least one of the gloves.

Under the circumstances, it seemed a waste of time to send Wylie off to the Pagetts' house to take hand swabs, but at least, as he had said to Boyce, he was going through the motions. 'And tell them it's just routine,' he added to Wylie before he drove away, making the stipulation largely for Mrs Pagett's benefit. He was less bothered about Pagett's reaction.

Millbridge, when they finally arrived there, was a small country town which began and ended abruptly. Even from its central market cross it was possible to see the farmland which surrounded it on all sides and from where it drew its trade to the two narrow streets of shops which formed its heart and where it was still possible to buy tin kettles, long-sleeved woollen vests and stone hot-water bottles.

The branch office of Dunbar and Hamilton was above an estate agent's, both accommodated in a former private house, and was reached up a steep flight of lino-covered stairs. Mr

Chitty occupied what had once been the main bedroom with its Victorian fireplace, sash windows and plaster cornice in the form of acanthus leaves still in place.

The setting suited Mr Chitty. He was in his seventies, long due for retirement but hanging on, Finch suspected, to this little kingdom of his with the tenacity of an ageing monarch who regarded any attempts to remove him as treason, although he was full of praise for David Hamilton.

'A charming young man,' he told Finch. 'I was deeply shocked to hear of his death. Ralph rang me. Dreadful business! He'll have to pull his socks up; Ralph, I mean. He relied far too much on young Hamilton. Utterly dependable. And to think that I was speaking to him only a couple of days ago.'

'That's what I wanted to ask you about,' Finch put in. 'I gather he was here on Tuesday.'

'He came every Tuesday,' Mr Chitty corrected him. 'It was Dunbar's idea; thought I was getting past it. But I can still handle a conveyancing or the drafting of a will and it's that sort of business which is our bread and butter. And, despite what Ralph says, a lot of the farmers round here still prefer to deal with a solicitor who knew their fathers – and their grandfathers too, in some cases.'

'So what business did Mr Hamilton deal with?' Finch asked.

'Divorce,' Chitty said promptly. 'Personally, I won't touch it with a barge pole. It's even spreading out to the villages.' From his expression of distaste, he might have been speaking of some unpleasant and virulent disease. 'Young Hamilton also took over the more complicated property sales or any litigation which involved briefing counsel, most of which would be transferred to the main office in Framden. I'd arrange preliminary appointments for those clients here in my office so that Hamilton could interview them. He also handled any correspondence relating to their affairs.'

'So he kept normal office hours?'

'To the dot. As I said, he was utterly dependable. He was here at nine o'clock sharp and left at half-past five; said he had to get home. Well, I could understand his keenness, a young married man with that lovely young wife of his.'

'He always left at half-past five?' Finch asked casually,

avoiding Boyce's glance for the Sergeant had looked up from his notebook.

'Yes; at least, he had been in the habit of doing so since September. He asked me not to make any appointments for him after half-past four.'

'And he said he was going home?' Finch persisted. 'Can you remember his exact words?'

Mr Chitty looked affronted. 'Really, Chief Inspector, I can hardly be expected to remember word for word a conversation which took place nearly two months ago. Hamilton merely remarked that he'd appreciate an early evening at home once a week. Reading between the lines, I gathered he often had to put in extra hours at the Framden office which, knowing Ralph's tendency to shuffle off as much responsibility as he could on to young Hamilton, didn't surprise me in the least. As our list of clients wasn't all that long, I had no trouble in arranging it to suit David's request, which seemed perfectly reasonable to me. He was very grateful. But I really can't see what relevance all this has to his death.'

'We're simply checking on Mr Hamilton's movements,' Finch said with deliberate vagueness. 'Did he leave at the usual time last Tuesday?'

'Strange you should ask that,' Mr Chitty replied. 'He didn't seem in quite so much of a hurry, although it couldn't have been much later than a quarter to six before he went.'

'And did he ever speak to you about getting a meal out on the way home, at a restaurant or pub?'

'No; why should he?' Mr Chitty countered. 'I assumed from what he said about an early evening at home that he would be dining with his wife. That seemed the whole object of the exercise. At least, that's the impression he gave me.'

'Thank you, Mr Chitty,' Finch said, rising to his feet and putting an end to the interview before Chitty who, for all his years, was clearly as sharp as a needle, could ask any more awkward questions; although, as soon as they emerged into the street, the Chief Inspector expressed to Boyce the query which was uppermost in his own mind.

'Why the hell did Hamilton lie, Tom? He knew damned well his wife wouldn't get back from Framden until at least quarter to eleven on Tuesday evenings, so why lead Chitty on to believe he wanted an early evening at home?'

The questions were merely rhetorical. He already knew the answer which Boyce also had evidently guessed for he replied, 'For the same reason most men tell lies, I suppose – another woman.'

'Exactly; but which one? So far we haven't turned up a likely candidate although, whoever it is, the pair of them must have kept the affair very quiet. Everyone we've spoken to so far who knew the Hamiltons well, like Dodie Pagett, seemed to think the marriage was ideal.'

'If Hamilton was having an affair, it'd give Mrs Hamilton a motive,' Boyce pointed out.

'Not only her. There's Napier as well. You've seen for yourself how close he is to his daughter. He's quite capable of going to any lengths to protect her. So, if we count out the conspiracy theory and assume that they weren't working together to provide each other with an alibi, Napier looks the more promising candidate of the two.'

He had already explained to the Sergeant his objections regarding this particular theory the previous day after he had timed the walk from the gateway to the telephone-box on the Framden road, Boyce agreeing with him that it was too complicated and that some simpler explanation was more feasible.

'Is he?' Boyce didn't sound too convinced of that line of argument. 'But what about the timing? If he shot Hamilton just before quarter-past ten – and I'm going on the assumption that Bradley's innocent, and therefore wasn't lying about the time he heard the shot – then I can't see how Napier managed to get back to his own house a minute or so later in time to take the call from his daughter at sixteen minutes past. It's just not possible.'

'It could be, Tom, although he'd be cutting it very fine. After all, we only have Napier's word for it that she rang him at ten-sixteen. If you remember, she said in her statement that she didn't know what the time was when she got to the call-box. The only timing she could verify was when her father picked her up at half past ten. Working back from the deadline, Napier had just over a quarter of an hour in hand from the time Bradley heard the shot to the time he arrived at the gateway to pick his daughter up. Assuming he committed the murder, he'd have taken about four or five minutes to get from the scene of the crime back to his house which brings the timing up to about ten-nineteen, or even later. Now supposing his daughter rang him, not at ten-sixteen as Napier stated, but at ten-twenty, shortly after he arrived home? He'd still have about ten minutes in hand, long enough to drive to that gateway in the Framden road by half-past ten. In other words, there's about four or five minutes not accounted for in his statement and that's enough time for him to have committed the murder and got home.'

'Yes, I see your point,' Boyce agreed, although he still didn't seem all that convinced. 'But what about Bradley's clothing? I can see Napier could have had the opportunity to take it on Tuesday morning when he was out with the dog. But when the hell did he dump it? If, as you say, he was cutting it fine anyway, he'd've added a couple more minutes on his timing to drive along Gade's Lane after the murder and stop off along that pathway to get rid of it.'

'Perhaps he didn't dump it then,' Finch suggested. 'He could have kept it concealed in the back of the Range Rover and left it by the side of the path this morning on his way into Framden.'

'Pretending to find it on the way back? It's possible, I suppose,' Boyce admitted. 'It still leaves a hell of a lot of ifs. For a start, if your theory's right, Napier couldn't have known his daughter would ring him up so I suppose we have to put that down to chance. But he would have known she'd go home and find her husband's body. If he was, as you say, so damned keen on protecting her, would he have put her through an ordeal like that?'

'I think he might have done,' Finch replied, 'if it was to save her from something worse – the knowledge of Hamilton's affair and the likelihood of a divorce. From what we know of Hamilton, he wasn't the type of man to go in for a bit on the side, which makes me suspect that his affair with this other woman, whoever she was, was serious. Napier may have guessed that, too; may even have known the identity of the woman. Weighing it all up, he could very well have decided that Hamilton's death was better than his daughter's betrayal, as he'd see it.'

'But what about Mrs Hamilton herself? Wouldn't she have as strong a motive as her father for wanting Hamilton dead?'

'I can't see she had the opportunity, Tom. If we discount the conspiracy theory but assume she's guilty, then Napier must be innocent and was therefore telling us the truth when he said that his daughter rang him from a pay-box at ten-sixteen, one minute after Bradley heard the shot. There's no way she could have got to the one on the Framden road in that time, although she might have made it to the phone-box in the village. But, as that one was out of order, we know she couldn't have used that particular kiosk, which leaves the next nearest, the one on the Framden road. It's just not possible when you consider that, in addition, she'd have to dump Bradley's clothes on the way. She certainly didn't have them in the car with her. Marsh searched it. There was nothing in it except for some shopping and her own clothes which she'd changed out of for the evening class in Framden.'

'So, if we rule out Elizabeth Hamilton, what about the Pagetts? Are they out of the running as well?'

Finch tried to hide his exasperation at the Sergeant's literal-mindedness.

'No, I'm not saying that. I'm simply pointing out that it's possible Napier could have had the motive as well as the opportunity for shooting his son-in-law. So, too, could Bradley or the Pagetts. None of them is in the clear yet; not even Elizabeth Hamilton, although I admit she seems the least likely of any of them.' To cover up his impatience with Boyce, he added, turning some of it on himself, 'It's my fault for not checking up on Hamilton's movements earlier. If I'd done that straight away, we'd be a lot nearer finding a solution.'

'You can't do it all,' Boyce had the grace to point out, although he seemed cheered up by the Chief Inspector's admission of his own shortcomings as, starting the car, he asked, 'Where to now?'

'Back to Woodstone. I want to go over their statements again with Napier and Mrs Hamilton; Napier in particular. I'm curious to find out just how he accounts for that four or five minutes he had in hand before he arrived to pick his daughter up on the Framden road. I also want to confront the pair of them with the lies Hamilton told Chitty. It'll be interesting to see their reactions.'

17

Felix and Elizabeth were seated on either side of the drawing-room fire, both silent and both pretending to read when Finch and Boyce arrived.

The dog heard the car first, raising his head as he lay stretched out between them.

'Damn!' Felix said, putting down *Emma*, the pages of which he had merely been turning, catching a phrase here or a fragment of conversation there. 'That's probably the police.'

Although he had said nothing to Elizabeth about finding Bradley's clothes, he had been half expecting Finch and his Sergeant to call and question him about their discovery and had been turning over in his mind what he would say to them about Bradley. But only part of his thoughts had been occupied with his decision to clear Bradley's name. The rest had been taken up with more personal worries concerning Kate and Elizabeth.

He still regretted Kate's loss, recalling again and again their meeting that morning and trying to remember what he had said or done that could have caused her to withdraw from the relationship, but could think of nothing.

As for his daughter, Felix hardly knew where to start. He had been distressed when, on returning to the house, he had found Dodie gone and Elizabeth alone, and although it appeared that Elizabeth herself had asked Dodie to leave, preferring her own company, it had done nothing to relieve his deep concern for her.

She had been in a strange restless mood ever since, which had increased his anxiety, going from room to room or starting conversations, largely about the past which she never normally referred to, as if trying to recapture some long-ago state of happiness, before breaking off and falling silent.

Now, as Felix remarked that the visitors were probably the police, she got hurriedly from her chair, throwing aside the magazine she had been looking at. 'In that case,' she said, 'I'm going out for a walk.'

'But my dear Elizabeth,' Felix began in protest.

It was nearly five o'clock; too late in his opinion for her to think of leaving the house on her own. It would soon be dusk.

'I don't feel up to facing that man Finch again,' she replied from the hall where she had gone to fetch her coat from the downstairs cloakroom. Coming back into the room, she put it on. 'I'll go out by the back door so he won't see me.' Noticing Percy scramble eagerly to his feet, his tail wagging, she added, 'I'll take the dog with me.'

Felix followed her into the hall where the front door bell was already ringing. 'Supposing he wants to ask you some more questions?'

'I've told him everything I know,' Elizabeth replied. 'I can't bear to keep going over and over it all. What else can I possibly say to him?'

The bell rang for a second time and, hurriedly kissing the tips of her fingers, she laid them against Felix's cheek before letting herself out by the kitchen door, Percy at her heels.

After waiting for a few moments to give her time to disappear from sight round the far side of the house, Felix went along the hall to admit the callers, still feeling the place warm on the side of his face where she had touched him.

He was right. Finch and his Sergeant were standing on the doorstep.

'We'd like to talk to you and your daughter,' Finch began.

'I'm afraid Elizabeth's out,' Felix explained, showing them into the drawing-room where he indicated chairs.

'Oh?' Finch sounded disappointed although he quickly recovered his bland expression. 'Then, in that case, Mr Napier, perhaps you wouldn't mind answering a few questions. I'd like to ask you first about the clothing you found this morning. Could you tell me exactly how you came across them?'

It was ridiculous, Felix thought, that in giving the Chief

Inspector his account he should feel so damned guilty. After all, there was nothing suspicious about the circumstances, although as he recounted the details – the visit to the bank, the drive home, the walk with Percy along the path – he found himself hesitating as if he were making it up as he went along.

It was partly caused by Elizabeth's sudden decision to go out, he realized, but mainly because of the omission in his statement of any reference to Kate Denby.

Finch listened in silence, his expression giving nothing away although he seemed to exude an air of scepticism which hardly helped to restore Felix's confidence.

'I reported finding the clothes,' he concluded, 'and returned to point the place out to the constable who was on duty at the mobile headquarters. Then I came home.'

'So the dog found the clothing?' Finch asked. 'Why did you choose that particular path for your walk?'

'Because I'm familiar with it,' Felix replied. 'It's near Paddocks, where I used to live.'

'I see, sir.' Finch still sounded unconvinced, although he appeared about to drop the subject and move on to other matters. Before he did so, Felix hastened to add a last remark of his own.

'About the clothes, Chief Inspector. I assume they belonged to Bradley?' Taking Finch's silence for assent, he hurried on. 'In that case, I'd like to make it quite clear that, in my opinion, Bradley had nothing to do with David's death. I know there may have been some disagreement between them over the right of way but I feel I may have misled you over its importance. I'm quite sure David and Bradley would have come to some amicable agreement . . .'

He left the rest unsaid, realizing it was a waste of time to continue. Judging by the Chief Inspector's expression, he wasn't impressed.

'Yes, I see, sir,' he replied and then, after a small, polite silence, he continued with the interview as if there had been no reference to Bradley at all. 'We called to see Mr Chitty this afternoon at the Millbridge branch. He told us that Mr Hamilton usually left the office at half-past five because he wanted to spend the evening at home with his wife.'

He spoke in a deliberately off-hand manner as if what he was saying was only the beginning of a much longer statement, leaving it to Napier to pick it up if he wished.

He reacted immediately.

'But that's absurd, Chief Inspector! David knew Elizabeth was in Framden every Tuesday until quite late. Why should he tell Chitty he wanted to get home early?'

His surprise seemed genuine.

'The same question crossed my mind, Mr Napier,' Finch replied. 'Why should your son-in-law bother to lie to Mr Chitty, unless he had something to hide?'

'I don't understand,' Napier said. 'I've never known David to be deceitful over anything. He's been rather tired recently but I put that down to overwork. Apart from that . . .'

He broke off as if he had nothing more to add and yet Finch, who had been watching Napier's face closely, saw his expression change in some subtle way which was difficult to define. It was suddenly veiled. The blue eyes went on regarding him with the same direct gaze but the focus had shifted slightly to a point where they no longer quite met the Chief Inspector's with equal candour.

'You can think of nothing, Mr Napier?' Finch asked.

'No, I'm sorry. I'm afraid I can't,' Napier replied, his voice firm and dismissive.

The man clearly had something himself to hide but it would be pointless, Finch realized, to try to force him to admit it. Whatever it was, Napier had recovered himself sufficiently and the opportunity had been lost.

Sitting back in his chair, Finch nodded to Boyce to take over the interview, a tactic they had agreed between them on their way to Napier's house. That way, Finch could concentrate his attention on watching Napier, interrupting with questions of his own whenever it seemed advantageous.

Boyce took Napier step by step through his statement, beginning with his movements on the morning of the murder, an account which Napier repeated with no sign of stress that Finch could detect until he came to the point where Miss Denby had arrived when his manner grew more stiff and formal.

'She came, as I've already stated, at about three o'clock and left at five.' Breaking off, he turned to Finch in protest. 'Is this really necessary, Chief Inspector? I've already gone over this at least once and I can't see it has any relevance to my son-in-law's murder.'

Finch merely gestured to Boyce to continue.

'And then, sir?' the Sergeant went on.

'I spent the rest of the evening alone, until my daughter telephoned me just before sixteen minutes past ten.'

'You're quite sure of the time?'

'Yes, I am; quite positive. As I told you before, I'd glanced at the clock shortly before the phone rang. It was then a few seconds past ten-fifteen.'

'And when exactly did you leave to pick up your daughter?'

It was the crux of the interview, not that it would have been possible to guess this from Finch's attitude. He was leaning back in his chair, legs crossed, relaxed and comfortable, his expression pleasantly non-committal and registering no reaction when, for the second time, Napier showed signs of stress. On this occasion, it took the form of an angrier response.

'How on earth do you expect me to know that?' he demanded. 'I didn't time myself. I was anxious to get out of the house as soon as possible. I knew Elizabeth would be waiting for me to pick her up; wet through, no doubt, having walked to the phone-box and then back to the car, although I suggested she wait in the kiosk. But as there was no light in there, she preferred not to. Even so, I had to put on my outdoor clothes and shut the dog up in the kitchen as well as get the car out of the garage . . .'

Boyce interrupted to ask, 'All the same, Mr Napier, I'd like some idea of the time it would have taken you.'

'Three minutes? Four minutes?' Napier made the suggestions in the same abrupt, staccato manner. 'I really have no idea. I only know I got there as fast as I could, given the driving conditions on Tuesday night. You've already been told the time I arrived; it was half-past ten.'

Boyce made no sign that Napier's answer had any significance. Without so much as a glance in Finch's direction, he turned to the next page in his notebook and continued the interview with the same dogged persistence as if Napier's subsequent actions had as much relevance to the investigation as his previous movements.

Finch, too, listened to the questioning, maintaining his impassive air until its conclusion, rising to his feet as Boyce finally closed and put away his notebook.

There was still no sign of Mrs Hamilton, which was a damned nuisance. It meant they would have to return to question her on another occasion. But at least the interview with Napier had established one vital point – it was possible Napier could have had the opportunity to murder his son-in-law, a conclusion he put to Boyce as they left the house.

'Although God alone knows how we prove it,' he added gloomily. 'He had at least four minutes in hand, long enough by my reckoning but, unless we can come up with some more concrete evidence, I don't see that we can even hope to make an arrest. All we have at the moment is a strong suspicion, but that's not going to be enough to satisfy the DPP, let alone a jury.'

It was exactly the same situation with the other suspects in the case, he might have added, although he kept the thought to himself. Like Napier, both Bradley and Pagett could have had the opportunity but the evidence was also too circumstantial to establish guilt beyond any reasonable doubt. As for Elizabeth Hamilton and Dodie Pagett, the case against them was even flimsier. Dodie Pagett seemed to have no motive; Elizabeth Hamilton no opportunity, if Bradley's evidence on the timing of the shot was accepted.

Which left him, Finch thought, his gloom deepening, with damn-all except a dead body and a lot of unanswered questions.

He was in no better mood when, later that evening, he returned home; certainly not in the right frame of mind to listen with any concentration to what his sister had to say to him after she had cleared the supper things from the table and had joined him in the sitting-room.

'I want to talk to you, Jack,' she announced.

He tried to rouse himself, aware that whatever she had to say to him must be of some importance, at least to her, for she was sitting up very straight in her chair, her hands clasped in her lap, her expression oddly different although Finch was hard put to it to decide what it was about it that made it appear so changed. It was, he decided, the unaccustomed brightness about it which suggested a complexity of emotions – embarrassment, defiance, combined with an appeal for his sympathy but, above all, it was the happiness it contained which caught his attention. She had not looked so vital and alive for years.

'Well?' he asked, aware that what she had to tell him was not important just to her but, he suspected, to him as well.

'I don't know how to tell you, she began. 'It's about Frank . . .'

'Frank?' he repeated. He knew of no one called Frank.

'Frank Goodall,' she explained. 'You remember he gave me a lift home from the church social on Tuesday evening when you were called out on that case?'

Finch sat up, suddenly alert, and, as he listened to what she had to say, it came as no great surprise to him after all. He had, he realized, already read the signs but had chosen to ignore them, pretending they were of no real significance.

It seemed she had met Frank Goodall on a couple of occasions since that Tuesday evening, for coffee that morning and for tea on Wednesday, the day, Finch remembered, he had tried to phone her from the call-box on the Framden road and had got no answer; and although she was anxious, too anxious, it seemed to Finch, to assure him that the relationship was only a matter of friendship, that unfamiliar glow about her suggested otherwise.

She was saying, 'The point is, Jack, that Frank's asked me out to dinner with him tomorrow evening, but I'd prefer to invite him here for a meal so that you can get to know him better. You've only met him once or twice, haven't you? I said I'd ring him tomorrow morning to let him know; that is, if you could get home in good time for the meal?'

'Yes, of course,' Finch agreed almost automatically; but his mind was not so much on his promise, difficult thought that would be to carry out in the middle of an investigation, nor on Frank Goodall whom he remembered vaguely as a pleasant enough man, a widower in his late fifties, active in church affairs, which was presumably how Dorothy had first got to know him, and with a small business of his own – a newsagent's, wasn't it? – which he ran in partnership with his son. It was not even on the implications behind Dorothy's proposal that she invite the man home for dinner which suggested to Finch that, whatever Dorothy might say about it, her relationship with Frank Goodall must have progressed to a stage where it had become intimate enough for the man to be introduced into the family.

His thoughts were still largely on that telephone call he had made to Dorothy from the telephone kiosk on the Framden road the previous afternoon. Something was not quite right about it and he was not just thinking of his sister's unexpected absence from the house, although he seemed to hear the phone ringing and ringing as he had stood there, the receiver to his ear, looking out through the small, dirty panes of glass at the little row of houses, the garage, closed for business, and the car drawn up alongside its forecourt with Boyce at the wheel, the side-lights on because it was getting dusk.

And suddenly he had it.

It was so damned obvious that he couldn't understand why he hadn't picked it up as Boyce was taking Napier through his statement that afternoon.

Dorothy was still talking, saying something about the meal she would prepare for the following evening, and he heard her out, pretending to listen although he was seething with impatience to get to the phone and ring Boyce.

'And one of my lemon meringue pies to follow. What do you think, Jack?'

'It sounds fine to me,' he replied. 'But you've always been a good cook, Dot.' The compliment and the use of his childhood name for her pleased her, as he had intended. After all, who was he to spoil her happiness? Getting to his feet, he added, 'I'll supply the wine, by the way. There's no need for you to buy it.' It was another sop to soften his final remark. 'I must go and phone Tom up. There's something I have to discuss with him straightaway about the case we're working on. It's going to mean I'll have to go out again, I'm afraid.'

As he went into the hall to ring Boyce, he hoped she wouldn't take his departure as an attempt on his part to avoid any further discussion about Goodall. If she did, it couldn't be helped; although it stuck him as ironic that, while they had both been deceiving each other over their separate relationships, his with Marion Greave, hers with Goodall, it was his sister, not himself, who seemed to have found the happiness he had so ardently longed for.

Was he envious? he wondered, dialling Boyce's number; and surprised himself by answering, Yes, he was.

And supposing they married? What would happen to him?

But there was no time to go into such selfish considerations. Boyce had picked up the receiver and he heard himself saying hurriedly, 'I want to discuss the Hamilton case with you, Tom. I think I know who killed him. Meet me at headquarters as soon as you can.'

18

'I want to talk to you, Elizabeth,' Felix said at last.

He had been postponing the moment ever since she had returned from her walk with Percy, nearly an hour after Finch and his Sergeant had left, finding various excuses for the delay: first his own anxiety over her long absence even though the dog had been with her, then her obvious tiredness when she had finally come home, and lastly the need to prepare and eat a meal.

Neither of them was in the right frame of mind to settle down to a serious conversation, Felix had persuaded himself – although he was aware that the main reason for his hesitation was a reluctance on his part to speak out loud what had to be said.

How in God's name was he to find the words?

It was only after dinner had been eaten and cleared away and they returned to the sitting-room, where the drawn curtains and the fire blazing in the hearth with the dog stretched out in front of it had given the room a semblance of normality and cheerfulness, that he found the courage to speak. Even so, he poured brandies for them first, carrying Elizabeth's glass over to where she was sitting by the fireplace, her legs drawn up under her.

'Talk to me?' she repeated. 'What about?'

'It's about David,' he replied. 'Finch spoke to Chitty this afternoon. It seems David always left the Millbridge office at half-past five on Tuesdays, telling Chitty that he wanted an early evening at home.'

He waited for her reaction and, when none came, he continued, trying to maintain the same neutral voice and expression as Finch when he had put the same question.

'Why did he lie, Elizabeth? He knew you were out in Framden until at least half-past ten. There was no need for him to hurry back.'

'I don't know,' she said.

She was holding the glass of brandy between both hand and looking at him, her eyes very wide and yet with a dazed, opaque expression in them as if she were not focusing on him properly.

For his part, he saw her only too clearly – the fair hair glistening under the lamps, her face bright with the glow cast up by the burning logs. She seemed more than ever a creature of light, as if it were she who formed the nucleus from which the lamps and the fire drew their radiance.

'I think you do, my dear,' he said gently. 'You've always had the gift of reading other people's moods, mine as well as David's There was very little you missed. And all the signs were there; I realize that myself now, although I thought David was merely tired and overworked. But you realized the truth, didn't you? You were much too close to David not to be aware of what was happening.'

He did not add, as he might have done, that he, too, should have read the signs which had pointed to her, and if he hadn't been blinded by his love for her, he himself might have reached the truth much earlier.

But perhaps, he thought, he hadn't wanted to. Until Finch had presented him with the fact of David's deceit, forcing him to recognize that imperfection in his son-in-law, he had chosen to ignore all the other lies and deceptions, however obvious they might be to him now. It was as if Finch's revelation of that one untruth had acted as a bright beam of light, making it possible to see all the others.

She said, 'What do you want me to do?'

'To tell the truth,' he replied. 'The police think that Bradley may have been involved in David's death. You must make sure his name is cleared.'

His own was of no importance. Although he had been aware during the interview with Finch and his Sergeant that their suspicions had been directed towards him as well, the realization had only strengthened his resolve to establish Bradley's innocence.

She had finished her brandy and was holding out the empty glass towards him.

'I need a little more courage first,' she said, adding, as he took the glass and carried it over to the decanter, '"If you tell the truth, I shan't be angry with you." Do you remember you used to say that to me, darling?'

'Yes, I remember,' he replied, his back towards her. It was one of those phrases which he supposed most parents must use to their children at some stage in their lives. Turning to face her, he saw her expression contained the same clear directness which it had held then, her 'owning-up' look as he and Helen used to call it. 'And I shan't be very angry with you now,' he continued, handing her the glass.

Boyce said, 'But what the hell put you on to her?'

'The kiosk light,' Finch replied.

'I don't get you,' the Sergeant said heavily.

He had made tea for them both, using the electric kettle which Finch kept in the cupboard for such out-of-hours discussions and, as he spoke, he spooned the tea-bags out of the mugs, dropping them, still steaming, into the waste-paper basket.

'In his interview this afternoon, Napier said that he arranged to pick his daughter up at the car because she didn't want to wait in the phone-box. There was no light in there,' Finch explained, taking one of the mugs which Boyce had carried over to the desk.

'So?'

'But there was, Tom. Do you remember after I timed the walk from that gateway where she left the car to the kiosk, I made a phone-call? The light was working then, and the bulb wasn't a new one. It was covered with dust, so it must have been there for months. She lied, in other words; and, once you accept that fact, her whole alibi starts to come to pieces.'

He spoke quickly not only to explain himself but to take his mind off the other events of the evening – the conversation with Dorothy about Frank Goodall and his feeling that he had been blind not to see that deception as well, if deception was the right word.

'And it was her alibi which fooled me' he continued. 'I couldn't see how she had the opportunity to kill her husband. She simply didn't have the time. The rest fitted in all right: she had access to the gun; she knew the layout of Bradley's premises next door; she could even have seen Bradley wearing that jacket and gloves as he cleared the spinney. She could also have had the opportunity to take the clothing. We only have her word for it that she left the house on Tuesday morning to drive to Framden before Bradley himself went out. All she had to do was watch him set off in the car before going round to the kennels by the back garden and helping herself to the stuff in the shed. Since we spoke to Chitty this morning, we now know that she had a motive – her husband was having an affair, although I blame myself for not picking that up earlier. I could have done. All the signs were there.'

'What signs?' Boyce asked. 'I didn't notice any.'

'In Hamilton's behaviour. Even before we learned from Chitty that Hamilton had lied to him about wanting to get home early, there were two other pieces of evidence which should have warned us he had something to hide. Firstly, he decided not to give permission for that right of way to be closed. As Bradley said, it was unreasonable. The Hamiltons hardly ever used the path. Even Napier seemed surprised that his son-in-law had changed his mind when he had seemed in favour of it only a couple of weeks earlier. But something must have happened to make him withdraw and I think I know what it was. Hamilton had decided to end his marriage and he didn't want to involve his wife in any possible legal hassle over the right of way which could have added to the stress of a divorce.'

'And the other bit of evidence?'

'Hamilton had changed his mind about something else,' Finch explained. 'I didn't pick that up either at the time although I should have done because it gives us the identity of the woman Hamilton had fallen in love with and was meeting every Tuesday after he left the Millbridge office.'

As he gave Boyce the name, he could see in the Sergeant's face the astonishment which he himself had felt when he had first arrived at that conclusion.

'*Her?*' Boyce exclaimed.

'Yes, her,' Finch replied. 'I know it seems unlikely but there's no one else who fits the pattern of Hamilton's actions before he was murdered. And if you're surprised, Tom, think how much greater the shock must have been for Elizabeth Hamilton. She had built up a carefully maintained façade of the ideal marriage, the pair of them sharing in the happy-ever-after which all her friends, even her father, believed in and which she, too, may have thought was real – only to have it come tumbling down around her. I'm not sure if Hamilton told her, or if she put two and two together for herself, but, once she realized that her husband had fallen in love with someone else and with that woman in particular, I think she decided to kill him, not just for revenge, although that may have been part of the motive, but to spare herself the humiliation of a divorce. She hoped, you see, that we'd go along with the theory that Hamilton had been shot by an intruder who'd been trying to burgle the house, thinking there was no one at home. Napier fell for it and we were supposed to as well. But, as I see it, Elizabeth Hamilton had been so used to getting her own way all her life that it just didn't cross her mind that, where her husband's murder was concerned, she couldn't cajole or persuade everyone into thinking that she had nothing to do with it.'

'I was certainly fooled by it,' Boyce pointed out with a rare admission of weakness. 'But she was taking a hell of a risk, wasn't she, in pinching Bradley's clothing? Once we knew that jacket and gloves were missing, the intruder theory no longer stood up.'

'It was a gamble she must have been prepared to take. Don't forget, she'd have picked up enough knowledge about guns from her father to realize that powder marks could be left on hands and clothing, so she knew she'd have to find some protection. The gear Bradley had been wearing as he cleared the spinney must have seemed ideal. There was a good chance, too, that it wouldn't be missed straight away. She may have hoped that by the time Bradley wanted to wear the clothes again there'd be too big a time gap for him to connect their theft with the murder. Or she may have counted on retrieving them at some later date and returning them to the shed before they were missed. And she might have got away with it, too. If Bradley hadn't had a guilty conscience himself about piling up the debris in that opening, he wouldn't have gone to the shed on the following morning to fetch the fork. Of course, once the clothing was reported missing, and was later discovered in the ditch where she'd hidden it, she had no opportunity of taking it back.'

'It's bloody ironic when you think it was her own father who found the stuff,' Boyce remarked with an air of gloomy satisfaction as if such events proved the sheer cussedness of fate. 'But I still don't see how she managed to shoot her husband, put in that call to her father and be waiting at that gateway along the Framden road when he turned up at half-past ten. If she didn't ring him from that box, where the hell did she phone him from?'

'I'm not sure myself,' Finch confessed, 'and I think the simplest solution is to go and ask her.'

It took more than an hour for his daughter to finish her account and for most of the time Felix Napier listened in silence, interrupting her only occasionally to ask a question. Otherwise he made no comment but sat, hands clasped between his knees, leaning slightly forward in his chair, his face turned towards the fire.

From time to time, the logs shifted in the grate, sending up small spurts of flame, or the dog, stretched out between their chairs, stirred and grunted in his sleep.

Otherwise, there was only the sound of Elizabeth's voice, modulated, controlled, calm, as if, Felix thought, she had reached some high place and was looking down over what had happened, seeing the events stretched out below her like the view from the end of the garden, distanced in both time and place.

When it was all over, she said, 'What are you going to do, daddy?'

He roused himself from his contemplation of the fire.

'I think you know that, my darling. I shall have to let Finch know the truth.'

'Yes, of course,' she agreed quickly. 'That seems the best thing to do.'

'You'll wait here?' he asked.

She nodded, putting one hand down to touch the sleeping dog as if gaining strength and comfort from the contact.

Avoiding her eyes, Felix got up and, leaving the room, went along the hall towards the study where he closed the door. It was better, he decided, to use the extension in there, rather than in the hall. She would not be able to overhear what he said.

As he dialled the number of Divisional Headquarters in Chelmsford, it crossed his mind that it was unlikely that Finch would be there at that time in the evening, and he regretted the consequent delay there would be in contacting him at home.

The phone was answered, and as Felix asked to speak to Detective Chief Inspector Finch an anonymous male voice at the other end of the line confirmed his fears. The Detective Chief Inspector had been in the office but had left about half an hour earlier. Was there any message?

Felix hesitated, and as he did so he heard the drawing-room door open and Elizabeth come into the hall. She moved quietly but it was still possible for him to pick up the small sounds and to interpret them as he might have done the faint rustles of movement in the undergrowth when he was out on a shoot. She was turning the handle to the downstairs cloakroom where the gun-safe was kept and, as he registered the tiny click of metal on metal which followed, he remembered that he had left his jacket with his keys in it in the drawing-room.

'Are you there?' the voice at the other end of the line was asking.

Felix cleared his throat and drew himself up. 'My name is Felix Napier,' he said. 'N-A-P-I-E-R.'

In the time it took to spell it, she had passed the study on her way to the front door.

'Yes, I've got that, Mr Napier,' the voice replied. 'What's the message, sir?'

Felix waited a moment until he heard the front door close. Then he continued, 'Tell Detective Chief Inspector Finch that I have some important information regarding the murder of my son-in-law, David Hamilton.'

'I see, sir.' The voice, trained not to show any emotion, nevertheless seemed to Felix's ears to contain a faint note of surprise. 'I'll see he gets the message as soon as possible and contacts you.'

'Thank you,' Felix said.

As he spoke, he heard her start the MG and the sound of the engine in reverse gear as she backed into the lane.

Replacing the receiver, he stood listening as it gathered speed on the long hill which led down to the village.

Bradley poured himself a whisky and carried it over to the desk where he put it down next to the telephone almost as an act of defiance.

I am not bloody well going to ring her, he told himself.

All the same, as he wrote out a couple of cheques and stuffed them into envelopes, his eyes kept straying to the receiver where it sat, squat and looking oddly defiant itself, among the scattered bills and invoices.

The sound of the shot when it came a few seconds later was faint but recognizable. It could, Bradley thought, have been mistaken for the sound of a car back-firing. The barking of the dogs which followed close upon it was much louder, a cacophony of high-pitched, semi-hysterical yelps mixed in with the deeper, spaced-out tones of the larger animals.

With the sense of having done it all before, Steven Bradley got to his feet and, stopping only to collect his coat and the torch, let himself out by the back door.

Somewhere at the far end of his land, beyond the spinney, the headlamps of a car were visible – Elizabeth Hamilton's MG, as he discovered when he walked towards them and stepped through the gap in the hedge.

It was parked in the opening, with Elizabeth Hamilton at the wheel. At least, he assumed it was her. Flashing the beam of the torch briefly in at the driver's window, he had only enough time to register the fair hair before he saw the gun propped up between her knees, the double barrels pointing upwards.

Switching off the torch, he backed away and then began running towards the house, the noise of the dogs following him. He could still hear them as, letting himself into the sitting-room, he picked up the phone.

19

Finch, too, peered in at the driver's window, although he let the beam of his torch rest for several long moments on the body before he straightened up.

The call, initiated by Bradley through the emergency service, had been relayed on the car radio by Divisional Headquarters as he and Boyce were on their way to Woodstone and had followed only minutes after another message informing him that a Mr Felix Napier had telephoned in to say he had information regarding his son-in-law's murder.

The one event had evidently come hard on the heels of the other, but too late to make any difference. Elizabeth Hamilton was dead and Finch didn't need Pardoe to tell him that, nor to inform him that it was almost certainly suicide, although he stepped back from the car to allow the small figure of the police doctor to make his examination.

'And she made damned sure of it, too,' Pardoe added.

Finch didn't even bother to reply. He had seen that much for himself as well.

Turning away, shoulders hunched, he surveyed the scene in silence for a few moments.

Gade's Lane had probably never witnessed so much activity. An ambulance was already there, drawn up on the far side behind his own vehicle, with Pardoe's car parked a few yards away, their headlamps illuminating the leafless hedges and the bare branches of the trees which formed a backdrop to the small scene centred on Elizabeth Hamilton's red MG and the huddled shape behind the windscreen, all that could be seen of her, thank God.

Felix Napier's Range Rover was waiting on the outer edge of this lighted circle, its headlamps switched off, Napier presumably seated behind the wheel although it was impossible to make out any details in the darkness.

He had arrived shortly after Finch but had so far made no attempt to get out of his car for which Finch was also profoundly grateful.

Boyce came up to announce, 'I've got on to Headquarters. They're sending a breakdown van to tow away the car. Anything I can do in the meantime?'

'Yes,' Finch told him. 'Get a statement from Bradley.' He jerked his head towards the spinney where Bradley could just be seen standing on the footpath under the trees, also distanced from the centre of illumination but incapable, it seemed, of moving further away, drawn perhaps by its brightness and the activity round it.

'And you?'

'I'm going to have a talk with Napier,' Finch replied, adding, as Boyce moved away, 'Tell Pardoe I don't want the body moved until he's gone.'

Boyce nodded in reply before, skirting round the MG, he picked his way through the gap in the hedge to join Bradley.

As if the action had already been decided between them, Napier leaned across and opened the passenger door as Finch approached, indicating to the Chief Inspector to climb into the seat beside him.

For a few seconds both men were silent, looking out through the windscreen at the scene taking place some twenty yards ahead of them, isolated in the surrounding darkness like a peepshow.

Then Napier said, 'You'll want a statement from me, I suppose, Chief Inspector?' The voice was dry and formal.

'If it won't cause you too much distress, sir,' Finch replied.

'Better to get it over and done with,' Napier said, 'although I think may have suspected at least some of it. It was Elizabeth who shot David. She had guessed several weeks ago that he was meeting someone else, when she phoned him one Tuesday evening from Framden and there was no answer; although it wasn't until fairly recently that she realized who the woman was. She knew then that it wasn't a meaningless little infidelity but a serious love affair. Knowing David, I realize myself that it couldn't have been otherwise. He wasn't the type of man to play fast and loose with other people's feelings. It was the thought of being set aside for someone else that Elizabeth couldn't accept, and for that I blame myself. She was so used to being loved all her life that she came to look on any form of rejection as a terrible betrayal. And I can sympathize with that. What I can't understand or accept is her decision to kill David, and the way she went about doing it; not in a sudden passion but quite calmly and deliberately, planning it stage by stage.'

He paused and glanced sideways at the Chief Inspector, inviting his comment, but Finch made no direct response except to remark in a non-committal voice, 'Yes, I see, sir.'

After all, it wasn't his place to point out to Napier that his daughter must have possessed, under the physical attractiveness and the charm, a ruthless, calculating quality which she might never have had cause to reveal had not events gone against her.

'About an hour after you left, Elizabeth returned from her walk,' Napier continued. He was staring straight ahead again and all that Finch could see was his profile with its high, thin nose. 'I had already guessed what must have happened from what you told me. You see, David so rarely lied that I knew he must have had some important reason for deceiving Chitty. I also knew that Elizabeth must have been aware of it. She had this gift, you see, of responding to other people's moods. It was part of her charm.'

The last remark was spoken in a wry tone as if Napier had finally seen through it all and had reached the truth at last.

At the same time, it occurred to Finch that Boyce had been right after all. A large part of the reason for Hamilton's murder had been that honesty and decency of his which Napier had mentioned. If he had been a little more adept at lying, a little less transparent in his deceit – in other words, as Boyce had put it, not so bloody *nice* – Elizabeth Hamilton might not have found out about his betrayal nor felt so deeply humiliated by it that his murder became the inevitable consequence.

'She noticed that David had left the gun in the hall after we'd come back from rough-shooting that Saturday a couple of weeks before,' Napier continued. 'It was then that the idea occurred to her, although she told me that at first it was nothing more than a desire for David's death; an accident with the gun, perhaps, as he was cleaning it. She had no plan at that stage, except the thought that if he died she would be spared the public disgrace of his leaving her for another woman. But, once the seed was there, the idea grew until, as she admitted to me, it became an obsession. She had to make sure of his death herself before he rejected her.

'To begin with, there seemed little opportunity. David removed the gun from that container in the hall, took the cartridge out that he'd left in the breach and returned the gun to the safe in the study.' As he spoke, Napier glanced quickly in Finch's direction. 'You suspected that's what had happened, didn't you?'

'I thought it a little strange that your son-in-law had left a loaded gun lying about the house,' Finch admitted, 'particularly when all the other signs – the way the papers were arranged on his desk, for instance – suggested that he was competent and well-organized. But when you said that he wasn't very experienced at handling a gun, I thought it was possible he'd forgotten about it.'

'So I persuaded you otherwise?' Napier asked and, when Finch hesitated, he went on, half to himself, 'I should have seen the truth right from the beginning! If I hadn't been so blind . . .' He broke off, resuming his account in the same level, unemotional voice, 'But because David had left the gun in the hall for a couple of days, it gave Elizabeth the idea of passing off his murder as a crime committed by an intruder and, once that idea was established in her mind, the rest followed as if the events themselves took over. I'm quoting my daughter almost word for word, by the way, Chief Inspector. She seemed to think that his murder was inevitable because everything fitted into place exactly as she wanted; that storm on Tuesday morning, for example, which put the local phone-box out of order . . .'

'She knew about that?' Finch broke in to ask.

'Yes; someone had hung a sign on the kiosk door. She noticed it that morning as she drove through the village on the way to Framden. The storm also meant that Bradley stopped work on the spinney. She had gone upstairs to close the windows when it began to rain, and she saw him coming past the kennels wearing that padded jacket and carrying the gloves. She had already decided that a Tuesday was the best time to carry out the murder, when she would be out of the house until late in the evening. When she saw Bradley putting the clothes into the shed which he didn't bother to lock and later heard his car leaving, it seemed to her that the opportunity was there; she only had to seize it.'

'So she took the clothing?'

'Yes, and put it in the boot of the car together with the gun which she'd already taken from the gun-safe in the study, using her own keys. After that, she left for Framden. The rest followed as she had planned. It was already her intention to arrange an alibi in which I was to play a part. I was also to support her by agreeing to the theory that David had been shot by someone who had entered the house by the back way, thinking that, because the lights were out, the place was empty. And, I'm afraid, Chief Inspector, that she succeeded. I went along with both deceptions because I was too ready to be persuaded by her, as I've always been.'

And she knew it, Finch added to himself.

'How was the alibi arranged?' he asked out loud. It was the

one aspect of the case which he and Boyce had not been able to establish. How the hell had she managed it?

'She made a tape-recording of the sound of the pay-signal and the coin dropping at a public phone box somewhere in Framden on Tuesday afternoon. I'm not sure which one,' Napier explained, hesitating as Finch shifted involuntarily in the seat beside him.

Bruton Street, of course! he was thinking, remembering the details of that ordinary little side road where Kate Denby had caught a glimpse of Elizabeth Hamilton walking in the rain. Until that moment, he had dismissed that particular piece of evidence as irrelevant. But he saw now that it, too, was part of the pattern. Elizabeth Hamilton had been on her way to the sub post-office in Bruton Street, which must have contained a pay booth, where she had made the recording of the sounds she had needed to convince her father that when she rang him later that evening, it had been from the kiosk on the Framden road.

'She used a small recorder which she'd bought earlier in the day and which fitted into her handbag,' Napier was saying. 'The phone was in a corner, and by turning her back to the counter she was able to hold the recorder up to the receiver without anyone noticing what she was doing. Later, after the evening class in Framden, she drove straight back to the house, parking the car in the opening which leads off Gade's Lane before putting on Bradley's gloves as well as his jacket which was big enough to fit over her own coat. Then, taking the gun with her, she let herself in by the back door.'

'And the lights were on, of course?' Finch asked the question although he already knew what the answer would be.

'Yes; in the kitchen and the hall but not upstairs,' Again Napier turned his head briefly in Finch's direction. 'You suspected they might have been, didn't you?'

'I thought it unlikely that the whole house, apart from the study, was in darkness but . . .'

'I again persuaded you that it was possible,' Napier finished the sentence for him. 'I see now that Elizabeth put the idea into my mind along with the whole intruder theory. I should have questioned it myself, of course, but it never crossed my mind to do so because I trusted her and because the truth was so terrible that it was totally unthinkable.

'After she had shot David, she rang me from the telephone in the hall, using the tape-recording she had made that afternoon. It was entirely convincing. I heard the pay-signal and the sound of the coin dropping. When she said she had a puncture and was calling me from the kiosk on the Framden road, I had no reason to think she was lying.'

'Wasn't she cutting the timing very fine,' Finck asked. It was another aspect of the case which he had discussed with Boyce.

'Not really,' Felix Napier replied in the same wry tone. 'She knew my habits, you see, Chief Inspector. At that time of the evening, I'd be at home, thinking of going to bed. It would take me several minutes to change out of my slippers, put on a coat and get the car out of the garage. Besides, the drive down the lane into the village would add another two or three minutes on to my own timing, long enough for her to get back to her own car, switching off the lights in the house as she left. The noise of the shot had, of course, disturbed the dogs next door at the kennels and she guessed Bradley might come out of his house to find out what was going on but that wasn't a problem for her. It was raining hard and was too dark for Bradley to see anything; and in fact the noise of the dogs barking covered up the sound of her car as she drove away down Gade's Lane, although she was careful not to turn on her headlights until she was well clear of the place. Once she reached the pathway, it only took her a few seconds to hide the clothing. It was ironic, of course, that it was I who found them later.'

'She had intended returning them?'

'If that was possible. But she had counted more on them not being missed for at least a week. Bradley only worked on clearing the spinney on a Tuesday, the day the kennels were closed. She thought that by the time he realized they were missing, he wouldn't make the connection with David's murder and so wouldn't report the theft. As everything had gone just as she planned, she seemed to think in some strange way that she was immune from disaster.'

Because she'd never had to face it, Finch thought. Kate

Denby had said of Elizabeth Hamilton that she had seemed the type of woman who was born to be cherished. With such an upbringing, she must have been conditioned to believe that luck would always be on her side.

'Once she got rid of the clothing,' Napier continued, 'she only had to drive to the gateway along the Framden road, turn the car round so that it was parked on the verge facing in the direction of the T junction to make it appear she'd just driven from Framden, and then force a nail into one of the tyres. You'll find the tape recorder and the hammer, by the way, in the pond in the adjoining field. She walked the few yards along the road to throw them in. She then waited by the side of the car in the rain until she saw the headlights of my car approaching. That was to make me believe she'd walked to the kiosk and back. I arrived about three minutes after her and, at her prompting, confirmed the time so that her alibi was established. The rest, about returning to the house and finding David's body happened exactly as I described it to you, although I see now that she knew I would offer to drive her home and agree to go into the house for a night-cap. It was her intention all along that it should be I, not she, who would discover David was dead. She returned there this evening, by the way.'

'Where?' Finch asked. He had lost the threat of Napier's statement.

'To the pathway. She didn't know I'd found the clothing, you see. I hadn't told her. But she overheard a conversation I'd had this morning with Dodie Pagett about Bradley's clothes being missing and that the police were going to search for them. It's the reason why she left the house when you and your Sergeant arrived. She wanted to check that the gloves and jacket were still where she'd left them, and move them to a safer hiding-place. When she found they were gone, she realized her plan wasn't working out as she'd intended, and that made her afraid. I've never seen her frightened before. That's why, after she came home and confessed to David's murder, I let her go.' Napier hesitated for a moment, before adding, as if choosing the word with care, 'It was *cleaner* that way. I guessed where I'd find her though, once it was all over. Knowing her, I realized she'd come back to the place where she'd left the car on the night she shot David. It was her way of expiating a little of the guilt.'

As he spoke, Pardoe got into his car and, turning it, began to drive towards them along the lane, his headlamps lighting up the interior of the Range Rover. In the sudden brightness, Finch caught a glimpse of Napier's face. It was still in profile, the lips pressed together and the expression so full of pain that Finch, who had been about to ask what Napier had meant by the last part of his statement, thought better of it and kept silent.

The next moment, when Pardoe's car had gone past, he said quietly, 'Go home, Mr Napier. There's nothing you can do here.'

'No,' he said simply as if no more needed to be added, although, as Finch opened the passenger door and climbed out, he asked, 'You knew it was her, didn't you? What put you on to her?'

There seemed no point in refusing to tell him. 'The light in the telephone box,' he explained. 'You told me this afternoon that your daughter had said the light wasn't working, but it was.'

'I didn't notice that,' Napier admitted, 'even though I drove past the kiosk on Tuesday night. I was too anxious, I suppose, to get to her as quickly as possible. But how absurd!'

'Absurd?' Finch repeated. It seemed a strange word to choose.

'It was such a little lie,' Napier replied and, leaning across, shut the passenger door before he started the engine and drove away.

Finch stood in the lane watching as the Range Rover headed off in the direction of the village, and then walked towards the parked vehicles, drawn up along the verge.

It was time to find Boyce and, once the body had been removed, to carry out the last interview.

20

Ruth Livesey might have been expecting them, for she showed no surprise at finding them standing at the front door.

'Come in,' she told them, going ahead of them into a small sitting-room, its shabby furniture in as much contrast to what Finch remembered of the elegance and style of Elizabeth Hamilton's drawing-room as the women themselves, although he preferred not to recall in too much detail the last occasion on which he had seen David Hamilton's wife, concentrating his attention on this other woman, his mistress.

She had gone to stand by the fireplace, a small figure, her neat head with its short, dark hair tilted defiantly and her fists jammed down hard into the pockets of the long cardigan jacket she was wearing.

It was largely a pose, Finch suspected. All the same he was forced to admire her courage and that sense of her own integrity as an individual which he supposed had drawn Hamilton to her in the first place, for she possessed few of the obvious physical attractions which most men look for in the women they choose to love.

Before he could open his mouth, she said, 'I know why you're here. It's about David's murder, isn't it? I'd made up my mind that I was going to come and see you tomorrow as soon as I'd given Dr Wade my resignation.'

She nodded towards the desk where two white envelopes were propped up against the lamp, one in front of the other, the topmost one addressed to Dr Wade, as Finch could see as he followed her glance.

'I realized,' she continued, 'that I couldn't keep quiet about my relationship with David after I saw Steven Bradley yesterday. He told me that you'd been questioning him and that some clothing of his had been stolen. Then, later this morning, I saw the posters that you'd put up round the village asking for information about the clothes. It was then I realized that David hadn't been killed by someone who'd broken into the house. For everyone's sake, including Steven Bradley's, I decided that I'd have to tell the truth although I couldn't see how it would help in finding David's murderer. It wasn't Steven Bradley, was it? He had no reason . . .'

'It was Elizabeth Hamilton,' Finch told her quietly. 'She confessed this evening before committing suicide.'

For a few seconds her face was expressionless with the blank look of the totally deaf as if she had not heard a word of what had been said to her. Then Finch saw the whole structure of her features begin to disintegrate, the mouth falling open, the line of her jaw trembling.

'But she didn't know!' she cried out passionately before, turning away so that they could not see her face, she began to weep.

Behind her back, Finch caught Boyce's glance and shook his head.

Better to leave her alone, the gesture indicated. Boyce nodded in agreement, although he stood awkwardly, fidgeting from one foot to the other and examining the pattern on the carpet until she had herself under control and turned to face them.

'I'm sorry,' she said. 'It's all over now.'

She could have been referring to her brief breakdown which, Finch suspected, was caused by an accumulation of grief built up since Hamilton's murder and unexpressed until that moment, although the words could also have signified the finality of it all, not just the ending of her relationship with Hamilton with his death but his wife's suicide as well.

'I'm afraid Mrs Hamilton realized what was happening,' Finch told her.

He was relieved to see that, although the tears still glittered under her eyelids, her chin had gone up and her head had resumed the same challenging angle.

'Of course, I should have guessed that,' she admitted. 'It was stupid of me not to have seen it. Elizabeth was an intelligent woman and too aware of what was going on around her not to have known about David and me. We fooled ourselves into thinking that, because we'd been so careful and so discreet, no one, least of all Elizabeth, could find out about us. I can see, too, that she wouldn't have been able to face giving David up, certainly not to me.'

It was cruelly honest of her and Finch put in quickly, anxious to spare her any more distress, 'If you prefer, I could postpone taking your statement until tomorrow?'

'No; it's better to get it over and done with, Chief Inspector,' she replied, using very much the same words, Finch realized, as Napier had done only a little earlier. Indicating the two armchairs, she continued in the same flat, dispassionate voice which she was to use for the rest of the interview, 'Please sit down. I'll make it as simple and straightforward as I can.'

She herself took her seat by the desk, turning the straight-backed chair which stood in front of it to face them so that the interview assumed a formal air, deliberately contrived on her part, Finch suspected, in order to remove from the situation any opportunity for further emotion.

'David and I had known each other ever since I came here about eighteen months ago as Dr Wade's assistant,' she began, 'although we didn't fall in love until last summer. Neither of us wanted it to happen, and at first we tried to avoid meeting each other, although in a small place like Woodstone that wasn't easy. David's main concern was Elizabeth. He didn't want to hurt her; nor her father-in-law. He was very fond of Felix and he knew a divorce would cause them both a great deal of pain, even though, from his point of view, the marriage hadn't been entirely satisfactory for some time before we fell in love. It may seem unkind of me to say this now that Elizabeth's dead, but she needed people round her all the time, the constant stimulus of admiration and excitement. He preferred a simpler life. Besides, he wanted children and Elizabeth refused to have any. So the marriage was already failing, although he kept up the pretence, largely for Elizabeth's sake. He knew it was important to her that it seemed successful. She couldn't admit to failure, certainly not where her personal relationships were concerned.

'We began meeting each other secretly two months ago, in September when Elizabeth started going to an evening class in Framden every Tuesday. It was the same day that David went to the Millbridge office, and as I wasn't on call on Tuesdays it seemed a God-given opportunity to meet somewhere away from Woodstone, where we weren't known. So David arranged to leave the Millbridge office at half-past five. Meanwhile, I'd drive over from Woodstone, leave the car at some quiet place we'd previously arranged, and wait for him to join me. At first, we merely went for country walks, finishing up at some village pub where we'd have a meal together before he had to go home in time for Elizabeth's return from Framden. Later,' and here she looked down at her hands which were clasped together in her lap, 'we became lovers.

'I have some friends in London who own a week-end cottage at Brookend which they agreed to let me use. It's by itself, a short distance from the village, so there seemed little danger that David and I would be seen going there together. I ought to add,' she continued, raising her eyes to look directly at Finch, 'that it was my idea we went to the cottage. David wanted to make the break with Elizabeth before we began our affair. His sense of right and wrong in such matters was much more keenly developed than my own, which was why he insisted on transferring to another GP in Framden. Although he was on Dr Wade's list of patients, there was always a chance, he felt, that, should Dr Wade be off duty or out on another call, I might be asked to treat David if he ever become ill. He was scrupulous, perhaps too much so, where such matters as professional etiquette were concerned.'

Finch merely nodded as if accepting her remark, although he intended the gesture also to acknowledge, for Boyce's benefit as well as his own, that it was Hamilton's transfer to another doctor which had led him to the identity of Ruth Livesey as Hamilton's lover. As he had pointed out to the Sergeant, the answer had been there in front of him all the time, in Hamilton's behaviour during the weeks immediately preceding his murder.

'But you didn't meet last Tuesday,' he said. He had learned that much from Wilfred Chitty that afternoon. As Chitty had stated, Hamilton had not seemed so anxious to leave the Millbridge office promptly at half-past five on the day he was murdered.

'No,' Ruth Livesey agreed. 'David and I had talked the

whole matter over the week before. He was unhappy about the situation, and the fact that on Saturday Elizabeth was going to have the party to which I'd been invited. He felt the deception had gone too far and was becoming too complicated. He was worried, too, that Elizabeth would guess the truth sooner or later. So we decided not to meet on Tuesday. Instead, I was to go to London and talk to the friends of mine who owned the cottage, explain what was happening and ask if David could move in there temporarily, until he could find a flat or a room in Framden where he could live until the divorce was settled. Once that was arranged, he was going to take Felix into his confidence before talking to Elizabeth. In the meantime, I was to hand in my resignation to Dr Wade and apply for another post. He wanted the separation to be as straightforward as possible. As a solicitor, he's handled divorce cases and, knowing the unhappiness they could cause, he wanted to spare Elizabeth as much pain as possible.'

'And that's why he changed his mind over the right of way?' Finch asked.

'Yes; he was anxious not to involve Elizabeth in any legal discussions with Bradley after the separation. Besides, he felt he had no rights over the property. Once he had left her and the arrangements for the divorce had been started, he intended making no claims on the house whatsoever. It would have been hers outright.' She gave a rueful smile. 'I'm afraid Steven Bradley caused more than one complication without meaning to.'

She left it there, and out of respect for her reticence Finch made no reference to Bradley's attempt to establish his own relationship with her, passing on instead to the more serious matter which had brought him to see her in the first place.

'After David Hamilton was murdered, why didn't you come forward and tell us about your relationship with him, Dr Livesey? You knew you had important information which could have made a great deal of difference to the investigation of the case. You realize you could be charged with withholding evidence?'

She accepted the rebuke, even the threat of legal action, without flinching, looking him straight in the face as she replied, 'Yes, I'm aware of that, Chief Inspector.' Turning towards the desk, she picked up the second of the two envelopes which was propped up against the lamp and passed it to him. As he took it, Finch saw that his name was written across the front. 'I drew up a statement earlier today. If you hadn't called this evening, I would have brought it to you tomorrow but, since you're here, I preferred to tell you about David and myself face to face. You'll see that, in the statement, I explain why I didn't come forward earlier. It was to protect Elizabeth Hamilton. Absurd, isn't it? But David was so anxious that she should't be hurt that I decided to keep silent. You see, after Felix Napier rang me on Tuesday evening and I went to the house and found David dead, both he and Elizabeth seemed so convinced that he'd been shot by an intruder that it didn't occur to me there was any other explanation for his murder. Nor was there any reason why I should suspect Elizabeth. As far as I was aware, she had no idea that David and I were lovers, so what possible motive could she have? She seemed so shocked, too, by David's death that I didn't want to add to her distress.'

'It couldn't have been easy for you,' Finch commented. After all, she'd had to examine David Hamilton's body as well as cope with his widow, hiding her own grief and shock at the same time. As for Elizabeth Hamilton's distress, that had probably been genuine enough. She, too, had undergone her own ordeal, part of which must have been the presence of Dr Livesey herself, the woman for whose sake she had, less than an hour before, murdered her husband.

'No, it wasn't easy,' Ruth Livesey replied simply. She paused for a moment before continuing, 'Later, when Steven Bradley's clothes were taken and it seemed likely there was some other explanation for David's murder, it still didn't occur to me to suspect Elizabeth. You seemed to be concentrating your attention on Steven, so there was no reason then to come forward and admit that David and I had been lovers. Besides, talking to Felix Napier on Tuesday evening and learning what had happened, it seemed that Elizabeth had an alibi and that, too, convinced me she'd had nothing to do with her husband's death.'

Finch got to his feet, putting her statement into his pocket as he did so. A report would have to be made, of course, and submitted to the DPP, although he doubted if any legal action would be taken. After all, he too, had been convinced of Elizabeth Hamilton's apparent lack of opportunity, and if it hadn't been for that small, unnecessary lie about the kiosk light which had led him to suspect her, evidence which Dr Livesey couldn't have known about, he himself might not have discovered the truth.

All the same, it struck him as ironic that Ruth Livesey had been at such pains to protect, however unwittingly, the woman who had murdered her lover out of her own sense of guilt and honour.

He held out his hand.

'Thank you for being so frank with me, Dr Livesey,' he said, adding a little awkwardly, 'And may I wish you good luck for the future?'

He meant it sincerely and, for a moment, he saw in her face a little of the distress which she herself must have been suffering, for it gathered between the level brows in a sharp crease of pain.

The next moment it had gone and, as they shook hands, she said, 'Thank you, Chief Inspector,' in a cool, wry voice which reminded him of Felix Napier's as he had made his own parting comment.

'So that's that,' Boyce remarked with an air of finality as they emerged from the house and got into the car.

God alone knew what he meant by it, Finch thought sourly. It was true the case was concluded. Two people were dead and, for them at least, it was all over.

But for those left behind, Napier and Ruth Livesey, even Steven Bradley and the Pagetts to a lesser extent, he doubted if it would ever be finished and done with, although he supposed they would eventually pick up the pieces of their lives and fit them together again into some semblance of normality.

21

Dodie sounded so distraught over the telephone when she rang on Friday morning that Kate could hardly understand what she was saying, except that it concerned Elizabeth Hamilton and was so dreadful that Dodie couldn't bring herself to talk about it coherently. 'Oh, Kate, Kate!' she kept saying. 'I just can't believe it.'

At this point she broke down in tears. Listening to the muffled sobbing at the other end of the line, Kate came to a decision.

'Stay where you are,' she told Dodie. 'I'm coming over straight away.'

As she fetched her coat and the bottle of whisky from the drinks cabinet, it crossed Kate's mind to wonder if Dodie's distress was caused solely by whatever tragedy had happened to Felix Napier's daughter, and if Mike wasn't also partly to blame; a suspicion which seemed confirmed when, half an hour later as she drew up outside Dodie's house, she saw Mike came slinking out of the side door and make for the barn. He was obviously avoiding her, which suggested guilt. His ducked head and furtive manner added to the impression.

In this, she had guessed correctly. Dodie was still deeply distressed by Mike's betrayal and would have remained at her sister's if he hadn't rung her the previous evening to tell her of the visit of a detective constable who had taken his fingerprints as well as making tests on his hands.

'The police seem to think I had something to do with Hamilton's death,' he had added, sounding frightened and close to tears himself. 'Oh, God, Dodie, I can't face it on my own.'

Of course, it had been foolish of her to agree to go back. Both Fran and her husband had told her so and, deep down, Dodie realized it herself. And yet, what could she do? She knew he wouldn't be able to cope with the situation alone, however absurd the suspicions against him might be. All the same, on the drive back to Woodstone she had been filled with a sense of her own weakness and that, in giving way, she was betraying herself. It had left her feeling exposed and vulnerable as if her last protection had been stripped away.

The news that morning of Elizabeth Hamilton's confession to her husband's murder and her subsequent suicide had come as a final shock. It seemed to Dodie that everything that had once appeared so stable and worthwhile and beautiful was shattering into pieces round her.

She tried to express this to Kate although she said nothing about Mike, pouring out only Elizabeth Hamilton's story, talking, talking, talking as the tears ran down her face, the glass of whisky which Kate had given her held unnoticed in her hand.

Kate heard her out in silence, aware that Dodie needed to express her grief and despair although she still doubted if all of it was entirely due to Elizabeth Hamilton's death, tragic though that was.

'And God knows what Felix must be suffering,' Dodie continued. 'I rang him this morning as soon as I heard. He sounded – oh, I can't explain it, Kate – so *distant* on the phone, I just didn't know what to say to him. There'll have to be an inquest, of course, and I suppose she'll be buried once that's been held. I shall have to go. I know it may mean having time off school but that can't be helped. I simply can't let Felix face the funeral on his own.'

'Of course,' Kate agreed and hesitated before adding, 'I suppose I ought to write to him.'

It was the least she could do, although she was reluctant to be drawn again into any involvement, having made up her mind to remain aloof, and was even less sure that she was right to go back on that decision when she saw Dodie's expression light up, her tears momentarily forgotten.

'Oh, I wish you would, Kate! He said he'll stay on here, but even so he's going to be desperately lonely. He'll need all the support he can get from his friends. And I know he liked you. I could tell when I introduced you to him that Sunday. Remember?'

'Yes, I remember,' Kate replied. She got to her feet. Dodie

seemed to have recovered a little, buoyed up, Kate suspected, by the prospect of a renewal of her own relationship with Felix Napier and all that this implied in visits to Woodstone and shared friendships, as if the possibility of some happy-ever-after ending had given her fresh hope for the future.

But then, Kate thought, Dodie always had believed in somewhere over the rainbow.

Yes, she would write to him, she decided, expressing her commiseration and suggesting that she call on him one afternoon to return his edition of the Jane Austen letters. And, despite her reservations, she felt oddly appeased. She had committed herself and, after all, it seemed the right choice to make.

Stooping down to kiss Dodie's cheek, she said out loud, 'I shan't come to the funeral myself but I'll send flowers.'

'No; don't do that,' Dodie told her. 'Felix made that quite clear on the phone this morning. He's going to put an announcement in the local paper – *No flowers, by request*. But don't you think that's a shame, Kate? I think Elizabeth would have wanted flowers.'

But not her father, Kate thought, pausing on the doorstep as Dodie hugged her, before crossing the forecourt in front of her house to her car. Opening the door, she glanced up the lane to where the tiled roof of Felix Napier's house could be seen above the trees.

No, he wouldn't want flowers and, in a strange way, Kate could understand why. He had too strong a sense of what was fitting to allow his daughter to be buried with any ceremony apart from the simplest rites. And in that, she was inclined to agree with him.

With the dog at his heels, Felix let himself out of the house and walked down the lawn, past the rosebeds where a few last flowers were still struggling into bloom although the buds were too mildewed by the rain to open properly.

They'd need pruning soon, he thought. If the weather held out, he might even make a start on them after lunch, trimming them back to prevent wind-rock in the winter gales. It usually helped.

Yes, he'd tackle the roses first and then he'd take the dog for a long walk. And in the evening . . .

But he wasn't too sure about that.

Decide later, he told himself. There's no point in looking too far ahead. Little by little was best. Little by little.

Like the view. He couldn't yet bear to look at it. Now that most of the leaves were off the trees, he was able to see too clearly Elizabeth and David's house, as well as Paddocks. But with the coming of another summer, he might find the courage to look out again towards the village and those familiar rooftops, to the distant prospect of woods and fields. Nothing was impossible.

Turning abruptly before he reached the terrace and calling to the dog to follow him, Felix walked slowly back up the long slope of lawn towards the house.

Steven Bradley managed to busy himself outside all the morning, keeping well clear of the office as much as possible. It was not only to avoid the telephone and the temptation to pick up the receiver and dial Ruth Livesey's number but also to escape from Jackie, his young girl assistant, who ever since her arrival could hardly wait to pass on the gossip, barely giving him time to unbolt the office door before rushing into her account.

It seemed the news was all over the village about how Dr Livesey had been having an affair with David Hamilton which was why Mrs Hamilton had shot her husband and wasn't it awful?

The girl was agog with it.

He was thankful that, in her excitement, she appeared not to notice his silence although, as he listened, pretending to busy himself for the arrival of the first clients, he was careful to keep his face turned away from her.

'Imagine, Dr Livesey and Mr Hamilton!' the girl added with the amused, casual cruelty of the young. 'I mean, it's not as if she's good-looking.'

Bradley tried not to picture them together nor to recall his own fumbling attempts to establish a relationship with her.

What a bloody fool he must have seemed.

Well, it had taught him a lesson. He'd never make the same mistake again by trying to get in touch with her, although he realized he couldn't have given her up entirely when he heard himself asking, 'So what's going to happen to Dr Livesey now?'

'Oh, she's leaving,' the girl replied. 'Haven't you heard? It seems she's given in her resignation and Dr Wade's told her she can leave as soon as she likes. He's going to get someone else to replace her as a temporary until he can advertise for a new assistant. So she's clearing out this weekend; going to stay with friends in London, or so I've been told. Well, you can understand Dr Wade's point of view, can't you? Who's going to want to be treated by her? I know I wouldn't.'

'No,' he said, meaning that he hadn't heard and that he negated as well her other comments, although she seemed to take his reply as an agreement for she went on, 'And good riddance, too. I've never liked her.'

It was then that Bradley said, 'I'm going out to repair the fence round the exercise pen. Let me know if anyone phones,' and made his escape.

Not that he expected Ruth Livesey to ring him, and when he returned to the office at lunch-time he wasn't really surprised to find there was no message from her. After all, it had been so faint a possibility that he had been foolish to pin any hopes on it.

It was half-past five, as Finch verified, glancing at his watch, as he pulled the last page of his report on Elizabeth Hamilton out of the typewriter and shut it up in the folder along with the other official statements which were just beginning to come in – Kyle and Marsh's on her movements in Framden on the day her husband had been murdered, Sergeant Benson's on the discovery of Bradley's clothing; all too late to be of any use in the investigation but which had to be filed away nevertheless.

For his own part, he was pleased with his sense of timing. He could now knock off and go home with a clear conscience, although he wasn't much looking forward to the prospect of

meeting Goodall and of spending an evening in company with him and Dorothy.

God knows what he'd say to the pair of them over dinner.

He was uncertain also about the letter he had written to Marion Greave earlier in the afternoon, which he had left in its envelope, as yet unaddressed, by the side of the typewriter.

Should he send it? He wasn't sure, doubting his motives for writing it in the first place. It was a friendly letter merely, passing on his news and asking for hers but making no reference to either Dorothy or Goodall, even though he suspected that they were the main reason behind his impulse to write to her. In some obscure way which he was only half aware of himself, he had wanted to persuade himself that he wasn't quite alone and that it was possible for one contact, at least, to be maintained simply by picking up a pen. He was asking, in other words, for assurance that she was there and might still care a little about him.

It was absurd but, all the same, as he laid the folder to one side, he picked up the envelope and quickly wrote her name and address on the front before, finding a stamp, he stuck that on as well, almost as an act of defiance, putting the letter into his inside pocket. He was committed now to posting it.

Wine, he reminded himself as he went out of the building towards the car-park. He had promised Dorothy he'd buy the wine for dinner.

There was a parade of shops on the way home where it was possible to park and where the supermarket was still open for late-night shopping. At the off-licence counter he bought two bottles of wine in a sudden surge of generosity, white for Dorothy, red for himself. As for Goodall, he'd have to make his own choice; Finch had no idea of his preferences.

Turning away, he saw bunches of chrysanthemums crammed into a green plastic container by one of the check-out desks and, bending down, he picked out two of those as well; not so much out of generosity this time as a sense of guilt, as if he were making good a half-remembered omission on his part of something he should have done if only he had been aware of it at the time.

'Having a party?' the girl at the till asked him, seeing him

approach with the wine and the flowers, and, because she had lank hair and bitten nails and yet seemed pleased with the idea that someone had reason to celebrate, he smiled at her and said, 'Yes; just a bit of a family get-together.'

'Nice!' she replied, calling out after him as he walked away, the bottles in a plastic carrier bag and the flowers tucked awkwardly under his arm, 'Enjoy yourself!'

Enjoy yourself!

Well, he bloody well would, too, or at least, he'd put on a good show and, as he paused outside the sub post-office on the corner to drop the letter to Marion Greave into the box, he felt his spritis rise.

There was, after all, something to celebrate and something to look forward to as well, for she would reply to his letter eventually, maintaining the contact which, however tenuous, was a damned sight better than nothing.